MY HEART'S A DANCER

Melanie's marriage had ended before it had begun – but happily it was not long before she found herself in love once again. Yet even now happiness looked like eluding her, when her career as a ballet dancer began to come between her and the man she loved.

MY HEART'S A DANCER

by

ROBERTA LEIGH

MILLS & BOON LIMITED
17–19 FOLEY STREET
LONDON W1A 1DR

First published 1970
This edition 1971

© *Scribe Associates* 1970

*This book appeared in serial form with the author's
pseudonym of Rachel Lindsay.*

ISBN 0 263 71183 8

Made and printed in Great Britain by
Cox & Wyman Ltd, London, Reading
and Fakenham

CHAPTER ONE

THE last haunting notes of the violins throbbed into silence and the red velvet curtain swept down, temporarily muffling the thunderous applause. Pale arms relaxed and heads lowered, stiffening into position again as the curtains rose to give the audience a final view of the dancers.

'How much longer?' Melanie thought, and darted a quick glance at the wings. Her eyes met Madame Verenskaya's piercing black one, and she stiffened into position again, knowing that even a momentary relaxation at the very end of the performance would be treated with the same severity as if it had occurred at the beginning. Not for nothing was the Verenskaya Ballet renowned throughout the world; and if this brought with it the autocracy of Madame herself, it also brought the cachet of belonging to a Company that ranked second to none.

Finally the curtain fell for the last time, and with a swirl of white net skirts the corps de ballet ran off the stage, leaving the principal dancers to take their solo calls.

Standing in her place at the long dressing-table, with its naked light bulbs, Melanie listened to the excited chatter around her and tried not to think that this was the last time she would be dancing with the Company; indeed, if truth were told, it was the very last time that she would be dancing at all. Tomorrow everyone would be going to Australia to commence a three months' tour and she herself would be beginning a new life as Mrs. Timothy Ransome.

'Hey there, stop dreaming,' said Anna, the girl who shared the dressing-table on Melanie's right.

With a start Melanie came back to the present. 'Sorry. I was thinking about the future.'

'It doesn't need much thinking about – it's twenty-two-carat gold! Honestly, I never thought *you'd* snazzle a man like Timothy; loads of money and as handsome as—' Words failed Anna and she pulled a face. 'It just isn't fair!'

Melanie grinned. 'For the first month I met him I didn't think he had a bean.'

'He was just putting on an act to make sure you loved him for himself!'

'I suppose so,' Melanie said thoughtfully, and remembered her surprise when, after four weeks of penny-pinching, with suppers in cafeterias, he had suddenly burgeoned out and money had been no object. Only once had she questioned him about it, but his reply had been so evasive that she had not asked him again. No matter whether Timothy had been rich or poor, her feeling for him would have been the same, but if by pretending to have nothing he had convinced himself of her love, she was too intelligent to mind. What mattered was that she was now his wife. The thought was so wonderful that she closed her eyes and relived the simple wedding ceremony that had taken place that morning – with two dancers their only witnesses – culmination of a whirlwind courtship that had changed her life.

'I hope you won't hate being done out of a big wedding?' he had asked when he had produced the special licence.

'I'm delighted,' Melanie had confessed. 'I'm just sorry your mother won't be here to meet me first.'

'You'll see her the moment she gets back from Jamaica. Anyway, you've nothing to worry about. She'll love you as much as I do.'

'Won't she be upset that you've married a dancer? Men of your background don't usually—'

'Stop it!' Timothy had silenced her with a kiss. 'Mother may be old-fashioned about some things, but she isn't a snob.'

Although at the time Melanie had been reassured by his confidence, she was not so sure now, and wondered whether in his eagerness to marry her, Timothy had been too optimistic.

'You'd better hurry up and change,' Anna said. 'Verenskaya will be furious if you're late for your own wedding party.'

'Particularly as she's giving it!' the girl on Melanie's left added.

Hastily Melanie unhooked her tutu. There was the sound of tearing net and she looked down and saw that her diamond engagement ring had caught in her skirt.

'Darn it!' she said. 'I've completely ruined it.'

'I wouldn't let it worry you,' Anna shrugged. 'It's the last time you'll be wearing it.'

'I was going to keep it as a memento.'

'To show to your grandchildren?'

Melanie laughed. 'I hadn't thought that far ahead. I just wanted it as a reminder of the years I've spent here.'

'I wouldn't have thought you'd need reminding of that,' Anna said dryly. 'You're lucky to be leaving this. I'd give my eye teeth for an easier job than this one.'

'What's stopping you from finding one?'

'I'm crazy about dancing!'

Melanie laughed. Only too well she knew that this attitude applied to all the girls around her. One could not go through years of arduous training and continual daily practice unless one did it from choice; to be a ballet dancer was not something one did for money; it was a vocation, stemming from a need to express emotion by dance.

'Hey there!' Anna said. 'You're dreaming again.'

'Melanie's always dreaming,' a guttural voice said, and there was silence in the dressing-room as the girls turned to see Madame Verenskaya in the doorway. The old woman rapped on the floor with her ebony and silver cane.

'You've had long enough to change. I want to speak to Melanie alone.'

Quickly the room emptied and as the door closed behind the last girl Verenskaya stepped forward.

'So,' she demanded with the accent she had not lost in over thirty years in England, 'what does it feel like to be a bigamist?'

A flush stained Melanie's cheeks. 'I don't understand.'

Verenskaya snorted. 'This morning you married Timothy Ransome. Yet I had always believed you were married to the ballet.'

Melanie smiled. 'Luckily it was a marriage that could be annulled!'

'Not as easily as you think,' came the answer. 'Dancing has been your life since you were a child; you will not find it easy to give up.'

'I know,' Melanie admitted, 'but Timothy wouldn't be happy if I were dancing each night.'

'Ballerinas do not dance every night.'

'I'm not a ballerina,' Melanie grinned, 'just a cog in the corps de ballet. And that means I would have *had* to dance every night.'

'One day you would have been a prima ballerina,' came the answer. 'You have talent, my child. It only needs more time.'

'It's too late now,' Melanie said firmly. 'I've already made my decision.'

'If Timothy loved you – the *real* you – he would realize that dancing is a part of your life. To take you away from it is taking away the core of your existence.'

'He doesn't see it that way.'

'I know. He looks at you, but he sees only himself.' The dark eyes narrowed. 'Anton believes you will come back to the Company.'

Melanie crossed the room and touched Verenskaya's arm. 'It's no good, Madame. I have already made my decision.'

Verenskaya's crêpey lids lowered, but not swiftly enough to hide the tears that dimmed her eyes. 'I am a stupid old woman to go on at you this way. But it is not only because I see you as a dancer. To *me* you have been like a daughter; and now I am losing you.'

'You haven't lost me,' Melanie said swiftly. 'I'll never forget the way you took care of me when my parents were killed. If it hadn't been for you, I would have been in an orphanage.'

'Your parents were dancers in my company,' the old woman said brusquely. 'I could do no less.'

'You did more than anyone could have expected. You brought me up and gave me a home.'

'It was my pleasure to do so.' A gnarled hand stroked Melanie's cheek in an unaccustomed gesture of affection. 'It is not surprising Timothy loves you.'

Melanie smiled, 'A moment ago you said he didn't love me at all!'

'Love has many meanings,' came the answer. 'To me it means allowing a person to achieve their fulfilment. To dictate what they should do is to destroy them as personalities.'

'Timothy didn't ask me to give up dancing,' Melanie protested. 'I'm doing it because I know it's the only way our marriage can work.'

'Then his love is too shallow. Dancing is a part of you. You will regret your decision, my child. Not now perhaps – but in six months or a year. . . .' Verenskaya moved to the door. 'It is better if we do not discuss this any more. Make yourself beautiful, Melanie. The party is for you and it will be your last entrance with the Verenskaya Ballet Company!'

Left alone Melanie finished dressing. Nerves made her clumsy and her fingers trembled as she drew her dark hair smoothly away from her face and fastened it into a low chignon at the nape of her neck. The simple style accentuated her wide brow and high cheekbones, emphasizing her faintly foreign and exotic appearance. An unaccustomed flush tinged her ivory skin, giving depth to slanting aquamarine eyes fringed by lashes so long and thick that she had never had to wear false ones on stage. Yet an observant onlooker would have known that the sophistication was merely a veneer, product of years of training that served to hide an unawakened spirit.

For an instant as she looked at her reflection Melanie was sombrely aware of her inexperience, and as she left the dressing-room and raced down the narrow spiral staircase, she sent up a silent prayer that she would be able to make her marriage work.

'Where are *you* rushing to?' A soft voice halted her flight as she reached the bottom step, and she drew back to see a thin, sallow-faced man looking at her. It was Anton Marek, leading male dancer and second-in-command of the Company. She should have known he would not let this day pass without telling her what he thought of her behaviour!

Although not much taller than herself, Marek had a sinewy grace that gave him the appearance of great strength. As his name indicated he was of Polish descent, a fact made visible by soulful brown eyes marked by high-winged brows. His sharp chin was softened by a sensual mouth that was now stretched into an angry thin line, and as he tilted his head to look at her, his beige blond hair, worn long and thick, fell back from his forehead.

'What's the rush?' he asked again.

'Verenskaya's waiting for me.'

'So she'll wait a bit longer.' Though Anton's voice was quiet, Melanie sensed the tension in him and diplomatically said nothing. If her lateness caused comment, he was well able to take the blame.

'You won't be missed,' he continued. 'At least not by your devoted bridegroom. He's too busy playing havoc with the female section of our corps de ballet!'

'Is that supposed to make me jealous?' Melanie asked.

'Doesn't it?'

'No. I happen to trust my husband.' Pushing past him, she ran down the corridor to the rehearsal room and opened the door. The heat and noise hit her as though it were a physical force and for an instant she longed for the peace of the dressing-room. Then the mood passed and she went in, scanning the throng for sight of a blond head. She saw Timothy at the same moment he saw her, and he pushed his way through the crowd to her side. His face was red and as he bent to kiss her she was enveloped in a cloud of alcohol.

'I'd forgotten I had such a beautiful wife,' he whispered. 'Come and say hello to my friends. Until they actually see you they won't believe I'm married!'

Following his glance she saw a group of unfamiliar faces at a table near the buffet. 'You didn't tell me you'd invited anyone.'

'It was a surprise. Come and meet them.'

She held back, unexpectedly afraid. 'I hope they like me.'

'Why shouldn't they?'

'Because I'm not their sort. I haven't led their kind of life. I'm a working girl and—'

'For heaven's sake! You're my wife now, Melanie, not an unknown little dancer.'

Hurt by the remark, she withdrew her hand from his and followed him across the room. Although she could understand his desire to show her off, she could not help wishing he had chosen another time and place for her to have met his friends.

But then there was no more time for thought, for she was surrounded by more than a dozen people all pumping her hand and talking at once. It was not until the flurry of introductions was over that she was able to pick out his friends individually, recognizing many of them from remarks he had occasionally let drop. How well they fitted his description, and how closely they followed the pattern she had anticipated: elegant, charming, smooth; the conversation typical of the Jet Set. '... and that month in Gstaad was fabulous – much better than Bermuda. ...'

'I said if he couldn't fly over from Canada to see me, he shouldn't bother calling me again. ...'

'I *still* think St. Laurent's passé. But there's a super Italian designer. ...'

The voices droned on around her, none of them bringing her into the conversation, and all of them increasing her feeling of being the odd one out.

'You're not at all what I expected,' a low voice drawled, and Melanie swung round to see a willowly blonde girl beside her. 'What *were* you expecting?' she asked.

'Someone who looked like a chorus girl.' The rudeness was so unexpected that Melanie was speechless.

'I do hope you're not angry with me,' the girl went on hastily. 'I suppose there *is* another name for what you do, but I don't know it.'

'I'm in the corps de ballet,' Melanie said shortly, 'but it doesn't matter. I *am* a girl and I *am* in the chorus.'

'It must be frightfully exciting. Timothy said something about your being born in the wings.'

Melanie glanced round to see where he was and he caught her eye and came over to her. 'So you've met Bibsie already?' His voice was more slurred than before, his face unbecomingly flushed. 'I hope you're going to like each other. Bibsie was my first girl-friend, darling. We met in our respective prams!'

A blare of music made it impossible for Melanie to answer, and even as she wondered frantically how much longer she and Timothy would have to stay here, the girl he called Bibsie pulled him on to the small area of floor that had been cleared for dancing.

In a moment they were swallowed up in the crowd, and as Melanie turned away, intent on finding Verenskaya, a young man pushed a drink into her hand.

'Don't take any notice of our little kitten,' he said. 'She's just sore *you* married Timothy instead of her.'

'It's nice to know there was a reason for her bad manners!'

'There's never any reason for bad manners. It's stupid and bad-mannered!'

She laughed and he laughed with her.

'Are you a friend of Timothy's too?' she asked.

'We went to school together, so I suppose that *must* qualify me!' He looked at her with undisguised admiration. 'I can see why Timothy kept you hidden, though. If *I'd* met you first I'd have done exactly the same.'

'You're too flattering.'

'No pretty girl should say that!' He continued to talk aimlessly, and only half aware of what he was saying – for she was waiting anxiously for Timothy to return – she gave monosyllabic replies.

The music seemed to go on interminably and she was again wondering desperately how to slip away when Anton appeared by her side like a Genie.

'Verenskaya's waiting for you to cut the cake.'

'I must tell Timothy.'

'I have already done so.'

Catching her hand, he pulled her after him through the crowd to where Verenskaya was standing by the large wedding cake which had been given pride of place on the buffet table. Timothy was already there and he caught her hand and drew her close.

'Where did you disappear to?' he whispered.

'I should ask *you* that.'

'Just a duty dance,' he reiterated, and gave her arm a squeeze. Instantly she was happy again, and as Verenskaya signalled for the music to stop, Melanie picked up the knife to cut the cake.

The next hour passed in a blur of congratulations, yet all the time she was aware that Timothy was still dancing exclusively with the blonde girl. No doubt he felt as out of place with the ballet Company as she herself felt with *his* friends, and she wondered how long it would be before they could – without hurting anyone's feelings – leave for the peaceful quiet of Timothy's flat where they were spending the night before flying to Madeira for their honeymoon.

Their honeymoon. The thought made her so acutely aware that she was his wife that she knew an intense longing to be held in his arms and reassured that in marrying him after so swift a courtship she had not done the wrong thing. If only the Australian tour had not precipitated her decision; but on learning she would be away a minimum of three months – possibly even six – he had refused to let her go.

'It's out of the question,' he had protested bitterly. 'If you love me as much as you say, you *can't* go. I need you, Melanie. If you're so many miles away I'll. . . .' he had stopped abruptly and, pulling her into his arms, kissed her so passionately that all her doubts had subsided. Timothy was her love and he needed her. She would have to stay.

Anxiously she searched the dance floor, but there was no sign of him and she wondered whether he was showing the blonde girl what the theatre looked like from the wings; it was a sight many people liked to see.

As the music stopped she managed to slip from the room, and she was speeding down the corridor to the wings when her name was called. With a sigh of exasperation she turned and saw Anton by the door of his dressing-room.

'Going to make a sentimental farewell to the boards?' he asked sarcastically.

'I'm looking for Timothy. Have you seen him?'

'He's the last person I'd want to see! Only a Philistine would have made you give up dancing.'

'Oh, not again!' she exclaimed, and turning her back on him, ran towards the stage. But it was deserted and shrouded in darkness; just bare boards and canvas flats with a desolate air that would only be relieved when the lights came on and dancers filled the stage.

For a moment she paused, breathing in the atmosphere and fighting back an overwhelming sense of loss. Then blinking back the tears she retraced her steps, pausing to see if Timothy was in the wardrobe room where the costumes were kept. But this too was empty and one by one she entered the workshop, the dressing-room of the leading ballerina and the largest make-up room. But nowhere was there any sign of him.

She paused, wondering if he had returned to the rehearsal room. In front of her was the door leading to Madame Verenskaya's private office and without knowing the reason why – almost as if she were returning to the womb – she went in. The room was in darkness and she switched on the light.

Instantly two figures closely twined together sprang apart and she found herself looking at Timothy and the blonde. But now the girl was no longer soignée: her face was flushed and the bodice of her dress was undone.

Melanie drew a shuddering breath and with shaking body turned and groped for the door.

'Melanie!' Timothy called and stumbled towards her. The sound of his footsteps acted as a spur and she rushed headlong from the room, intent only on flight. Behind her she heard his footsteps, and afraid he might gain on her she swung round the nearest corner. In front of her was Anton's dressing-room and without hesitation she pushed open the door and rushed in.

He was sitting in front of his dressing-table and, seeing her face through the mirror, he swung round. Without a word she stumbled towards him, collapsing on the floor and resting her head in his lap. Outside in the corridor Timothy could be heard calling her name, but Anton made no move to answer for her, silently stroking her hair until Timothy's voice grew fainter and disappeared. Only then did Anton speak.

'What's happened?' he asked quietly.

13

She shuddered, tried to answer him, but found it impossible to speak. Gently he lifted her away from him and placed her in an armchair. Then he walked over to a cupboard and returned with a glass of brandy. 'Drink this,' he ordered. 'It will make you feel better.'

She obeyed him and swallowed the contents in a gulp. The liquid burned her throat and brought tears to her eyes. She tried to blink them away but they fell faster, increasing until she could no longer control the sobs that racked her body. Timothy, Timothy. His name was a silent cry inside her, burning into her brain like fire. For a long while she continued to cry, but eventually exhaustion took over and she lay back in the chair and closed her eyes.

'Now then,' Anton said, 'tell me what happened. I've got to know.'

Still keeping her eyes closed she answered him. 'It's over,' she said dully. 'You and Verenskaya were right. I should never have married him.'

There was a momentary silence, broken only by Anton moving back to the cabinet and pouring himself a drink. 'Isn't this a rather unexpected change of mind?' he said at last. 'What's caused it?'

Still she could not answer him, and suddenly she felt his hands on her arms, drawing her up so that she was standing in front of him, his face so close to hers that she could not look away. 'What's wrong, Melanie? You've got to tell me.' She shuddered and would have fallen if his hands had not been gripping her arms like a vice. '*Tell me*,' he commanded. In a voice so faint that at times it was barely audible she did as he asked, but only as she reached the final point in her story – the discovery of Timothy in another girl's arms – did her voice break down completely.

'Is that the only reason you're upset?' Anton said. 'Because of a kiss?'

'No,' she cried. 'It was more than that! He knew her before he married me – since they were children.'

'What's that got to do with it?'

'Everything. He knew he'd made a mistake marrying me and he turned to her.'

'Rubbish! He was drunk and he wanted a woman. You weren't there so—'

'You're making it worse!' she cried. 'He's not an animal

14

that's got to turn to the nearest. . . .' She could not go on and Anton shook her roughly by the shoulders.

'When men are drunk they often become animals. He wanted to make love and – and – well, it was unfortunate you weren't there.'

'Unfortunate!' she gasped. 'Is that all you can say? Do I have to follow him around all the time to make sure I am there when he wants to make love? Hasn't he any control – any sense of what's right?'

'No man has sense when he's drunk,' Anton reiterated.

She shook her head, unconvinced by his reasoning. 'Not on his wedding night – not the first day we're married.' Unbidden, Verenskaya's warning came to her mind and involuntarily she glanced round the dressing-room, taking in the pots of grease-paint lying haphazardly on the table, the brilliantly lighted mirror and the disarray of costumes. 'Verenskaya was right,' she murmured. 'I was crazy to have married him.'

'Crazy or not, you *are* married.'

'No. It means nothing to him.'

'But it means something to you.'

'All the more reason to end it then.' She looked him in the face. 'Do you think I can forget what I saw tonight? Do you think I can ever trust him again?'

'Yes.'

'Then you don't know me.' She pulled away from him and moved over to the mirror. 'I want to go on the tour with you. It's where I belong.'

'You're crazy. By tomorrow you'll have changed your mind.'

She shook her head. 'I know exactly what I'm doing. I had a dream, Anton, but now I've woken up.' Even in her own ears her voice sounded calm, filled with a detachment that must have communicated itself to him, for he stared at her for a long moment before he nodded, 'Very well. I'll tell Verenskaya you'll go home with her. Then at least you can still change your mind in the morning without anyone in the Company being any the wiser!'

'I won't change my mind,' Melanie repeated, 'and I won't go home with Verenskaya. That's the first place where Timothy will look for me.'

'Then you'll have to stay with one of the girls.'

'No! I couldn't. It would mean having to give some sort of

explanation and I ... and I. ...' She put out her hand in a pleading gesture. 'Help me, Anton. Help me!'

'Talk to Timothy first.'

Angrily she flung away from him. 'You're the last person I expected to hear defend him!'

'That's why I'm doing it,' he rejoined without any humour. 'I'm trying my damnedest to be fair!'

'Stop wasting your time. I know exactly what I'm doing.' Her voice trembled and she walked nervously around the small room as she continued to talk, half to herself, half to him. 'In the last hour I feel as if I've lived a lifetime ... a whole lifetime. It wasn't just seeing him with another girl – it was the way he acted the whole evening ... it was as if I were seeing him with different eyes. He made me realize how far apart we were. He's a spoiled boy with too much money and not enough sense. We're worlds apart and we should have stayed that way!'

She swung round and came over to Anton's side. 'You've got to help me get to Australia. If you don't I'll – I'll run away!'

'Stop being so dramatic,' he said crossly. 'If you're determined to go, I'll do what I can to help. I just wanted to make sure you knew exactly what you were doing.'

'Are you convinced now?'

'For the moment. Though you may well think differently in the morning.' He gave a rueful smile. 'Have you got your passport?'

'Yes. And I've had all my shots too.'

'Then it's just a matter of fixing you up somewhere tonight and getting you on our flight in the morning. If you won't stay with Verenskaya or one of the girls, you'll have to doss down with me. Will that be okay?'

She nodded, afraid to speak in case she burst into tears. Silently she watched as he took a thick cardigan out of the wardrobe and handed it to her.

'You'd better not risk going up to the dressing-room for your coat. Come on, let's get going before I change my mind!'

Grateful to leave the thinking to someone else she followed him down the corridor to the stage door. At every corner she expected Timothy to pounce on her, and not until they were out of the theatre and speeding in Anton's car towards his flat was she able to relax. But with relaxation came a return of emotion, and in an effort to ward it off she forced herself to make conversation, knowing it was trivia but knowing too that it was the only way of preventing herself returning to the theatre and Timothy.

'I've never seen your flat, you know,' she said quickly. 'I've often wondered what it was like.'

'Different from Verenskaya's.'

'In what way?'

'You'll see for yourself in a minute.' He drew up outside a tall house and pointed his hand towards it. 'Top floor left,' he said. 'A conversion, of course, but the rooms are bigger than you'd find in a modern block.'

Guiding her as he spoke, he led her up to the front door, unlocked it and shepherded her to a small lift that glided swiftly to the fourth floor and a small but exquisitely furnished studio flat. At the touch of a switch several lamps came on, illuminating the modern paintings on the walls and the few, but choice, pieces of sculpture.

'Put on the electric fire and sit down,' he ordered. 'I'll make some coffee.'

He left the room and, still wrapped in his cardigan, she went over to the window. Below her a street lamp shimmered upon a Bayswater square, but the sky was already lightening above the rooftops with the approaching new day. Yet for her it signified a return to the old life and, acknowledging it, she vowed that for no man – no matter how much she loved him – would she ever again give up dancing. It was part of her life – the one source that would never fail her.

'Coffee's up,' Anton said behind her, and with a start she turned and saw him placing a tray on a table in front of the electric fire, which was now glowing red. 'When you've finished your coffee I suggest you have a rest on the couch.'

'Where will *you* sleep?' she asked.

'I've another room off the kitchen. A glorified larder actually; but I hardly eat in, so I've turned it into a guest room.'

'Let me stay there.'

He shook his head. 'You do as you're told. You'll be less of a nuisance in here. Anyway, neither of us will have time for more than a couple of hours' rest. I've got to talk to Verenskaya as early as I can.'

Yawning, Melanie set down her cup and curled back on the settee. Only then did she realize how tired she was, and though certain she would only be able to cat-nap, the moment she closed her eyes she fell into a deep and heavy slumber.

The ringing of a bell brought her sharply back to consciousness and as she sat up and rubbed her eyes she saw Anton cross to the door and open it.

Verenskaya swept into the room, the folds of her long black coat sweeping behind her as she advanced forward. 'So,' she said, glaring at Melanie, 'not content with upsetting everybody by marrying the wrong man, you now want to upset us all again by unmarrying him!'

'It's not that at all,' Melanie protested. 'Hasn't Anton told you—'

'Yes,' Verenskaya intervened. 'I know everything. But coming to Australia won't solve your problem.'

'At least it will give me time to think.'

'Not very much time.' The ringed fingers flashed in the air. 'He's rich enough to follow you round the world and back, my child. Run away from him today if you wish, but in the not too distant future you will *have* to see him.'

'At least let me try and get a breathing space ... time to decide what to do.'

'So be it,' Verenskaya glanced at Anton. 'I have packed all she will need for the trip. The luggage is downstairs in the taxi.'

Anton glanced at Melanie and half smiled, his look giving clear indication that the battle was won.

During the journey to Australia Melanie felt as though she were two separate people; one who was able to pretend to be calm and rational, the other who looked down on the scene and knew it to be merely a mirage that would eventually crack and release the torrent of emotion being held in check. She was grateful that no one had made any comment on her unexpected arrival at the airport, and guessed at the dire threats that Verenskaya must have made in order to silence a group of dancers who were the most avid gossipers in the profession!

During the last lap of the journey the plane was buffeted by an electric storm that reduced the majority of the passengers to nauseated silence or fear. Only Melanie was incapable of fright, and lay with her eyes closed as the aircraft plummeted and rose like a bird in a hurricane, knowing that death, if it came now, would be a fitting end to the tragedy of her brief marriage.

But within an hour the storm passed and blue skies, bright sunshine and a battery of press photographers greeted their arrival in Sydney.

'We've never had publicity like this,' one of the girls whispered excitedly. 'It's fantastic!'

'It's normal,' Anna corrected. 'Aussies aren't used to celebrities, so they give 'em all royal treatment.' She grinned. 'That's why so many has-beens try and make their comeback here. When you're top of the pops you don't go touring the outback!'

'We aren't a has-been company,' Melanie interrupted. 'If Verenskaya kow-towed to the Establishment we'd have been given a decent grant and—'

'Hey,' Anna protested, 'what's the matter with you! I'm a member of the company too. I was only making a comment.'

Instantly Melanie regretted her outburst. 'Sorry,' she apologized. 'I'm a bit on edge at the moment.'

'I know. Verenskaya said something about it.'

'I'll tell you the whole story later . . . when I can talk about it clearly. For the moment I can't. . . .'

'You don't need to talk about it at all,' Anna said. 'I'm just glad you're with us again. It's where you *belong*.'

The words were an echo of Verenskaya's, and Melanie wondered whether a ballet dancer, once she had committed herself to a full training, could ever have a life of her own. Of all the professions in the world, it was one which seemed to require an overwhelming determination and single-mindedness, so overwhelming that everything paled into insignificance beside it. Yet for Timothy she had been willing – even eager – to give it all up. How wrong she had been.

With usual White Russian lavishness Verenskaya had booked them into Sydney's best hotel. 'If we wish to be judged as first-rate,' she said as they entered the lobby, 'we must act first-rate!'

But the gesture was more hollow than it appeared, for only the principal dancers were allocated rooms of their own, and everyone in the corps de ballet shared a bedroom between two or three. Melanie was the only one to be given a room by herself, though this gesture was explained away by Verenskaya as being due to the unexpectedness of her arrival.

'But you'll be sharing with Anna next week – if you're still with us.'

Without replying Melanie turned and followed the last of the girls to the lift, but as she was half-way across the lobby a young pageboy ran after her to say someone was calling her from London.

Instantly Melanie knew it was Timothy. She flashed a look at Verenskaya, but reading no response in the dark eyes, knew she must make the decision herself.

'I won't accept it,' she told the pageboy. 'Ask your operator to tell Mr. Ransome I won't take any calls from him *ever*!'

But despite her emphatic refusal to speak to him, Melanie was realistic enough to know that Timothy would not be easily dissuaded; ego alone – to say nothing of conscience – would make him whitewash his behaviour. Yet she was unprepared for the ceaseless persistence of his calls and cables, and at the end of four days, when she could bear it no longer, she went to Verenskaya for help.

'*You* talk to him,' she pleaded. 'Tell him to leave me alone.'

'That's something you must tell him yourself.'

'I don't want to hear his voice.'

'Are you afraid?'

'Of course not!' It's just that. . . .' Melanie turned and walked over to the window. She was in Verenskaya's bedroom, no larger than her own but filled with masses of flowers, gifts from the Russian emigrés who seemed to swarm around Madame whenever she set foot in a strange city. 'It's hard to put my feelings into words,' she went on, 'but I feel as if – as if my marriage never happened.'

'You are still in a state of shock,' came the guttural reply. 'That is why it is important that you speak to Timothy. I do not tell you to go back to him. That is something you must decide for yourself. But at least hear what he has to say. Until you stop running away from the past you will never be able to build a future.'

'Right now I'm not interested in building anything. All I want to do is live in the present.' She turned from the window. 'And also to get my marriage annulled. That's more important than anything.'

'Perhaps so. But there is a right and wrong way of doing it. And the way *you* wish to do it is wrong. You are behaving like a heroine in a Victorian melodrama!'

'How would you have felt if you'd seen the man you'd just married making love to another woman?'

'It would depend whether or not I married him with my eyes open or closed! And as far as Timothy was concerned, *your*

20

eyes were closed tight!'

'Well, they're wide open now, and I don't want to see him again!'

'Then you could never have loved him.'

'On the contrary. I loved him too much.'

Verenskaya shook her head. 'Love cannot be turned on and off like a tap. It may dry up – I grant you that. But even then, it would take time.'

'What are you trying to make me do? You're behaving in the same way that Anton did. You didn't like Timothy, yet you're defending him.'

'Only because I care about you. Talk to him, child. Hear what he has to say, and then . . . then if you still feel the same, I will not discuss it any more.'

Knowing herself beaten, Melanie sighed, 'Very well. Next time he calls, I'll speak to him.'

But to Melanie's surprise there was no further word from Timothy that day or the next, and for the first time since her arrival in Australia she dreamed about him and woke up with tears on her face.

Anxious to leave the solitude of her bedroom, she bathed and dressed and went down to have breakfast in the busy and noisy grill room. She was drinking her second cup of coffee when a pageboy came in and handed her a cable. Quickly she opened it and read the message, the words dancing madly in front of her eyes before they finally settled and made sense.

'By time you get cable will be on my way Australia. Stop. See you soon. Stop. All my love. Timothy.'

Pushing back her chair Melanie ran from the room, reaching Verenskaya's bedroom just as the woman was coming out.

'I've heard from Timothy,' Melanie gasped. 'He's coming here. He's already on his way.'

Taking the cable, Verenskaya read it and then folded it carefully into four. 'I expected this. Personally I am surprised he waited as long as he did. I would have thought he would have taken the first plane he could.' The dark eyes glittered. 'You know what this means, don't you? He'll be here today.'

'I know. But I can't see him. It's impossible.'

'Rubbish! The sooner you meet, the sooner you'll settle the whole thing!'

'It's already settled,' Melanie replied.

'For you perhaps, but not for him. You have to see him

21

whether you like it or not.'

'Then he'll have to meet me at the theatre,' Melanie said slowly. 'We'll be rehearsing nearly all day today.'

'You won't be able to dance while you're waiting for him. Besides, your anxiety will affect everyone else. It will be better for you to stay here.'

Recognizing the wisdom of the order Melanie gave way, though as she stood on the hotel steps and watched the Company leave, her fear of meeting Timothy increased to panic. Yet to run away would serve no lasting purpose, for as Verenskaya had rightly said, she and Timothy would have to meet and discuss their future.

Forcing herself to a semblance of calm, she re-entered the lobby and asked the clerk at the reception desk to find out what time the flight from London arrived at Sydney.

'I'll need to know which airline, lady,' he replied.

'I don't know. But it's from London.'

'I still can't help you. All I can do is give you the arrival times of all the planes that could connect with the London flight.'

'That won't be much help,' she said. 'I'd better wait in the hotel. If Mr. Ransome should call or arrive here, please let me know.'

Alone in her room, Melanie relived all that had happened since her marriage, and for the hundredth time wondered if she had been wrong to run away without giving Timothy a chance to talk to her. Yet for the hundredth time she knew that nothing he could have said would have served as a satisfactory explanation for his behaviour, and knew too that if she were faced with the same situation again, she would still make the same decision.

The morning dragged past and by noon the monotony of remaining in her room was so intolerable that she decided to go for a walk. Leaving word at the desk, she strolled outside, unaware of the heat and the crowds and conscious only that before the day was out she would be seeing Timothy. Somehow the thought had no reality, and though she could see his face clearly in her imagination, she could not feel any emotion at the thought of him. Was it a self-defence mechanism? she wondered. Nature's way of ensuring that she would not be hurt again? But here too the answer eluded her and she knew that only when she actually saw Timothy in the flesh would she be able to judge her feelings.

After an hour she retraced her steps to the hotel, perspiration clinging to her forehead. The heat had made her so drowsy she could hardly keep her eyes open. A cool shower was what she needed to revive her. She crossed the lobby and was about to enter the lift when a pile of newspapers on the bookstand and their large black headlines caught her eye:

SYDNEY-LONDON JET EXPLODES. NO SURVIVORS.

She stopped and stared at the words disbelievingly. People pushed past her, but she was unaware of them, seeing only the line of heavy black type advancing and receding in front of her. Was this the flight Timothy was on? Did the words NO SURVIVORS include him?

With a gasp she ran to the reception desk and asked the clerk to contact the airline office

'Which one, ma'am?' he queried.

'I don't know. But a plane just crashed and I – I think my husband. . . . The name's Ransome, Timothy Ransome.'

'I'll find out right away,' he said, and picked up the receiver.

Melanie's heart was pounding so loudly in her ears that she could not hear what he was saying, but she saw his lips moving, saw too the way the colour ebbed from his face as he replaced the receiver.

'Mr. Ransome's name *was* on the list of flight passengers,' he said slowly. 'I'm terribly sorry, lady.' Melanie swayed and he leaned over the desk and caught her arm. 'Can I get you anything? Would you like to see a doctor?'

'No. . . . No . . . I'll be all right. If there's any news, let me know at once.'

'I'm afraid there won't be. The explosion was so bad that they haven't even sighted any wreckage.'

With a gasp Melanie turned away, longing for the solitude of her room. But even when she reached it the tears would not come and she lay on the bed and stared at the ceiling. There was no longer any need to wonder what she would say to Timothy when they met. Fate had made the decision for her. Her husband was dead and she was a widow without ever having been a wife.

CHAPTER TWO

OVERWHELMED by the shock of Timothy's death, Melanie's first thought was to run to Verenskaya for comfort. But only the knowledge that the Company were giving their first performance tonight prevented her from doing so. Nerves would be strained to breaking point without herself adding to the tension. All she could do was to wait here alone with her grief and her guilt. Not until tonight, when the performance had ended, would anyone have time to read the newspapers and learn of the plane crash.

But in this Melanie was proved wrong, for the blue sky was slowly turning purple when there was a rap on the door, followed immediately by Verenskaya's entrance.

'My poor child!' she said swiftly, and crossing over to the bed gathered Melanie into her arms. 'I came back as soon as I heard. Why didn't you come to me? It was crazy of you to stay here alone.'

'I didn't want to upset you before the première,' Melanie said shakily.

'The première!' Veranskaya snorted. 'It was nothing! Just one more performance in a new city. For you to bear *this* alone – it was crazy!'

The sympathy in the guttural voice brought tears to Melanie's eyes, but they only blurred her vision, for when she blinked her lids, her eyes were dry again. 'I can't even cry,' she whispered. 'I don't feel anything . . . it's so unreal.'

'That's why you cannot cry,' Verenskaya said prosaically, and released her. 'Even myself – I cannot believe it is true. It is like some nightmare.'

'But it's true,' Melanie moaned, and rested her head in her hands. 'It's true and it's all my fault. I killed him, Madame, do you know that? I killed him!'

'Nonsense! It was an accident.'

'He wouldn't have been on the plane if it hadn't been for me.' She gave another moan and swayed backwards and forwards. 'If only I knew what he'd been thinking when it happened . . . what was in his mind. But knowing he thought I hated him – that I never wanted to see him again. . . .'

'He never thought that for a moment,' came the firm reply.

'That's why he was coming here. Don't you see that for yourself? Timothy was convinced that once he had you in his arms everything else would be forgotten.'

'If only I could believe that,' Melanie whispered. 'But I keep remembering the way he looked at me the last time I saw him. . . . The pain in his eyes.'

'You're torturing yourself for nothing! Timothy was a boy and he thought like one. It never entered his head that he wouldn't be able to talk you round once you were together. He didn't die believing you hated him. He believed you loved him!' Verenskaya pulled Melanie into a sitting position. 'And can you be so sure that you didn't? Do you know exactly how you would have reacted when you'd met?'

'No.'

'Well then,' Verenskaya said triumphantly, 'that proves my point. Timothy may well have been right.'

'I can't be as sure as you.'

'Perhaps not today, but wait till later – when you can think more clearly.' Verenskaya stood up. 'I've brought Anna back with me. She's waiting outside. I've asked her to stay with you tonight.'

'It isn't necessary.'

'Maybe not. But she's your friend, and if you feel like talking she'll be here to listen.'

'A father confessor?' Melanie asked dryly.

'Unfortunately you don't need one. If you weren't so innocent you wouldn't feel so guilty!' Verenskaya paused by the door, and with her hand on the knob, turned round again. 'I want you at the theatre in the morning for rehearsal.'

'I can't!'

'You must. From now on you will concentrate on your work. It's the one thing that will never let you down.'

'I wish I was as sure as you.'

'I speak from experience. In time you will be able to think of Timothy and your marriage as something that never happened.'

'That's your Russian optimism speaking!' Melanie retorted.

'It's my feminine logic! I may be old, but I'm still a woman and I've had a great deal of experience. You'll be surprised how quickly memories dim. You're young, my child, and you only knew Timothy a few months.'

'Long enough to fall in love with him.'

'But not long enough to forgive him when. . . .' Verenskaya did not finish the words, but Melanie finished them for her.

'When I found him making love to someone else?' She sat up and leaned forward, her expression anguished. 'Yet a moment ago you said I might have forgiven him.'

'And so you might. But it's an answer you'll never know now.'

'That's what I find so unbearable.'

Verenskaya gave an exclamation of anger. 'You cannot live with regret – it's the one thing he wouldn't want. He loved life, my child, and he wouldn't want you to throw yours away.'

Melanie nodded and sighed, remembering the plans he had made for them; the things they would do, the countries they would visit, the family they would raise. But this was all over and her future was – as Verenskaya had said – one that must be filled with work.

More quickly than Melanie would have believed possible she settled back into the routine of dancing: not that she had ever left it for long enough to get out of the habit. It was strange to realize that the last time she had danced had only been ten days ago; so much had happened to her in the interim that it seemed like a lifetime since she had stood on the London stage and heard the audience applaud.

Once more she resumed her place in the corps de ballet, practising for the usual five or six hours a day and snatching whatever time she could to sunbathe on Bondi Beach.

The Sydney audiences were vociferous in their welcome and, despite the unexpected fatigue engendered by the extremely hot weather, not one person in the Company regretted Verenskaya's decision in arranging for them to go there.

But all too soon their stay in Sydney came to an end and they set out on a series of one-night stops, dancing at small towns and settlements along the coast.

Slowly the weeks turned into months and the lengthening time dimmed Melanie's memory of Timothy, until all that remained to remind her of her brief marriage was the pearl necklace he had given her and the enormous diamond engagement ring which she had always been nervous to wear.

Gradually she realized that Verenskaya's opinion – expressed on the day Timothy had died – had not been based on optimism alone. She *was* forgetting him; she *was* finding that their courtship and marriage had been part of another life and – most important of all – she no longer felt bitter towards him.

Analysing the reason for her change of attitude she wondered whether the self-analysis to which she had subjected herself – in order to reach an acceptance of Timothy's death – had not only given her a better understanding of his behaviour, but had also served to increase her own self-knowledge. But whatever the reason, she could now accept his weakness and forgive him for it.

Concentrating all her energies on work, she found added confidence as a dancer, and was delighted when she began to get another part added to her repertoire, until there was hardly a ballet in which she did not appear. Not only had she improved technically, but her greater self-knowledge also added depth to her interpretation, enabling her to give a more sensitive portrayal of each part she danced.

'You'll be a prima ballerina yet,' Anton declared one Sunday in Perth as he came into the rehearsal room at the theatre and found her practising at the barre. 'But don't you think you should rest at least one day of the week?'

'Verenskaya wouldn't agree with you,' Melanie smiled.

'As it so happens she does. As a matter of fact she sent me here to bring you back to the hotel. You can't work without a break. You'll crack up.'

'If it hadn't been for work, I'd have cracked up a long time ago.'

'Maybe. But now it's time you took it easy. Too much practice will make you stale.' Suddenly he pulled her round to face the long mirror at the end of the room. 'Look at yourself, Melanie. What do you see?'

'A scraggy female who needs to gain weight!'

'*I* see a beautiful girl who should start behaving like one.'

She swung round to look at him. 'Why the flattery? Do you need your socks darning?'

He did not smile. 'I'm being serious. You're beautiful and it's time you realized it.'

'Why the interest in my appearance?'

'Because it's affecting your dancing.' He smiled at her look of surprise. 'Until you think of yourself as a woman you won't dance like one. It doesn't matter for the parts you're doing now, but when it comes to *Giselle*—'

'*Giselle!*' she interrupted. 'It'll be years before I dance that!'

'Don't be so sure.' He put his hand on her chin and tilted her face to look into her eyes. 'You've got great talent – everyone in the Company recognizes that – but you're still scared of emotion.'

'Do you blame me?' she asked bitterly.

'I do. You had a bad shock and it took courage to face it. But now you've got to think of your future. And that doesn't mean living like a nun and making ballet your whole life!'

She pulled away from him. 'When I married Timothy you were angry because I *hadn't* made ballet my life.'

'I said you should never give up dancing,' he corrected. 'But I didn't mean you to regard it as your lover!'

Angrily she walked back to the barre. 'Do we *have* to discuss my private life?'

'You haven't *got* a private life; that's what's wrong! If you had a lover it would at least—'

'Stop it!' she burst out, her voice choked with anger. 'I don't *want* a lover. I want to live my life alone.'

'You can't. You're too young.' He caught her by the shoulders. 'Haven't you taken in anything I've said? You're an iceberg, Melanie, and it shows in your dancing. It's your only drawback.'

'If loving Timothy didn't help me to melt,' she retorted, 'nothing will.'

'On the contrary. Your love for Timothy was the feeling of a child for a boy.'

'Is that why his death affected me so much?'

'It was guilt that affected you,' Anton said. 'You know that as well as I do.' Once again he caught her shoulders, his breathing so fast that she could feel it on her face. 'Do you know the meaning of love, Melanie? Have you ever ached with desire for a man? Have you ever known the joy of complete fulfilment?'

A hot wave of colour flooded into her face and, seeing it, the tenseness vanished from Anton's expression, making him look his usual puckish self. 'So you're still the virgin bride! I'd never have believed it.'

'How dare you speak to me like that!' Anger gave her the strength to pull away from his hold. 'Do you find it so difficult to understand that two people can be in love without wanting to do anything about it until they're married?'

'Not difficult to understand – just incredible! If you'd been engaged to *me*—'

'We don't have the same standards,' she retorted.

'Standards!' he exclaimed. 'If two people love each other they *want* each other. What have standards got to do with it?'

'I don't happen to believe in the permissive society!'

'I prefer to call it behaving realistically!'

Determined not to show her embarrassment, she resolutely continued with her practice.

'What wonderful control you have.' His voice was directly behind her, low and mocking. 'I can see it will require a man of great courage to break you down.'

'You make it sound like a battle,' she said tartly.

'Getting you to give in *would* be a battle!'

'Which I suppose *you'd* be prepared to do as a duty to the Company,' she said sarcastically. 'To help me become a better dancer.'

'How blind you are!' Angrily he pulled her away from the barre. 'I love you, Melanie. Haven't you realized that?' The astonishment on her face was his answer, and he gave a wry smile. 'Yes, I love you. For two years I waited for you to grow up – waited till I thought you were ready – and then you fell for Timothy.' His voice grew deeper, harsher. 'I could have killed him!'

'Don't say that.'

'It's the truth. You don't know how I felt watching you throw away everything you'd worked for in order to marry a spoiled young man who didn't understand you.'

'I was equally to blame,' she answered quietly. '*I* didn't understand *him*.'

'Well, it's over now,' Anton said calmly, 'and you're free.'

'Not yet. . . . There are too many things I can't forget.'

'You will in time. And when you do, I don't intend to stand by and watch you make a second mistake.'

'There won't be a second time,' she said huskily.

'That isn't true. You were made for love, Melanie, and one day you'll want it.'

She was silent, unwilling to admit the truth of what he said, yet unwilling to lie to him. Deliberately she kept her eyes averted from his, but was aware of his touch upon her body, aware of him for the first time as a man and not just a dancer. Had it been naïve of her not to have guessed how he felt about her? Yet

29

how could she have known it when his behaviour during the last few years had kept the gossip columns fully occupied? For almost as long as she could remember, Anton had been surrounded by admiring women, his name linked with one beautiful girl after the other. But at no time had he allowed a love affair to impinge on his work, and it had become a standing joke with the Company that his lasting passion was reserved for ballet.

'Are you thinking of my reputation?' Anton asked with uncanny insight.

'You can't blame me,' she shrugged. 'I've never thought of you as a monk.'

'I'm a man, with a normal man's passion,' he replied. 'When I first knew I was in love with you, you were too young to be told.'

'I shouldn't have thought that would have stopped you!'

'It wouldn't have in the normal way – but Verenskaya was your guardian angel! She insisted I wait until you grew up.'

'You're digressing,' she said pointedly.

'Was I!' Once again there was the familiar glint of amusement in his eyes. 'As I remember it I was trying to explain why I didn't live in monk-like seclusion until you were ready for me!'

'I don't want any explanations,' she said quickly. 'I'm not interested in what you've done.'

'Thank goodness for that! But I hope you'll be interested in what I *intend* to do?'

'I wish you'd be serious, Anton.'

'I've never been more serious in my life.' His grip tightened. 'This is not a joke to me, Melanie. Remember that. Perhaps I've not chosen the best time to talk to you. Maybe I should have waited a few more months. But I was afraid that if I did I . . . I don't want to lose you again.'

There was a sadness in his voice she had never heard before, and unexpectedly she was touched by it. She would have liked to believe that everything he had said to her this afternoon had been a joke, but looking into his eyes she knew he had meant every word.

'I'm not your type,' she murmured huskily. 'We're too different. You're a sophisticate – a man of the world – and on your own admission I'm too innocent and too childish . . .'

'A child grows into a woman,' he said, 'and so will you. One day you'll need to be loved, and when that times comes, I hope you'll turn to me.'

Unexpectedly he released her, and walking over to the gramophone, he put on the music from *Giselle*. 'What about dancing part of this with me?' His voice was so normal that she was taken aback, and seeing her surprised expression he smiled. 'Don't look so startled, I've said what I wanted to, and I don't intend to repeat it. When you're ready to accept me I'll know. Until that times comes we'll just be members of the same company.'

'Then as the leading male dancer you shouldn't waste your time with someone as unimportant as me!'

'I'm not wasting my time. You're earmarked for bigger things. Come, Melanie, let us dance.'

'I don't know the steps,' she protested.

'You've watched them often enough. Stop pretending and dance.'

As the music swirled around her Melanie gave herself up to the rhythm. Anton was a superb partner and steps she had always considered difficult became easy to achieve with his grip secure around her.

For two hours they practised, Anton correcting her sharply each time she made a wrong step, making her repeat it again and again until he was satisfied she knew it properly. Neither by gesture nor look did he give any inkling that she meant any more to him than a dancer he was trying to train, and she could almost believe he had never uttered any declaration of love, nor told her he would always wait for her to turn to him.

Yet as the music came to an end and she moved exhaustedly to the door she suddenly found him standing beside her, his hand on hers. 'I meant every word this afternoon,' he said jerkily.

'I wish you didn't. You make me feel guilty.'

'Because I love you? That's *my* burden, not yours.'

'But now that I know it, you've made it mine.' She looked him directly in the face. 'You've made me feel embarrassed with you.'

'You didn't show it when we were dancing together.'

'That was different. I just felt you were my partner.'

'Then go on thinking of me that way,' he said. 'As your partner on stage.'

31

'On stage?' she said incredulously. 'I'll never be good enough for that.'

'I can guarantee that you will. I wish I were as sure you'll be my partner *off* stage.' Quickly he opened the door and stepped back, allowing her to precede him, but when she turned she saw he had closed the door without following her.

CHAPTER THREE

TRUE to his word Anton did not refer to their conversation again, and neither by look nor gesture could anyone have known he was in love with her. Sometimes, watching him from the wings as he danced, she wondered whether he had only said it in order to make her realize that she was still an attractive woman with a future in front of her.

It was Verenskaya who finally removed this doubt, talking openly about Anton's attitude on the night they returned to Sydney, a month before they were due to leave for England. She had come to see Melanie in her room, something she had only done on rare occasions during the tour.

'I'll be glad when we're home again,' the woman said, resting her ebony stick against the foot of the bed as she sat down. 'I'm getting too old for all this travelling.'

'You're ageless,' Melanie smiled.

'I don't feel it. If we hadn't needed the money I would never have come here.'

'But the tour's been a success, hasn't it?'

'From an artistic point of view yes, but financially. . . .' Verenskaya shrugged and dismissed the subject. 'But I didn't come here to bother you with my problems. I wanted to talk to you about Anton. You know he loves you?'

Melanie nodded and busied herself unnecessarily at the dressing-table in order to avoid the dark eyes that she knew were fixed on her. Despite spending her formative years with Verenskaya she had never become accustomed to the frank and detailed manner with which the woman discussed every detail of her own life and the lives of those around her, whether it were financial, emotional or domestic.

'What do you feel about him?' Verenskaya persisted. 'He would be right for you, you know. Soon you will be ready to dance bigger parts, and if you go on as you have been, Anton may well be your partner.'

This last remark brought Melanie swinging round. 'Me? You must be joking. I'm not good enough.'

'I'm a better judge of your talent than you are,' came the sharp answer, 'and also a better judge of what you need to give your dancing emotional depth.'

'*You* never got married,' Melanie retorted, 'and you were the best dancer of your generation!'

'I had lovers instead of a husband! But you are not the type to do the same. For that reason you should marry.'

'Anton?'

'Yes.'

'I can't think of marriage yet.' Melanie looked down at her hand. She no longer wore her wedding ring and it had been on her finger too short a time to leave a mark, yet she was still conscious of its absence. 'It's funny to think you can be tied by a marriage that was never real,' she murmured.

'Maybe it was too early for Anton to have spoken to you,' Verenskaya conceded, 'but I didn't want him to be too late again!'

'So you suggested he spoke to me?'

'Naturally.'

'Don't you ever get tired of interfering in other people's lives?' Melanie asked crossly.

'The Company is my family,' came the haughty reply. 'I wish to do what is best for them.'

'Perhaps they'd prefer to decide that for themselves.'

'If they did, they would not stay with me,' Verenskaya snorted, and picking up her cane, swept from the room.

Left alone, Melanie walked over to the window and stared down at the street far below. In the white hot glare of the sun the people were like ants scurrying across a grey desert; and yet each one carried its own burden of duty, of family ties, some even – like herself – of guilt. Yet one could not live with guilt for ever, and she was realistic enough to admit that one day she would feel the need to love and be loved; but whether it would be by Anton was something she found impossible to decide.

At the theatre that night she watched him again from the wings as he took a curtain call with Tanya Federovna; prima ballerina with the Company for the past three years, the girl had spent the last two of them feverishly pursuing him, despite the fact that all her advances had met with rebuttals. Even now she was plucking a rose from the bouquet presented to her by a footman, and placed it to her lips before handing it to Anton who, with studied grace, placed it to his own. But as he came off stage he dropped the flower to the ground and crushed it with his foot, a gesture which made Tanya give a dramatic exclamation of hurt.

'Wasn't that unnecessarily cruel?' Melanie said as Anton came abreast of her.

He shrugged. 'I'm tired of her chasing me.'

'You can't blame her for trying. And if she's willing to join the queue—'

'You sound as if you're jealous!'

'It's impossible to be jealous of a dozen different women. It's meaningless!'

'There'd only be one woman if you'd say the word.' In a quick gesture his hand touched her cheek and then dropped to his side. 'You haven't forgotten what I said to you, have you?'

'No, I haven't. But it's no use. The past is too close. I can't think about the future.'

'Then at least let me be part of your present.'

'You are; we both dance for the Company!'

'That's true,' he acknowledged dryly, and walked away.

The following day a crisis hit the Company. Two of the leading male dancers and several of the girls were taken ill with food poisoning, causing a hasty revision of the programme they were to dance that night. The performance of *Romeo and Juliet* was cancelled and a series of short ballets were arranged for the first half of the evening, with *Daphnis and Chloe* following after the intermission.

'I'm surprised we're doing that one,' Anna murmured to Melanie as Verenskaya ordered a rest telling them to report back within fifteen minutes. 'Tanya hates dancing Chloe.'

'I'm not surprised. She'd need to be a really great actress to play the innocent!'

Anna grinned. 'That's the first catty remark I've ever heard you make.'

'Sorry. It must be the heat. It makes me on edge.'

'Don't apologize for it. It's refreshing to know you're still human – capable of being jealous, I mean.'

'Jealous?' Melanie said quickly, and paused by the door,

'Why should I be jealous of Tanya?'

'Because of the way she makes a play for Anton.'

'You're crazy,' Melanie said more calmly than she felt. 'Why should I care what *he* does?'

Anna shrugged. 'Forget I said anything.'

'It's too late for that,' Melanie said. 'What made you say it in the first place?'

Her friend hesitated and then took the plunge. 'You've been watching him like a mouse watching a cat for the last month. That's why I was pretty sure he'd told you how he felt about you.'

'Felt about me?' Melanie echoed.

'He's in love with you,' Anna said frankly, then seeing the colour flood Melanie's face she added: 'Oh, don't look so worried about it – nobody else in the Company's guessed.'

'Then why did *you*?'

'Because I'm just a particularly observant friend and it makes me more conscious of the way you act. You've been pretty quick-tempered lately. That always happens when you're nervous.'

'I've had other reasons to be nervous,' Melanie said. 'I don't see why you should assume it's got anything to do with Anton.'

Anna looked at her quizzically. 'Am I really so wrong?'

Faced with such a direct question, Melanie found it impossible to lie. 'No,' she admitted, 'you're not. He did tell me he – he loved me. It was in Perth ... one afternoon when we were rehearsing. At first I didn't believe him, but now I'm not so sure.'

'He meant it all right; I'd take a bet on that.' Anna moved through the door. 'Come on, let's grab a cup of coffee before it's too late.'

As Melanie went to follow, Verenskaya called her name. 'After the break, report to the wardrobe mistress. You've got to be fitted for your costume.'

'What costume?'

'The one you'll be wearing tonight when you dance Chloe.'

'Dance Chloe? But that's impossible!'

'No, it isn't. You've been working on it with Anton.'

'But just as an exercise. Honestly, Madame, I couldn't. I'd never be able to dance the whole role.'

'It's either that, or returning the money for tonight's performance.'

'You'd be safer to return the money. I'd be the biggest flop of all time.'

'I don't agree with you,' Anton said directly behind her, and she swung round to see him by the door.

'I can't,' she protested. 'Honestly, Anton, I don't know the part.'

'You know it better than you realize. Anyway, I'll be your partner, and if you really do black out, we'll improvise!'

'That's not very funny.'

'Neither is the position we're in,' he said *sotto voce*. 'If we refund tonight's money we'll have to work our passage home.'

Melanie looked at him intently, and what she saw in his face told her he was speaking the truth. 'Very well. But heaven knows how I'll get through it.'

'You'll do fine,' he squeezed her arm, 'It's less nerve-racking to make your debut here than in London.'

'Maybe. But I hope there's a newspaper strike tomorrow!'

'You won't be as bad as that. We'll be rehearsing it for the whole of the afternoon anyway.'

'What can I do in four hours?' she asked bitterly. 'Four weeks would be nearer the mark.'

For the remainder of the day she and Anton rehearsed without pause. The first act was not so difficult for her and she was able to concentrate on the interpretation, but the last act – when she had to dance part of it alone – was the hardest thing she had ever had to attempt. Anton did not comment on any of her innumerable mistakes, but again and again went patiently over each step with her, murmuring in her ear when he felt her hesitate and sometimes forcibly guiding her with his hands.

At six o'clock they were both too exhausted to continue, though even so she was unwilling to stop. 'We'll be wasting our time if we don't rest,' he remonstrated. 'Lie down in one of the dressing-rooms – it's pointless going back to the hotel.'

'I'll be all right soon. If we could just go through the last act again. . . .'

'No. We can't get it any better – at least not tonight.'

'But it'll be a ghastly fiasco if—'

'Stop it.' He put his hand against her lips. 'It'll be all right. I promise you.'

Melanie repeated these words over and over to herself as,

later that evening, she stood in the wings waiting for her call. The change of programme had not worried the audience, who had greeted the first half of the performance with their usual rapturous welcome. But now the true testing time had come and her nervousness increased to the point where the trembling of her body almost made it impossible for her to stand, and the soft chiffon folds of her dress swayed visibly.

Then Anton was beside her, a smile on his face, his hands warm and comforting on her waist. 'You'll be all right,' he said firmly. 'Trust in me.'

The orchestra played the first chords and as the music floated back to them her trembling ceased and the fear that had gripped her ebbed away, leaving in its wake a calmness born, she afterwards realized, of despair. Her eyes took in the scene being enacted on stage where the dancers, bearing gifts of flowers and fruit which they deposited at the cave of Pan, could have been taking part in a ballet she had never seen or danced before. Then Anton was propelling her forward, and as they moved to the front of the stage with another throng of dancers the audience, recognizing Anton, greeted him with a burst of applause.

She stiffened visibly at the sound and he pressed her arm so tightly that she almost cried out. 'There's nothing to be afraid of,' he whispered. 'Relax.'

Forever afterwards, no matter how hard she tried, Melanie could not clearly recall her debut as a ballerina. She was aware only of Anton's hands and body as he guided her skilfully through the steps, steadying her when she faltered and occasionally leading her when he sensed she was at a loss.

If the first act was difficult, the second was doubly so, for Melanie had to dance a great part of it on her own. More than once she was overcome by terror, but luckily, the urge to run off the stage was so strong that it actually prevented her from moving, and the swaying of her body – caused by horror at her feeling of ineptitude – fitted in exactly with the part of the petrified girl she was playing. It was only when Anton came on stage again and they went into their final pas de deux that the numbness which had taken hold of her throughout the performance began to recede, and for the first time she was able to dance with feeling instead of only technique, having no need of any extra guidance from him and able to interpret the very spirit of the character she was dancing.

When at last the curtain descended there was a moment of complete silence; then deafening applause washed over them. But the vast auditorium in front of her was a faceless sea and only the man at her side held any reality for her, so that she gave him her hand spontaneously and looked into his face with all the gratitude of which she was capable.

'I'll never be able to thank you enough,' she whispered.

'You've nothing to thank me for; you did fine.'

'I was dreadful! If it hadn't been for you, I'd—'

'It's over,' he said, and pulled her forward so that the curtain could swish down behind them and allow them to take their bow alone. A footman came on stage carrying an enormous bouquet and, with an imp of mischief, she pulled out a flower, pressed it to her lips and handed it to him.

'I'll make a Tanya of you yet,' he said as he took the bloom and touched it to his mouth.

'Not unless you're Svengali!' she whispered back, and then turned to curtsey deeply again to the audience.

The sound of clapping was still echoing in their ears when they finally left the stage, and as they reached the wings Verenskaya was there to greet them, pulling Melanie forward and kissing her on both cheeks.

'You did better than I expected, child. But you must watch your elevation.'

'Isn't it enough that she danced?' Anton exclaimed. 'Leave the post-mortem till tomorrow.'

'There will not be a post-mortem,' said Verenskaya majestically. 'Tonight's performance was an emergency one and we will pretend it never happened!'

Melanie gave a shaky laugh, and as she did so the fear that had helped her to maintain her control disappeared and her laughter rose on a crescendo of hysteria which stopped abruptly as Anton's hand slapped smartly against her cheek.

With a gasp she stepped back, her face white except for the red marks where his fingers had struck her.

'I'm sorry,' he said gently. 'It was either doing that or having you go into hysterics.'

She gave a wan smile and impulsively leaned forward and kissed the side of his face. '*You* deserve the credit for tonight's performance. Without your help I couldn't have danced a single step.'

38

'Old dependable they call me,' he said lightly, and then added so softly that only she alone could hear. 'I'm always ready to help you, Melanie, in every way you want.'

CHAPTER FOUR

EXACTLY five months after leaving England the Company returned home. Melanie's fear that being in London again would revive her love for Timothy was not borne out by events, and more than ever she realized how foolish she had been to believe they had ever had anything in common. He had been her first love and, like so many first loves, it had proved to be an illusion. Her final acceptance of this reawakened all her feelings of guilt, and though she managed to fight it off during the day, when her mind was occupied with work, at night it returned with double intensity, making sleep impossible and sending her pacing the floor of her bedroom for hour after restless hour. Finally, as always, she took the problem to Verenskaya.

'It's knowing I never really loved him,' she explained. 'That's what I can't forgive myself for.' She looked around the large but shabby drawing-room of the Bayswater flat she had lived in with Verenskaya since the death of her parents. 'It's as though he never really existed – as if it were a dream.'

'Then stop turning it into a nightmare! Would you feel less guilty if you pretended to a sorrow you did *not* feel?'

'Of course not.'

'Then forget about the past. It's finished and nothing you can do can change it!'

'I know that. But it still doesn't stop me feeling guilty.' She hesitated, then said: 'Since I've been back in London I keep thinking about his mother. I suppose that's also made it worse for me.'

'That at least is something I can understand. Of all the people in this unhappy affair, *she* is the one who has suffered the most.' Hurt, Melanie turned away and Verenskaya continued chidingly: 'I do not mean to be cruel, my child, but for you the pain will pass. Already you admit it has! But for a mother – that is something quite different. All her life she will live with the heartache of his death.'

'Don't!' Melanie gasped. 'I can't bear it – and it won't do any

39

good either. There's no way I can help her.'

'You could go and see her.'

There was a silence so sudden that it heightened all the surrounding noises of traffic, the hiss of steam in the old-fashioned radiators and the steady whir of the grandfather clock.

'Go and see her?' Melanie echoed. 'I daren't! We've never even met!'

'All the more reason for you to do so. No matter what happened between you and Timothy, you're still his widow and *her* daughter-in-law. Think how *she* must feel; she knows you're in England again yet you haven't even spoken to her.'

Startled by Verenskaya's surprise emotion, Melanie was forced into the defensive. 'If you feel so strongly about it, why didn't you tell me to go and see her before?'

'I do not want to tell you *everything* you should do,' came the reproving answer. 'I was waiting for *you* to feel the need.'

'But what can I say to her? To try and explain why I left Timothy would be—'

'*Don't* explain. It isn't necessary. As far as his mother's concerned all you need say is that Timothy had agreed to let you go on the tour and that he was flying out to join you when he was – when he was killed.'

'I couldn't go through with such a lie!'

'Well, you can't tell her the truth. And if you tell her what I've suggested it will at least sound plausible.'

'I suppose so,' Melanie said slowly. 'Until I've seen her I won't be able to get her out of my mind.'

The following afternoon Melanie put on a dark dress and coat and went to see the stranger who was her mother-in-law. Timothy had lived in a flat in Knightsbridge and she had had to look up Mrs. Ransome's address in the telephone book. But even so she was unprepared for the grandeur of the large house off Belgrave Square, with its marble pillars rising regally either side of a beautifully polished mahogany front door.

Nervously she rang the bell and within a moment the door was opened by an elderly butler, his appearance as imposing as the surroundings she glimpsed behind him.

'I'd like – I'd like to see Mrs. Ransome,' she stammered.

'Do you have an appointment, madam?'

She shook her head, realizing how stupid she had been not to telephone first. 'If you could tell her it's Miss – tell her it's Mrs. Timothy Ransome.'

40

Well trained though he was, the man fell back a step.

Then he quickly opened the door wider and beckoned Melanie into a large, marble-floored hall. 'Please wait a moment,' he said, and crossed over to a door on her left. He closed it behind him but in a few seconds was in the hall again, beckoning her to go forward.

Melanie did so, and found herself in what she took to be a drawing-room. It was vast in size and elegantly furnished with French pieces, but beyond a fleeting impression of burnished wood and exquisite pictures on pale peach walls, her attention was held by an impeccably dressed woman sitting on a brocade-covered settee beside a fireplace. The lined face with its deep blue eyes was so like an older edition of Timothy's that Melanie felt herself grow faint, and it was more than a moment before she became aware that the expression with which she was being regarded was one of hatred.

'So you're the girl my son married. Why have you come here?'

'Because I – I just got back from Australia and it seemed the – the right thing to do.'

'Since when have you cared about doing the right thing?' The woman's voice was shaking, but her anger still came through it. 'My son is dead. Seeing you only serves to remind me of it. Go away!'

'Please don't!' Tears rushed into Melanie's eyes. 'I can understand how you feel – I was expecting it. But it isn't fair to blame me. It was an accident.'

'That's a matter of opinion,' a deep voice said, and Melanie swung round to see a tall man standing by the door. 'I'm Gregory Ransome,' he continued, and stepped forward.

So this was the cousin of whom Timothy had spoken with such resentment; an orphan since the age of ten, he had been brought up by his aunt and uncle, and had done his best to make them consider him their elder son. 'The mind of a computer and the emotions of an iceberg,' had been Timothy's description of him, and seeing the narrow face and steel-grey eyes under heavy brows, she could well believe it. But he was younger than she had expected, and totally unlike Timothy, having thick black hair and stern lines running down either side of his mouth.

'If my cousin hadn't been chasing after a runaway bride,' he went on, 'he'd still be alive today.'

Melanie caught her breath. So much for Verenskaya's hope that she could pretend nothing had gone wrong between Timothy and herself! Yet determined to see if she could retrieve the situation she tried to bluff it out. 'Timothy knew I was going on the tour. He agreed to it.'

'That doesn't tie in with what he said when he telephoned me the morning after you'd married him,' came the sarcastic rejoinder. 'He was practically out of his mind.'

Dismayed, Melanie was silent. To explain her actions would mean smirching Timothy's memory, and with his mother directly behind her, it was something she found impossible to do.

'Well,' the man said, 'where's your great defence?'

Clenching her hands, she turned to look at Mrs. Ransome, but the woman's face was marked by tears and Melanie knew it would be better for her to say no more. How stupid she had been not to consider the possibility that Timothy had told someone else of her sudden departure. Told them of it, yet omitted to give the real reason.

'It's no use my explaining,' she said tonelessly. 'It was silly of me to have come here. I'm sorry.'

Quickly she ran from the room, the dislike of the two people behind her so strong that her one thought was to escape from it. She raced across the hall, opened the front door and hurried down to the pavement. A bus drew into the kerb on the other side of the road and, lifting her arm to stop it moving off without her, she began to run towards it. Too late she saw a motorbike swing round the corner. It swerved to avoid her as she advanced into its path, but the edge of the wheel caught against her hip and sent her spinning to the ground. Her head struck the kerb, there was an agonizing flash of pain and she knew no more.

An incessant aching throb was her first conscious thought, and with an effort she opened her eyes. Everything was a blur of darkness edged with blinding light, but as it faded and the darkness turned to daylight, she saw she was lying in bed in an unfamiliar room. Its expensive furnishing and tall, graceful windows told her she must be in the Ransome house and she struggled to sit up, her one thought being to leave as quickly as she could. But the sudden movement caused another sharp stab of pain in her head and she gave an involuntary cry. The sound

42

brought a white-robed figure to her side.

'So you've come round at last!' a nurse said. 'That's excellent.' A firm hand raised her head and glass of tepid liquid was touched to her lips. Only then did Melanie realize how thirsty she was and she drank eagerly.

'How long have I been here?' Although she spoke in a normal tone she was surprised that the sound that emerged was a cracked, barely audible whisper.

'Three days,' came the reply.

'Three *days?*'

'That's right. And this is the first time you've been conscious.'

Melanie tried to raise herself again, but the sharp pain in her temples made movement unbearable and she lay back on the pillow. Three days. It was unbelievable. Even worse, it was untenable. The moment the throbbing eased in her head she would get dressed and leave; to stay here any longer was out of the question. Perhaps if she closed her eyes for a moment the pain would lessen. Of one thing she was certain: it certainly could not get worse.

When next she opened her eyes bright sunlight was streaming into the room and the nurse was standing by the bed.

'What a long sleep you've had! Feeling better?'

Gingerly Melanie moved her head. The pain had lessened considerably and even when she sat up it barely increased. 'Much better, thanks. I'll get up now.'

'Get up?' The nurse looked horrified. 'You can't do that for at least a week. The doctor would never allow it.'

'What doctor?'

'Dr. McAllister. Mrs. Ransome called him when you were brought here after your accident. Don't you remember seeing him? The first time you were unconscious, but yesterday he was here and spoke to you.'

'Spoke to me yesterday?' Melanie said incredulously. 'Did I answer him?'

'You certainly did! Most agitated you were too. Going on about having to leave at once and no one was going to stop you – not unless they knocked you unconscious again!' The nurse smiled. 'Still, don't worry that you've forgotten. It often happens in cases of concussion. You're lucky you're not worse. Heads weren't meant to hit kerbs, you know!'

Melanie sank back against the pillow. 'I can't stay here any longer. It's out of the question. If you could telephone Madame Verenskaya for me she'll ask one of the girls in the Company to collect me.'

'There's plenty of time to do that next week,' the nurse said soothingly. 'Right now you must stay in bed and do as you're told.'

Unexpectedly an overwhelming tiredness robbed Melanie of the energy to argue, and she closed her eyes. She was aware of the nurse moving about the room and found the sound of the starched apron strangely comforting. If only she were not in the Ransome home she would be content to stay in bed for ever. For ever and ever. 'What a funny thing to want,' she thought, and was puzzling over it when she fell asleep again.

Each time she awoke she felt increasingly stronger, but it was not until the fifth day, when she opened her eyes and saw Madame Verenskaya sitting by her side, that she felt almost her normal self.

'Thank goodness you're here. I was beginning to think you'd forgotten about me.' She held out her hands and Verenskaya patted them. Even in old age the woman still had the gracefulness of the ballerina assoluta she had been in her youth, and this elegance of movement contrasted oddly with the long black dress and dangling gold necklaces and bracelets which was her standard uniform. At the best of times she looked eccentric and exotic, but in this perfectly appointed room she looked so much like an ancient hippy that Melanie could not help smiling.

'And what is amusing you?' Verenskaya asked.

'Nothing,' Melanie said quickly. 'It's just that I'm pleased to see you. I hope you've come to take me home?'

'The doctor wants you to rest a few days longer.'

'I can rest at home. If we went back in a taxi I wouldn't even need to get dressed.'

'Maybe. But you're *not* going back in a taxi. Mrs. Ransome wishes you to remain here.'

'I hate being here,' Melanie expostulated. 'I should never have come in the first place.'

'You did your duty. When you leave, you'll be able to do so with a clear conscience.' Verenskaya looked at Melanie critically. 'It was a good thing you hurt your head and not your feet. By the end of the month you will be able to dance again!'

'That must be a relief to you,' Melanie laughed. 'If anything

44

happened to stop me dancing. I don't believe you'd even bother to come and see me any more!'

'Do not try to gain my sympathy,' the old woman said brusquely. 'Knocking your head has made you even sillier than usual. We will talk no more about it. When you come back you will have to rehearse twice as hard to make up for the time you have lost.'

'I'll work night and day.'

'The day will be quite sufficient.' Verenskaya stood up. 'Go to sleep again, my child, I will come and see you tomorrow.'

Left alone, Melanie puzzled upon Mrs. Ransome's insistence that she convalesce here, for she was certain that her presence in this house was as unpleasant for her mother-in-law as it was for herself. The woman had not come to see her even once, and though the nurse said she made daily inquiries as to her health, Melanie was sure they stemmed from a desire to maintain a front, rather than from a genuine concern over her welfare. Yet she did not feel bitter about it. Her actions immediately after her marriage had been judged from a false premise, and if she were Timothy's mother she would probably feel equally bitter. She was still conjecturing over the reason for Mrs. Ransome wanting her to remain here, when the woman herself came into the room. She was as elegantly dressed as on the first occasion they had met, but this time her expression was softer and there was no bitterness in her eyes.

'Good afternoon, Melanie,' Mrs. Ransome said hesitantly. 'How are you feeling?'

'Much better, thank you. But I'm sorry to have been such a nuisance.' Melanie's voice was shaky, her body trembling so much that she was afraid it would be noticed. 'I feel an awful fraud staying in bed. I'm sure I could get up and go home.'

'There's no need to hurry away. As – as Timothy's widow you have every right to stay here.'

The unexpectedness of the remark startled Melanie into tactlessness. 'That wasn't the impression I got the last time we spoke.'

Mrs. Ransome turned red. 'I'm afraid my nephew and I were rather hasty. It was unfair of us to blame you for – for the way Timothy died. Madame Verenskaya has told me the reason why you went to Australia.'

'She *what*?'

Mrs. Ransome did not appear to notice the horror in Melanie's voice. 'Yes. She explained that you'd given your word to go on the tour and that Timothy had agreed to it. It was wrong of him – though quite understandable, of course – to have changed his mind at the last minute. It must have been difficult for you too. As you'd given your promise, you couldn't very well break it.'

'No,' Melanie said huskily. 'I couldn't. But I'm glad you understand. I hated to feel that you were – that we were enemies.'

'I could never be an enemy of the girl my son had loved.'

This was the first statement Mrs. Ransome had made that was not based on Verenskaya's distortion of the truth, and Melanie was able to respond to it without any feeling of guilt.

'I was afraid you might have been annoyed that Timothy had married me without waiting for you to come back to England.'

'I was hurt,' came the admission, 'but not surprised. I always expected Timothy would do something like that. He was very impulsive.'

'I asked him to wait until I came back from Australia, but he wouldn't.'

'I don't blame him. He probably wanted to make sure you wouldn't be stolen by some millionaire sheep farmer while you were away!' Mrs. Ransome put out her hand in a gesture of warmth. 'I hope you'll forget our first meeting. I don't blame you for his death – I assure you of that. It was a tragedy for both of us.' She sat down in the chair Verenskaya had vacated. 'I'd like to think you'll look on this house as your home. Timothy would have wanted it that way.'

'You're very kind.'

'It isn't a question of kindness. You loved Timothy and so did I, and that gives us a mutual bond.'

Once again Melanie found it impossible to comment, but Mrs. Ransome took the silence as one of emotion and changed the subject by lifting up a leather album she was holding.

'I thought you might like to see some photographs of Timothy when he was a child.' She turned to the first page. 'He was only a month old when we took that one.'

The hour that ensued was one of the most nerve-racking Melanie had ever endured. Though she had accepted that what she had felt for Timothy had been infatuation and not love, seeing all the pictures of him – which ranged from babyhood to manhood – gave her such an intense feeling of pain that she wondered whether their marriage might not, after all, have been successful if she had not discovered him making love to another girl. But as always it was a question she could not answer, and she forced herself to put it from her mind.

For the rest of the week Mrs. Ransome was more in Melanie's room than out of it, regaling her with a succession of anecdotes about Timothy as a toddler, a child and then a young man.

'You must have been very close to him,' Melanie commented one afternoon when Mrs. Ransome was again in her room with yet another album of photographs.

'Not as close as I would have liked. In the last few years he was restless and unable to settle down. I suppose that's why I turned to Gregory. He's been as much my son as Timothy, and because he's older I've talked to him more about my problems.'

'Problems?' Melanie queried, and involuntarily glanced around at her luxurious surroundings.

Interpreting the look, Mrs. Ransome sighed. 'Having money doesn't mean one hasn't problems. My husband died very suddenly, you see, and there were many things to settle. He had a partner and that made it even more difficult. But Gregory was wonderful. He coped with everything.'

Melanie decided it would be wiser to maintain a diplomatic silence. It was difficult for her to see Gregory in any sympathetic light, for despite the change in Mrs. Ransome's opinion of her, his had obviously remained unaltered. Indeed he had not even observed the elementary courtesy of sending her a get-well message, let alone coming to see her. No, as far as that supercilious man was concerned she was evidently still very much *persona non grata*.

It therefore came as a distinct surprise when, a few days later, he did put in an appearance. It was the first time since her accident that she had dressed and gone downstairs, and she had just settled herself by the fireplace in the drawing-room when he came in.

'So you're better,' he said by way of greeting.

'Yes, thank you.'

'Good.' He walked over to a table, took a cigarette from a silver box and went to stand by the fireplace.

Without making any pretence of not doing so, she watched

him, and though he must have been aware of her scrutiny he did not appear concerned by it.

He was considerably taller and broader than she had remembered, emanating not only physical strength but a forceful personality as well.

'My aunt is out, isn't she?' he asked suddenly.

'Yes. She went to the hairdresser's, but she'll be back soon.'

'Actually I wanted to talk to *you*. How long do you think your recovery is likely to take?'

She hid a smile; so this was the reason for his call! 'I'm not feigning illness so that I can stay here. Your aunt has *asked* me to stay as long as I want.'

'You're even more clever than I gave you credit for.'

'I am not being clever.'

His laugh was short and disbelieving, but Mrs. Ransome, coming into the room at the moment, took it for one of amusement.

'How nice to hear you laugh, Gregory,' she exclaimed, and looked at Melanie. 'He's usually far too serious.'

'I can't believe it,' Melanie replied. 'I find him absolutely hilarious!'

Ignoring the comment, Gregory spoke to his aunt. 'I have some papers that need your signature. If you could come into the library. . . .'

'Of course. Will you be staying for dinner?'

'Not tonight, I'm afraid. Next week, perhaps.' From the doorway he glanced at Melanie. 'If I don't see you again before you leave, I'd—'

'Of course you'll see her,' Mrs. Ransome interrupted.

With a barely perceptible shrug he walked out, leaving Melanie with the unusual but pleasurable feeling that she had won a battle.

It was some fifteen minutes before Mrs. Ransome returned, the question on her lips leaving no doubt as to her perspicacity. 'What's wrong between you and Gregory? Don't bother denying it. Just tell me the truth.'

'I don't *know* what's wrong. I think he just dislikes me for having married Timothy.'

'Did he say so?'

'He made it obvious. I gather he thinks I married Timothy for his money and am staying here to ingratiate myself with you.'

'Oh, my dear, he surely didn't say *that!*'

'Not in so many words,' Melanie conceded. 'But he thinks it.'

'I'll have to talk to him,' Mrs. Ransome said. 'He really shouldn't be so cynical. Sometimes I think being in business spoils one's sense of values.'

'Your nephew would say it probably improves them!'

'Even so he's got no right to upset you like that.'

'He didn't upset me,' Melanie said quickly. 'I don't care what he thinks. It's *your* opinion that matters.' She hesitated, and then said in a rush: '*You* don't think I married Timothy for money, do you?'

'Not since I've come to know you.'

The simplicity of the answer touched Melanie more deeply than the most highly coloured compliment, and tears filled her eyes. 'Then nothing else matters. As long as *you* think that, I couldn't care less about your nephew.'

'But I want you to like each other,' Mrs. Ransome protested. 'He's behaving very stupidly and I will tell him so. You and he are the only two people I can call my family and I want you to be friends.' She moved close and rested against Melanie's shoulder, surprising her by the fragility of her body. 'You *must* be friends,' she reiterated.

'It might not be possible,' Melanie said. 'Gregory doesn't look the sort of person who easily changes his mind.'

'He will once he gets to know you.'

'Does he ever allow himself to get close enough to people to know them?'

Mrs. Ransome sighed and sank down into a chair. 'He was very close to Timothy at one time. But they were so different in character that. . . .' Momentarily her voice trailed away. 'He wasn't always so prickly and difficult – Gregory I mean. But he had an unhappy love affair a few years ago and it changed him completely.'

'I'm surprised he's even capable of falling in love!'

'Don't let prejudice blind your judgement,' came the chiding answer. 'When you get to know him you'll find him extremely understanding and kind. If he had fallen in love with someone like *you* it would have made an enormous difference to him.'

'He'd need a far stronger character than me.'

'I wouldn't consider you particularly weak-minded!'

'Verenskaya says I'm just obstinate!'

'That sounds like the pot calling the kettle black!'

Melanie laughed. 'It is a bit. She rules the Company with a rod of iron. But we all love her. If we didn't we wouldn't stay.'

'I'm looking forward to seeing you dance,' Mrs. Ransome said. 'Madame Verenskaya says you have great potential.'

'I shouldn't believe all she tells you,' Melanie replied quickly. 'She likes to think all her ducks are swans.'

'I hope I'll have the opportunity of judging for myself.' The woman looked down at her hands. 'I suppose you're anxious to get back?'

'I am rather. I feel guilty living the life of a lotus eater.'

'But you've only been here ten days!'

'That's still a long time.'

'Not for me, my dear. I'd like you to stay longer. Having you here makes me feel so much closer to Timothy.'

As always when Mrs. Ransome mentioned her son, Melanie was filled with guilt, and though she realized that as long as she remained here she would never have any peace of mind, she knew it would be a wrench to leave; not only because of the cosseting and the luxury to which she had grown accustomed but because of her growing affection for Timothy's mother.

'Still, we don't need to worry about your leaving yet,' Mrs. Ransome continued. 'I spoke to the doctor today and he said you mustn't think of starting work for at least another two weeks.'

'I bet you pushed him into saying that!' Melanie laughed.

'Only a gentle prodding!'

'I've a feeling I'll be getting *my* prodding from Anton,' Melanie said. 'He telephoned to say he's coming to see me tomorrow – and I'm pretty sure it's not just to see how I am.'

Melanie's surmise about the reason for Anton's visit was proved correct, for after a cursory inquiry as to her well-being, he changed the subject to work.

'It's time you started again,' he said, eyeing her critically. 'This sybarite existence is making you flabby!'

'I'm as skinny as a sparrow!' she protested.

'All the more reason to start rehearsing and toughen yourself up!'

'When is our season beginning?'

'In six weeks. If we *have* one.'

50

'What do you mean?'

'Simply that I don't know if we can keep the Company going till then. There isn't a penny in the kitty.'

Melanie could not hide her astonishment. 'I know the tour wasn't a success financially, but I hadn't realized it was as bad as that.'

'It wouldn't have been bad at all if Verenskaya hadn't insisted on our dancing at every single hamlet that asked us. You can't even meet your costs with an audience of a few hundred.'

'Ballet should be available to everyone who wants it,' Melanie said defensively. 'You can't blame her for believing that.'

'I do,' he said forcefully. 'Generosity can't be given by someone who can't afford it. And *we* couldn't. Those one-night stands cost us money.'

'What's the position now?'

'I've told you,' he said sourly. 'It couldn't be worse. I was at the bank this morning trying to persuade the manager to increase our overdraft, but he absolutely refused.'

'Isn't there anything else we can do?'

'No.' He picked up a delicate green vase. 'Pretty valuable, this.'

She dismissed the remark. 'Tell me more about the company.'

'There's nothing more to tell. We're finished. The only—' he stopped, and continued to study the vase in his hand with such intensity that she knew he was focusing on it in an effort to keep silent.

'What were you going to say just now, Anton? Tell me.'

'I was thinking how you could ... how *you* are the only person who can help us.'

'Me? What could *I* do?'

He set down the vase and his eyes moved to the Renoir over the mantelpiece. 'As Timothy's widow you're entitled to his estate. And if *this* place is anything to go by, he should be worth a packet.'

The remark was so crude and unexpected that she was speechless. But when at last she found her voice, it was icy with anger.

'You're out of your mind if you think I'd take anything from Timothy's estate.'

'You'd be out of your mind if you didn't!'

'I was never his wife – not in the real sense – and I wouldn't touch a penny of his. It would be cheating.'

'You're crazy!' Anton flung his arms wide. 'If you don't care about your own future as a dancer, at least think of the Company. It's Verenskaya's life.'

This last statement – undeniably true – robbed Melanie of her anger. Much as she disliked what Anton had said, she knew he was not saying it for self-gain; for a dancer of his repute would be welcomed by any other company, both here and in America. No, it was Verenskaya who would suffer most, and this made it imperative that she do everything in her power to help.

'How much do we need?'

'Ten thousand pounds.'

'That's a fortune!'

'Relatively speaking. If this house is anything to go by, Timothy was worth a packet. That Renoir alone is worth at least twenty thousand.'

'Don't!' she said sharply. 'I hate it when you talk like that.'

'We haven't time to be delicate,' he replied, and bent over her. 'Didn't Timothy ever discuss his position with you?'

'No.'

'But you must have known what he had.'

She shook her head. 'We didn't talk about it. He worked in the family business – that's all I know.'

'You mean to say he never spoke to you about money?' She shook her head again and he continued: 'Even so, he must have made some provision for you. You'll have to find out.' Her expression was one of such distaste that it seemed to provoke him to further anger. 'Damn it, Melanie, stop looking so priggish and horrified. I can't stand all this squeamishness about discussing money. It's so bourgeois.'

'I never pretended I was a sophisticate,' she retorted.

'Well, at least stop acting like a *baby!* If you're too squeamish to ask your mother-in-law, then find out who his solicitor was and ask *him!*'

'That's just as bad.'

'What's bad about trying to help the Company?' Anton shouted. 'Or don't you care any more?'

'Of course I care.'

'Then do something about it! We've got to get money and you're the only one who can do it.'

There was a long silence, broken only by the hissing of an ember as it flew out of the fire and died on the hearth.

'Very well,' she said at last, 'I'll see what I can do.'

'Thank goodness for that.' The words were spoken quietly, but there was a warmth in Anton's eyes that reminded her of the last intimate discussion they had had, and she knew without having to be told that he still felt the same way about her.

'I'm sorry I lost my temper,' he went on, 'but these past ten days have been a nightmare.' He drew her hand upwards and had just pressed it to his lips when the door opened and Gregory came in.

'I hope I'm not interrupting,' he said coldly.

Scarlet-cheeked, she pulled her hand free. 'Not at all.'

Quickly she introduced the two men, aware of the contrast between Anton in tight black trousers and black sweater, and Gregory in an impeccably cut grey suit.

'Are you also a dancer with the Company?' Gregory asked as he moved to the sideboard and picked up a whisky decanter.

'Yes.'

'I've often wondered what prompts a man to take up ballet as a career.'

'The same motivation that prompts a woman,' Anton replied. 'A need to express emotion by dance.'

'Indeed?'

'Indeed,' came the answer in Anton's dryest tone.

Though he must have known he was being mocked, Gregory gave no indication of it and lifted a glass. 'Would you care for a drink?'

'No, thanks.' Anton leaned forward and deliberately raised Melanie's hand again and pressed it to his lips. 'Call me the moment you have any news!' he said and, with a cool nod to the man by the sideboard, he went out.

Gregory Ransome pointed the decanter in Melanie's direction, and when she shook her head, he poured himself a drink and, glass in hand, came to sit in an armchair opposite her.

'Is your friend a good dancer?'

'One of the best. Haven't you heard of him? He's very well known.'

'I don't go to the ballet often. What did you say his name was?'

'Anton Marek.'

Gregory Ransome sipped his drink. 'I suppose he's anxious for you to start work again?'

Seeing his words as the opening she was looking for, she said quickly: 'I'm not sure there'll be any work for me to start. That's one of the reasons Anton came to see me.' She felt her cheeks grow warm with embarrassment but determinedly forced herself to continue. 'We're in trouble – at least the Company is. If we can't find the money to keep us going for another six weeks until the season starts, we'll have to disband.'

Only by a slight movement of one dark eyebrow did the man indicate he had heard her, and knowing that if she did not speak now she would never speak again, she blurted out: 'What was Timothy's position?'

The whisky slopped in the glass. 'I beg your pardon?'

'Timothy's position,' she stammered. 'I want to know what it was.'

'In life or in death?' he asked icily.

Perspiration dampened her palms, but she refused to be put off by his obvious disgust at her question. 'I've a right to know, whether you like it or not. He never spoke about the future. It didn't – it didn't seem necessary. Neither of us thought that. . . .' She stopped to moisten her lips, only forced into continuing by the knowledge of what it would do to Verenskaya if the Company had to disband. 'Now that Timothy . . . what I really want to know is my financial position.'

'Ah!' It was a satisfied sound. 'I was wondering when you would get around to that. A woman and money are never divorced for long!'

'I'm not asking for myself,' she said angrily. 'The Company's in trouble and needs help.'

'Spare me the excuses.'

'It's the truth!'

'I doubt if you know the meaning of the word.'

'How dare you!' Temper made her forget her embarrassment. 'From the moment we met you've been abominably rude.'

'I'm sorry you find the truth insulting.'

'Your idea of truth doesn't happen to be mine.'

'I suppose you expect me to believe you didn't marry my cousin for his money?'

The effrontery of the remark staggered her. 'That's the most disgusting thing you could have said,' she choked. 'You've no right to say that, no right at all.' She searched in her pocket for her handkerchief and when she couldn't find it, she rubbed the tears from her eyes with the back of her hand.

'Save your histrionics for my aunt,' he said calmly. 'They're wasted on me. I happen to know exactly what Timothy spent on you – down to the last penny.'

'What business is that of yours? You weren't his keeper.'

'More's the pity. He wouldn't have married *you* if I had been.'

She jumped to her feet and walked over to the window, putting herself as far away from him as she could. 'I don't intend to have a slanging match with you, Mr. Ransome. I'm sure you'd win. I just asked you a question and I want an answer. What is my financial position?'

'Exactly the same as if you were single.'

She swung round. 'That can't be true!'

'I assure you it is. Timothy had nothing to leave.'

'But the business . . . it was a family one.'

'He had no part of it.' Gregory Ransome set his glass down on the table beside him and came across the room until he was so close that she could have put out a hand and touched him. 'I'm telling you the truth. You'd be wise to accept it. The little money Timothy had, he spent on you.'

'I'm going to find out for myself.'

'You may do as you wish. The only thing I'd like you to bear in mind is the way my aunt feels about you. She's become attached to you since you've been staying here and I'd like you to at least try and spare her illusions. She has suffered enough already. To realize Timothy married a mercenary little—'

The slap of her hand on the side of his face stunned him into silence, and before he could say another word she stepped past him and ran out.

Upstairs in her bedroom she paced the floor, too angry to relax, too hurt to do anything except re-enact the scene that had just taken place. She had never had any doubt as to how Gregory Ransome regarded her, but not until now had she realized the depth of his dislike. Momentarily she wondered whether he had told her the truth about Timothy's position, but almost at once she dismissed the doubt; he was too clever to lie when it could be so easily found out. But where did that leave her now? She had promised Anton she would help Verenskaya, and no matter what happened she did not intend to break her word.

Backwards and forwards she walked; from the window to the door, from the bed to the bureau, but the more she pondered on the problem the more incoherent were her thoughts, and at last she picked up the telephone beside her bed and dialled Anton's flat. He answered so quickly that she guessed he had been waiting for her call, and briefly she told him of her conversation with Gregory Ransome.

'He's lying,' Anton said immediately she had finished. 'You must talk to your mother-in-law.'

'I can't. Not even for Verenskaya's sake.'

'Then we're finished.'

Dramatic though the words were, they were none the less true, and she sank down on the bed. The ring on her finger caught in the coverlet and she twisted her hand to set it free. Although she had found the diamond too cumbersome to wear regularly, she had put it on for her visit to Mrs. Ransome and had been wearing it ever since. Now, as she looked at it, she suddenly had an idea.

'What about selling my engagement ring?' she said into the receiver. 'I'm sure it would fetch enough to keep us going for a few weeks, and it would give you time to try and raise more money.'

'It's better than nothing,' Anton replied. 'I've already hocked everything of my own that's movable. Have you got anything else?'

'A string of pearls Timothy gave me. But I don't know what they're worth.'

'Where are they?'

'At the flat. I'll be leaving here in the morning and I'll give them to you.'

'Fine. But how come the sudden decision to go?'

'I'm getting flabby from resting!' she retorted, and hung up on him.

During dinner that evening Melanie announced her intention of leaving in the morning and was unprepared for the hurt look on Mrs. Ransome's face.

'I thought you'd be staying much longer. The doctor said—'

'What you wanted him to,' Melanie interrupted with a smile. 'But I'm perfectly fit and I must start rehearsing again.'

'Why can't you continue living here? When you're with me, I feel Timothy is so close.'

Mention of Timothy made Melanie realize the unpracticality of the suggestion. The idea of living permanently in this beautiful house was a temping one, but if she did so she would have to maintain the pretence of a heartbroken widow, and that would be impossible for her.

'Verenskaya would be upset if I didn't go back,' she murmured. 'I've always lived with her.'

'But you're not a child any longer – and you *are* my daughter-in-law.'

Melaine racked her brains to find another reason. 'It might be possible if I were doing any ordinary job with regular hours. But I never get back till midnight after a show and when we're rehearsing I have all sorts of odd hours.'

'What does that matter?'

'Quite a lot in a house like this. It all runs so smoothly that I'd disrupt everything.'

Mrs. Ransome carefully folded her napkin and set it beside her plate. 'I'm sure it would work if you wanted it to. But I understand your reasons for refusing. For me, Timothy will always be alive, but you're young and you want to try and make a new life for yourself. I don't blame you for that – it's the right thing to do – and if you lived here it would make that difficult.'

Wondering what Mrs. Ransome would say if she knew Timothy was already a memory that no longer held pain, Melanie said quickly: 'I'll come and see you as often as you wish.'

'I hope so. But don't ever wait for an invitation. I want you to think of my house as your home.'

CHAPTER FIVE

WITH mixed feelings Melanie returned to the Bayswater flat the next day. It was a far cry from the elegance of the house she had just left, and she was irritably aware of the shabby furniture and the clutter of photographs and knick-knacks covering the innumerable tables dotted around the living-room.

Anton was already waiting there for her and she hurried into her bedroom and returned with a small leather case.

He lifted the lid and stared at the pearls in surprise. 'I'll take a bet *these* aren't cultured.'

'They can't be real.'

'We'll soon find out.' He slipped the box into his pocket. 'I've already fixed to show them to someone in Hatton Garden. I'll let you know what I can get for them.'

Alone in the flat Melanie wandered restlessly from room to room. Unbidden, Gregory Ransome came into her mind and her depression dissolved into anger. How disgracefully he had behaved yesterday, and how greatly he had misjudged her. If only she could tell him the truth and make him retract every one of the bitter accusations he had flung at her. She was so engrossed in recalling his biting criticisms that she was startled when the telephone rang, almost afraid that she might – by some strange mischance – have conjured up a call from him.

But it was Anton, his voice high and jubilant. 'You'll never believe it, Melanie, but for the first time in years we're solvent!'

'How much did you get?'

'Ten thousand pounds.'

'You're joking!'

'I was never more serious in my life. But I need a letter from you authorizing the sale. Can you do it right away?'

'Yes.'

'Then I'll come back for it.'

In the living-room she searched for paper and pen, her thoughts racing as she tried to absorb what she had just heard. Ten thousand pounds! It was incredible. Remembering what Gregory had said about Timothy's financial position she wondered where he had found so much money. Here was one further instance of how little she had known the man she had married, and the knowledge increased the depression she had been fighting against all day.

She had just finished the letter for Anton when he returned to the flat, his sallow skin flushed with excitement.

'Isn't it wonderful?' he exclaimed, giving her a hug. 'Ten thousand pounds! It'll keep us going till the Season starts.'

'You'd better make sure we remain solvent after that,' she replied. 'I've nothing else to sell.'

He sobered instantly. 'You don't regret it, do you? I mean it's a lot of money for you to give up.'

'I don't care about the money. It's just that I never realized Timothy had spent so much on me.'

'He could afford it. I told you that before, but you wouldn't believe me.'

'I still don't. I'm sure Gregory Ransome wasn't lying.'

'Then where did Timothy get the cash? If we're getting ten thousand on a second-hand price, it must have cost him half as much again to buy it.'

'Do you mind if we change the subject?' she said wearily. 'Talking won't help me find the answer.'

'It would if you spoke to his mother. I'm sure Ransome's trying to do you out of an inheritance.'

'For heaven's sake, be quiet!' She walked over to the desk and picked up the letter she had written for him. He took it, glanced at it briefly and put it in his pocket.

'You're an angel, Melanie. When Verenskaya finds out—'

'Must you tell her? Can't you pretend you got the money from someone else?'

'What money?' a guttural voice asked.

They both swung round to see Verenskaya in the doorway.

'What money?' she repeated. 'Are you trying to hide something from me?'

Anton glanced at Melanie, shrugged and then looked at Verenskaya. 'I've sold Melanie's engagement ring and necklace. The money will keep us going till the Season starts.'

'I won't accept it,' Verenskaya interrupted.

'You can't turn down ten thousand pounds,' Anton said decisively. 'It's just what we need.'

Verenskaya stared at him incredulously. 'Did you say ten thousand pounds?'

'Yes.'

She sank into a red-plush armchair, its vivid colour heightening the whiteness of her face. 'So much money. . . . No. . . . No, I can't take it. It's a wonderful gesture, Melanie, but it's *your* security.'

'The Company is *my* security. What does it matter about selling my jewellery so long as it keeps us going? You said yourself a career is the only thing worth having.'

'You don't need the Company for that. You're good enough to get a job with the Royal Ballet.'

'But I need *you*.' Melanie knelt by Verenskaya's side. 'And you *are* the Company. No matter how much I give you I could never repay you for the way you took care of me when I was a child.'

'I don't want repayment for that. Such a word is wrong between us. You're like my daughter.'

'Then give me a chance of behaving like one and take the money.'

'No,' Verenskaya said. 'If we can't maintain ourselves by work, I should close down.'

'We'll be solvent once *I'm* financial director,' Anton intervened.

'Who says *you're* in charge?'

'You agreed to let me take control if I found the money to keep us going.'

'I said it because I never thought you'd succeed!'

Anton gave a wolfish smile. 'Well, I *have* succeeded, and I intend to keep you to your word. I'll guarantee that within a year we'll be able to repay Melanie every penny.'

'If only I could believe that,' Verenskaya said slowly.

'You can.' He moved to the door. 'I'll just finish this transaction and come back.'

'We will dine out and celebrate.' Verenskaya sprang to her feet, once more full of confidence. 'There's a new Russian restaurant – you must both come there as my guests.'

Anton glanced at Melanie, started to say something and then, seeing the warning in her eyes, stopped. 'Very well, Madame,' he said gallantly. 'Melanie and I will be delighted to be your guests.'

The following day Melanie returned to the theatre and from then on rehearsed daily for six or seven hours, returning to the flat in the evening too tired to do anything except have a light meal and fall into bed. It had been easier to become accustomed to being waited on than to become accustomed to waiting on herself, and time and again she thought back to the luxury of the Belgravia house, and wished that her conscience had allowed her to accept Mrs. Ransome's offer of a permanent home.

For the first few weeks she deliberately did not go to see her mother-in-law, determined to give herself a chance to settle back into her old life before laying herself open to temptation again, but on the third Sunday – her only free time during the whole week – she went to see Mrs. Ransome, experiencing a strange sense of homecoming as she crossed the marble hall and entered the warm, flower-filled drawing-room.

Mrs. Ransome seemed more tired and older than Melanie remembered, though she was not sure whether she was imagining it or whether absence had made her more perceptive. Yet her mother-in-law made no reference to being ill, and fussed happily over the tea-tray, plying Melanie with scones and crumpets and muttering about her thinness.

'I can't wait for your season to start. I'm longing to see you dance.'

'Why not come and watch a rehearsal?'

'Could I really? Do tell me when.'

'Next Tuesday if you like. We'll be dancing at the theatre.'

'Is it like an actual performance?'

'Sometimes it's even more exciting,' Melanie grinned. 'We haven't had a rehearsal yet where Verenskaya hasn't threatened to murder someone!'

By the time Tuesday arrived Melanie had forgotten her invitation, and not until she walked off the stage at the end of one of her solos and saw Mrs. Ransome talking to Verenskaya did she remember it and hurry over to greet her.

'Well, what did you think of it?' she asked eagerly.

'It was very interesting . . . very exciting.' There was such a tremor in Mrs. Ransome's voice that Melanie looked at her anxiously.

'Would you like to sit down? You sound tired.'

'I'll arrange for some tea,' Verenskaya interrupted, and hurried away.

'I don't want any tea,' Mrs. Ransome murmured, and Melanie saw she was clasping her handbag so tightly that the knuckles were white. 'I'm going home.'

'But the rehearsal isn't finished.'

'I can't stay – I'm too upset.'

'Why?' Melanie asked. 'What's wrong?'

Mrs. Ransome avoided her gaze. 'Do you need me to tell you? Don't you know?'

'About what?'

'The money. Madame Verenskaya told me about the money you gave her.' Mrs. Ransome's voice broke. 'How could you have sold *anything* my son gave you? Didn't the jewellery have any sentimental value – any meaning to you, or were you only concerned with what price you could get?'

Distressed at the woman's obvious hurt, and angry at Verenskaya's indiscretion, Melanie gave the first answer she could think of. 'Of course I cared about the ring – and the necklace too. But I had no choice. The Company was in trouble and I was the only one who could help.'

'You could have asked me.'

'I didn't like to. I thought you'd think I was . . .' embarrassed, Melanie could not go on.

'That I'd think you were behaving as Gregory had anticipated?' Mrs. Ransome broke the silence.

'Yes.'

'If you'd loved my son you would have come to me for help – gone to *anyone* so long as it would have stopped you from selling the things he'd bought you.'

'I can't feel sentimental about jewellery,' Melanie said desperately. 'Please try and understand.'

'I understand a lot of things.' Anger no longer gave strength to the weak voice and it was shaky and thin again, as though every word were an effort. 'I never believed the things Gregory said about you, but now . . .'

Tears filled Melanie's eyes. 'Because I sold Timothy's gifts doesn't mean I didn't care about him.'

'It wasn't only the fact that you sold them – it was accepting them in the first place – encouraging him to spend money he didn't have.'

The accusation was so like Gregory's that anger overwhelmed Melanie's normal reticence. 'You've no right to accuse me of being a gold-digger! I knew nothing about Timothy's affairs. I married him because I loved him, not because of what he had or what he could give me.'

'Melanie!' Anton called directly behind her. 'You're due on next!'

She swung round. 'I'll be with you in a moment.' She turned back to speak to her mother-in-law, but the woman was nowhere to be seen. With an exclamation Melanie pushed through the group of dancers and ran down the corridor. But this too was deserted and she returned to the stage.

As she took up her position with Anton she puzzled over Mrs. Ransome's remarks. When Gregory had called her a gold-digger she had believed his accusation to be based on a dislike due to snobbery; but her mother-in-law's statement could not be dismissed for the same reason, and she was reluctantly forced to admit that something – though she could not even guess what it was – had given the two people closest to Timothy an erroneous impression of her.

Another meeting with Mrs. Ransome was the only way to find out what this was, and she determined to go and see her immediately after dinner; if she delayed it, she might not pluck up the courage to go at all.

It was only as she stood outside the door of the Belgravia House at nine o'clock that evening that her courage ebbed, and with her hand raised to the bell she hesitated, wondering if it would not be wiser in the long run to cut her losses and never see Mrs. Ransome again. Yet to do that would be the coward's way out. She had not married Timothy for his money and she had come here to try and prove it.

With fast-beating heart she rang the bell, then waited as the door opened and the butler, with a welcoming smile, bade her come in.

'The family are in the drawing-room,' he explained as he took her coat.

'The family?'

'Mr. Gregory.'

With an effort Melanie controlled her dismay. It had been hard enough deciding to face her mother-in-law again without having to meet Gregory too! But it was too late to do anything about it now, and momentarily she held on to the door knob, summing up her courage before she turned it and entered the room.

'Melanie – thank goodness you came!'

The warmth of Mrs. Ransome's greeting was so unexpected that Melanie stopped abruptly, not sure what to say. 'I had to come,' she stammered. 'I wanted to – to explain – to try and make you understand that—'

'You've nothing to explain, my dear. Nothing at all. I'm the one who should do the explaining.' Trembling hands drew Melanie close. 'I don't know how to apologize for what I said this afternoon. It was a terrible mistake.'

Still bemused, Melanie glanced at Gregory, but Mrs. Ransome intercepted the look.

'I suppose you're wondering why I'm not upset any more? Well, you can thank Gregory. Though you can blame him too. If he'd told me the truth in the first place, none of this would have happened.'

Once again Melanie looked at the man by the fireplace, and this time he gave an imperceptible shake of his head, as though warning her to be careful of what she said.

'I've just told my aunt that *I* was the one who gave Timothy the money to buy your engagement ring and necklace.'

The remark was so obviously untrue – in view of his previous conversations with her – that she knew he had said it only to set Mrs. Ransome's mind at rest. But rest from what? The answer came from the woman herself.

'It was silly of me to have jumped to the conclusion I did. But when someone's been a gambler then you're always afraid they'll start again – even though they've promised they won't.'

With an effort Melanie gathered that Mrs. Ransome was referring to Timothy. 'He never gambled with me,' she said quickly. 'I didn't even know he liked it.'

'Thank goodness for that.' There was unutterable relief in the reply. 'When Madame Verenskaya told me how much your jewellery had fetched I immediately thought that Timothy had got the money from gambling. I mean he couldn't have got it from his allowance because we deliberately gave him a small one to make sure he didn't have anything to gamble with. I'd no idea he'd borrowed the money from Gregory. So when I learned the value of the ring and the necklace . . .'

'Timothy *never* discussed money with me,' Melanie said firmly, determined once and for all to clear her name. 'When I met him he was just another man who wanted to take me out. We didn't talk about his work and I didn't even know what he did beyond the fact that he said he was in the family business.'

'You've nothing to apologize for,' Mrs. Ransome said. 'If I'd been in England when you'd met, Timothy wouldn't have had to borrow anything from Gregory. I would gladly have given him what he wanted. After all, it was his own inheritance. If he – if he were alive today. . . .' Unable to go on, she caught Melanie's hand, clutching it in a tight grip as though by doing so she could force back her self-control. 'You must give me the name of the jeweller who bought your ring,' she continued huskily. 'That's the first thing we must get back.'

'It's too late,' Melanie said quickly. The last thing in the world that she wanted was to have the ring returned to her and be in Mrs. Ransome's debt for such an amount. 'It's already been sold.'

'So soon?'

'Yes,' Melanie lied. 'That's why I got such a good price.

Because there was a customer who wanted it.'

'Well, at least we can get back the pearls.'

'They've gone too.'

'Then I'll replace them.'

'I'd rather you didn't.' She hesitated, searching for an excuse. 'It wouldn't be the same – and it would only remind me . . .'

Mrs. Ransome sighed. 'I do wish you'd come to me in the first place. . . . If you ever need anything again . . .' Suddenly she gave a smile. 'But how silly of me. You'll have Timothy's share of the business now, and you won't be short of money again. I took it for granted you'd have known that already.'

'No,' Melanie said slowly, and looked directly at Gregory. 'I knew nothing of Timothy's affairs.'

'Then Gregory will tell you. I should have done so myself, but–' her voice broke and she lowered her head.

'There's no need for you to talk about anything,' Gregory Ransome said to his aunt, his voice so gentle that Melanie wondered at it. 'I'll see that Melanie knows all she wants to.'

Furious at such two-faced behaviour, Melanie glared at him. 'Why don't you tell me right now? Then we needn't discuss it again.'

Gregory looked at her. With his aunt to one side of him, he was able to let his expression speak for itself, and it held the same contempt with which he had always regarded her. But when he spoke his voice held exactly the same tone as before.

'An excellent idea. Tell me what you want to know.'

'Everything. But keep it simple. I haven't got a business brain.'

The venom in his glance gave her a feeling of triumph, and she sat back in the chair and waited for him to begin.

'Ransome Engineering was started by my uncle and Herbert Fenwick and they both had equal shares in it. My uncle put *his* shares into a family trust but left ten per cent directly to Timothy, which Timothy inherited when my uncle died.'

'It was that ten per cent which caused the trouble,' Mrs. Ransome intervened. 'If my husband had guessed what Herbert wanted to do he'd have kept all the shares in the trust. When I think of the trouble it caused, I–'

'There's no need to get upset,' Gregory said calmly. 'There's nothing Herbert can do now.'

As she listened to Gregory's soothing tones Melanie instinctively knew he was hiding something and determination made her direct her next question to her mother-in-law.

'What sort of trouble did Mr. Fenwick try to cause?'

'He wanted to change the whole concept of the business. Even before my husband died he was pressing him to bring in automation, but John wouldn't agree to it. Then when he died, Herbert started to put pressure on to Timothy.'

Melanie was now so out of her depth that she knew it was useless to pretend she understood what was being said, and she looked helplessly at the man sitting at the opposite side of the fireplace.

'Fenwick isn't quite the bogey-man my aunt makes out,' Gregory said. 'From a business point of view what he wanted to do was highly practical.'

'How can you say that!' Mrs. Ransome burst out.

'Because it's true. If Uncle John hadn't died he'd have been forced to realize it sooner or later.'

Gregory looked at Melanie again. 'Fenwick knew that automation would increase output by fifty per cent, though it would also have meant making twenty-five per cent of the staff redundant. It was for that reason that my uncle wouldn't agree to it.'

'John looked on the business as a family concern,' Mrs. Ransome intervened. 'He didn't want to fire anyone.'

'My uncle would have been forced to have given in eventually,' Gregory said, ignoring the remark. 'If he hadn't, he would have been out-priced by his competitors. But he died before anything could be decided.'

'That's when Herbert offered to buy Timothy's personal shares,' Mrs. Ransome spoke again.

'Why?' Melanie asked.

'Because the extra ten per cent would have given him control. But luckily Timothy refused to sell.'

'It wasn't very practical.' Melanie spoke automatically, not realizing – until she had done so – that her words were an implied criticism of Timothy's actions.

'It wasn't wise from a business point of view,' Mrs. Ransome agreed tremulously, 'but Timothy wouldn't sell because he knew I wanted to follow my husband's wishes for as long as possible. And while Herbert didn't have Timothy's extra ten per cent he couldn't outvote me.'

Melanie looked at Gregory. He was leaning back in his armchair, his face expressionless. The blackness of his dinner-jacket echoed the blackness of his hair, serving in some strange way to also heighten the strength of his features, and making him look even more arrogant and commanding than she had remembered. No need to wonder on whose side *he* would have been when it came to a vote! Success and money – no matter what personal relationship they destroyed – would obviously outweigh any other criteria he might have.

Mischief prompted her to ask him the question which tact would normally have forbidden. 'And whose side were you on, Gregory?'

Imperturbably he flicked ash from his cigar into the fire. 'I have no say in Ransome Engineering. I run my own company.'

'Gregory's in property,' his aunt said. 'John wanted him to join the firm, but he wouldn't. Even as a boy he was obstinate! Said we'd already done enough for him and that he felt he should make his own way in the world.'

'Commendable sentiments,' Melanie said dryly.

'*You* should know,' Mrs. Ransome replied. 'You're as obstinate as he is!'

'No, I'm not!'

'Of course you are. Obstinate and proud. But all that's over now. From now on you've got nothing to worry about financially.'

Melanie did her best to keep all emotion out of her face. Everything her mother-in-law was saying was a complete denial of all that Gregory had said to her earlier. She remembered how forcibly she had disagreed with Anton when he had said Gregory had been lying, and though she would happily have wished to believe it, she instinctively felt that what Gregory was saying *now* was the lie – and that he was only uttering it because his aunt was present. Only by speaking to him on his own would it be possible to learn the truth about Timothy.

The opportunity was given to her sooner than she had anticipated, for suddenly the colour ebbed from Mrs. Ransome's face and she fell back against the settee.

Instantly Gregory was by her side. 'I knew I shouldn't have let you hear all this. It isn't good for you to talk about the past. You must go to bed.' He glanced at Melanie. 'I'll take my aunt up to her room. Please wait for me.'

He bent forward, and to Melanie's amazement lifted his aunt

67

bodily into his arms. At the doorway he paused for her to turn her head in Melanie's direction.

'Do you forgive me for what I said to you at the theatre this afternoon?'

'I don't even remember it,' Melanie said staunchly, and kept the smile on her face until the door had closed.

Alone at last, she nervously paced the room, knowing there would have to be a showdown when Gregory returned, yet dreading what it might reveal. So immersed was she in her thoughts that she did not hear him come back, and only as he spoke did she swing round from the window to see that he had returned to his chair at the fireplace.

Still remaining where she was, she spoke to him. 'Don't you think you owe me an explanation?' He said nothing and after a few seconds' silence she spoke again, her voice louder. 'Either you were lying when you told me Timothy's position, or else Mrs. Ransome isn't telling me the truth. And I don't intend to leave this house until I find out.'

'I didn't think you would,' he said slowly, and then said no more.

Anger flared in her and she glanced round the room, unconsciously repeating Anton's gesture. 'If Ransome Engineeering can afford to keep my mother-in-law in this house, then ten per cent shouldn't be too bad for me!' She waited, expecting her outburst – deliberately made to provoke him – to arouse him. But still he said nothing, and with a sigh she came and sat down on the settee. 'Please tell me the truth. Tell me why you lied to me.'

'I've never lied to you. Timothy had a small allowance to stop him from gambling. I didn't tell you that because there was no point. But it was perfectly true that he didn't have enough money to buy you any jewellery.'

'Mrs. Ransome said she loaned it to him.'

'You're too intelligent to believe that, surely?'

Mortified, she nodded. 'Then where did he get the money?'

'Do you need to ask?' There was such fury in his voice that she was taken aback. 'Don't waste your time playing the innocent with me. You know damn well where he got the cash from.'

'I don't! And if you refuse to tell me, I'll ask your aunt.'

'You'll do nothing of the sort!' He jumped up and took a

step towards her, and she felt a stab of fear at the look of hatred on his face. 'Don't you think you've done enough harm already without trying to kill my aunt with shock?'

'Kill her?' Melanie echoed, astonished.

'Her heart's bad. Any worry or upset could give her another coronary.'

'I see.' There was a pause. 'Then I'm afraid *you* will have to answer my questions.'

'I'm afraid I will.'

To her surprise there was not the anger she had expected in his voice, only a sadness that was repeated in the expression on his face. No longer was it hard and tense, and the firm mouth had softened so that she could appreciate the curve of the upper lip and the full sensuality of the lower one. Taking a small crocodile case from his breast pocket, he took out a cigar, nipped off the end with a gold cutter and slowly lit it. The flame, so close to his eyes, reflected the same sadness as the rest of his face, and she knew that though he found it difficult to tell her the truth, it was not because of anger, but because the truth was hurtful to him.

'Timothy got the money to buy your jewellery by selling his shares to Herbert Fenwick.'

It took an instant for the words to sink in, but when they did she stared at him disbelievingly. 'But his mother said—'

'My aunt doesn't know the truth. If she found out ... I wouldn't like to think what the shock could do to her.'

'But *why*?' Melanie asked. 'Why did he do it?'

'Because of you!'

She ignored the reply. 'He wouldn't have sold out! I can't believe it. He'd have known his mother would find out ... what the shock would do to her. ... No, it isn't true. Timothy may have been – may have been wild, but he wasn't – he wasn't bad.'

'I don't think you realized your power over him.' Gregory's voice was still low and less harsh than usual. 'He was good-looking and had many girl-friends, but he was always unsure of himself. When you came into his life he was determined to do everything he could to keep you.'

'I asked him for nothing. What he gave me, he gave because *he* wanted to – perhaps because *he* found it necessary.' She stopped, seeing from his expression that it was a waste of time trying to make him see how badly he was misjudging her. Deliberately she changed the subject. 'But your aunt will find out sooner or later – about the shares, I mean. Mr. Fenwick won't want to waste time before putting his plans into effect.'

'I've managed to persuade him to wait a little while: to at least give my aunt a chance to get over the shock of Timothy's death.'

'You must have very persuasive powers!'

'I have,' came the cold reply, and though she was convinced there was more behind his words than he had said she knew he had no intention of telling her.

'Is there anything else you wish to know?' he went on, 'or is the catechism over?'

Again temper prompted her next question. 'How much did Mr. Fenwick give Timothy for his shares?'

'Fifteen thousand pounds.'

Melanie thought carefully for a moment. Gregory's answer had surprised her and instinctively she felt there was something wrong with the amount he had mentioned. Fifteen thousand pounds for ten per cent of the company. She glanced round the elegant drawing-room with a more appraising glance than she had ever given it before, seeing not only the Renoir and the exquisite French furniture, but also the small Matisse over the bureau and the jade figurines carefully displayed in a pair of cabinets.

'Does Mrs. Ransome own everything in this house?' she asked.

'Yes.'

'Then it's even more ridiculous than I thought!'

The man looked at her in astonishment. 'You'll have to be more explicit, I'm afraid.'

'Well, count it up yourself. Your aunt must be very rich. Extremely so if this house is anything to go by. I'm assuming that the money has all come from the family business, which means that ten per cent of it must have been worth far more than fifteen thousand pounds. It doesn't make sense that Timothy would have sold his shares for that amount – particularly as they'd have given Mr. Fenwick the control he wanted so badly.'

From the startled look on Gregory Ransome's face she knew it was a thought that had never struck him before, and she watched as he rubbed the side of his cheek with one long, slender finger.

'You're not as naïve as you first wanted me to think,' he said. 'I was mad not to have thought of it myself. But when Fenwick told me it came as such a shock – and so soon after Timothy's death that I just accepted it. ... I never thought about the actual price.'

'Then you aren't as businesslike as you led *me* to believe!' she retorted, and had the pleasure of seeing him change colour.

'It still doesn't affect my cousin's reason for wanting the money!' came the reply.

'For heaven's sake, can't you ever admit you're wrong!'

'About you? No, I can't.'

He jumped up and began to pace the room, his muttered words telling that he had already relegated her remarks into the back of his mind and was concentrating on something which he considered of far more importance: Timothy's shares.

'The only reason he would have sold them for so little is because he didn't want my aunt to find out. ... No, that doesn't make sense either. Once Fenwick had control, the truth would have come out the minute he started altering things at the factory.' There were further mutterings which were too softly spoken to be heard. 'Then why did he do it?' This time the question was almost a shout. 'There's got to be a reason.'

'Perhaps Timothy wasn't very good at business,' Melanie said.

'He wasn't,' came the terse reply. 'But he knew the value of things and he could always raise more money when he was at university than any of his friends! No, there must be some special reason.'

'Have you gone through his papers? Perhaps there's a clue there.'

Gregory shook his head. 'I doubt if Timothy kept any papers. He was pretty haphazard about that.'

'It might still be worth going to his flat.'

'Haven't *you* been back there yet?'

'No.' Sensing that he was waiting for her to continue, she added: 'I couldn't bring myself to go ... it was too painful.'

He frowned. 'It's not a bad idea to have a look there, though. I think I'll go over myself. There might be some papers lying around. It's a long shot but the only one I can think of.' His frown deepened. 'You won't say anything about this to my aunt, will you?'

'You already told me why I shouldn't,' she said icily. 'Credit me with *some* feeling even though you do think I'm a gold-digger!'

His look showed no embarrassment. 'I will arrange for you to receive an allowance each month.'

'That won't be necessary. If Timothy had nothing to leave, then I have nothing to get. You needn't feel you have to bribe me to keep my mouth shut!'

'I wasn't thinking of it as a bribe. I was merely thinking of my aunt. She has excellent taste in clothes, and if you intend to keep on visiting her – as you obviously do – then you'll have to come here wearing the sort of things she'd expect you to be able to afford.'

The pompous words made her laugh. 'How old-fashioned you are, Cousin Gregory! As I'm not the sort of wife anyone would have expected Timothy to marry, I honestly don't think that it matters if I wear haute couture or Marks and Sparks! Anyway, I happen to credit your aunt with more sense than you do. She won't expect me to follow fashion. If I did it's the one thing that *would* make her think I was behaving oddly.'

'I'll still arrange for you to have an allowance.'

'How?'

'That's my business,' he said coldly.

'You mean you'd pay me yourself?' she grinned. 'That's almost tempting me into accepting your offer!' She paused and waited for the look of triumph to appear on his face before adding: 'If you do send me one single penny, I'll go straight to Mrs. Ransome and tell her the whole story.'

His expression changed, the triumph replaced by a sardonic lift of his eyebrows. 'You really will go to extremes to show me how unworldly you are! Well, you've made the point. But if you do want money at any time, come to me. I don't want my aunt upset in any way.'

'Thanks for your offer, but I'd never take anything from you. I'd rather scrub floors!' She stood up. 'Anyway, Anton's running the financial side of the Company now, so I'm sure we'll manage.'

'You really are concerned about the ballet, aren't you?' he said with unexpected surprise.

'It's been my life.' She moved to the door. 'And now, if you don't mind, I'll go home.'

'There's no need.' Without answering, he held the door open for her, waited as she put on her coat and then preceded her outside. She shivered slightly as she felt the cold air, and dug her hands deeper into her pockets.

'You're not dressed warmly enough,' he remarked. 'You should have put on a fur.'

'Ballet dancers' allowances don't run to furs!'

'I'm surprised you didn't—' he hesitated and then said deliberately, 'that you didn't get Timothy to buy you one.'

She stopped on the pavement and looked up at him. In the darkness he seemed taller than usual, towering above her like a sceptre. 'If you go on making snide remarks at me, Mr. Ransome, I'll—' Abruptly she stopped and turned her back on him.

'You'll do what?'

She did not answer and when he continued, there was unexpected amusement in his voice. 'You can't be threatening to blackmail me when you've already turned down my offer of an allowance.'

'I'm not threatening anything. You know very well I'd never do anything to hurt Mrs. Ransome. You just happen to have an ability to make me lose my temper.'

'I could say the same thing about you.'

'I wouldn't have thought you capable of temper,' she said coldly, 'you're much too controlled to have any kind of emotion.'

He opened the door of the silver-grey Rolls and waited for her to make herself comfortable before going round to the other side. It was the first time she had ever been in such a car and she looked around curiously.

'It doesn't seem worth all the money,' she said aloud.

'What doesn't?'

'This car.'

'It's in the engine. That's something women don't appreciate. They choose a car because it goes with their favourite dress or happens to be the colour of the season!'

'And you?'

'I prefer performance and quality in everything – including women!'

She did not reply and watched as he overtook a car ahead of them. He drove in the way she had expected; with controlled speed, yet agility, and glancing quickly at his profile, she decided that this car – with its hidden strength and power – was very much like its owner.

'I know you live in Bayswater,' he said suddenly, 'but I don't know the address.'

'Just off St. Petersburg Place. Where do you live?'

'I have a flat in Mayfair, but I spend my week-ends at my place in Dorset.'

A Rolls, a country house and a flat in Mayfair. He must be very successful to maintain so much. Yet he was the sort of man who would be successful no matter what he did. It was implicit not only in his behaviour, but in his personality.

'You must tell me where to turn off,' he said.

She came to with a start. 'It's the next turning on the left.' She gave him the number and he drew up outside the tall, shabby house. 'Thank you for seeing me home.'

'Aren't you going to ask me in?'

She hesitated, surprised by the question.

'You can make me tea in a samovar,' he went on. 'There is a samovar, I suppose?'

She smiled involuntarily, and having done so was obliged to accede to his request. They walked up the worn steps and she fitted her key in the lock. She saw him look at the row of bells, each with a name above it, but he made no comment and followed her silently as she walked down a narrow hall and fitted a second key into a faded brown door. It creaked open and she switched on the light.

Dark crimson wallpaper flooded into view and she led the way into the living-room where red-shaded lights threw into relief the mahogany furniture, the signed photographs of ballet dancers and some satin slippers in a glass case.

'It's like a stage set,' Gregory Ransome said.

'Anton says the only thing it lacks is Mitsouko!'

'Mitsouko?'

She smiled. 'It was Diaghilev's favourite scent.'

'I see.' He peered at the faded photograph of a dancer. 'I can't understand the fever that ballet arouses in so many people. To me, it's purely an entertainment. I dislike it being treated like a religion.'

'With me, young man, it *is* a religion!'

They both turned in surprise and saw Verenskaya at the door. She advanced into the room, her dignity unassailable, despite her red flannel dressing-gown.

'I'm sorry if we woke you,' Melanie apologized, and quickly made the introductions.

74

'So *you* are Timothy's cousin,' Verenskaya said, her black eyes glittering. 'I am sorry you do not like my shrine. I realize it is archaic, but to me it represents the world I love. Transplant me and I would die!' She tilted her head and glared at him. 'But you are too English and unfeeling to understand such emotion!'

He smiled slightly. 'On the contrary, I understand it very well. My aunt also cherishes the past.' He looked at Melanie. 'I feel guilty at having disturbed Madame Verenskaya. I don't think I'll sample that tea after all.'

In silence Melanie escorted him back to the door, and only as he reached the threshold did he speak again.

'If I find anything in Timothy's flat, I'll let you know.'

'Please do,' she said, and waited until he had crossed to the main door and the street before she returned to the living-room.

'I'm sorry I frightened away your suitor!' Verenskaya said.

'Enemy would be a better word!'

'He would make a dangerous enemy,' the woman said, 'but a wonderful lover.'

'I'd prefer him as an enemy!' Melanie retorted.

'You are still young,' Verenskaya said slyly. 'You may change your mind.'

Melanie burst out laughing. 'You're incorrigible! All that rubbish about the English being unemotional. You were deliberately trying to annoy him.'

'That is the best way of gaining the attention of such a man.'

'Then I must have gained *all* of his!'

'Be careful then. *That* one is different from the cousin.'

There was no need for Melanie to ask why. Every meeting she had had with Gregory had increased her awareness of his intelligence, sarcasm and rigidity. Timothy's weakness had lain in his changeability – Gregory's strength lay in the exact opposite.

For a long while that night she mused over all she had learned, still finding it inconceivable that Timothy should have sold his shares to Herbert Fenwick. No matter how much he had wanted the money – her cheeks burned as she remembered the reason Gregory had given – he would surely never have obtained it if the only way of doing so had meant giving control of the company to the man who would have put into practice

75

the very ideas his father had fought so hard to prevent.

Yet there was so much about Timothy she had never understood; even his gambling had been a side to his character she had never seen. And if there was so much she did not know, how could she try and judge his motivations and behaviour?

She was on the threshold of sleep when she was jerked into complete wakefulness by a sudden memory that sent her starting up in bed. Her love letters! How could she have forgotten the letters she had written to Timothy each day of their courtship? What a fool she had been to suggest that Gregory search the flat without realizing that as he did so he would be certain to find them. Remembering the way she had poured so much of her heart into what she had written, her cheeks burned at the thought of Gregory – with his cold, logical mind – reading them, and she decided that first thing in the morning she would go to the flat and get them.

CHAPTER SIX

MELANIE'S intention to retrieve her letters from Timothy's flat was unexpectedly thwarted by Verenskaya's decision to call a full-scale dress rehearsal for one of their ballets.

Although Melanie tried hard to concentrate on her part she found it so difficult that she kept making mistake after mistake, and finally Anton called her over to one side and asked her what was wrong.

'I didn't sleep much last night,' she prevaricated.

'Sleepless nights haven't affected your dancing before.' He looked at her keenly. 'What's wrong?'

To disclose the real reason would have meant telling him what she had learned about the sale of Timothy's shares, which she had promised Gregory Ransome she would not do, and because of this, she tried to dismiss the question by feigning a yawn. 'There's nothing to tell. I'm just tired.'

'I don't believe you. Verenskaya said Ransome saw you home last night. Has he done something to upset you?'

'No. And I wish you wouldn't keep questioning me.'

'I'll question anything that affects your dancing. Every time you see either of the Ransomes it makes you so edgy you dance like an elephant! If you keep on as you are we won't dare put the new ballet in the repertoire.'

'Then find someone else to dance it.'

'Don't give me that!' he said angrily. 'The part was created for you.'

She put her hands to her head. 'I'm sorry, Anton, I just can't concentrate today. Everything's such a muddle.'

'Tell me what it is, and I'll try to help. You weren't reluctant to ask for my help before.'

She acknowledged the truth of the remark with a sigh. 'Gregory's going to Timothy's flat,' she confessed. 'He's looking for something, and I'm afraid in case he—' she hesitated and said in a rush: 'I used to write Timothy silly little notes each day and I couldn't bear if Gregory read them.'

'Then go to the flat before he gets there.'

'That's what I intended to do. But then this rehearsal was called and I couldn't.'

Anton glanced up at the wall clock. 'We'll nip along now. We can make it there and back in an hour.'

'Do you think so?' she said eagerly.

'I'll have a word with Verenskaya. Hurry up and change and I'll meet you outside.'

'There's no reason for you to come with me,' she said quickly.

'I don't fancy you going to Timothy's flat on your own – not in the state of nerves you're in,' he gave her arm a squeeze. 'The sooner you have those letters in your hands, the quicker you'll be able to get your mind back on the rehearsal!'

It was not until they were in a taxi speeding towards Kensington that Anton referred to Gregory again. 'If you didn't want him to go to Timothy's flat before you got there, you could easily have stopped him.'

'It wasn't until the middle of the night that I remembered the letters.'

'What does he want to go to the flat for anyway?'

The question was so point-blank that Melanie found it impossible to lie. After all, she had only promised Gregory not to tell Mrs. Ransome that Timothy had sold his controlling shares to Herbert Fenwick; it would make no difference if she told Anton the truth.

As briefly as she could, she recounted her entire conversation with Gregory, ending with her own belief that Timothy would never have willingly sold his shares in such an underhand way.

'I know he had faults,' she concluded, 'but he adored his mother. He would never have done anything to hurt her.'

'But he needed money to buy you things—' Anton held up his hand as she went to interrupt – 'Don't bother telling me you never asked him. I know that for myself, but it did give him a reason for wanting to raise some cash.'

'I thought of that, too, but I don't think he'd do it that way.'

Before Anton could reply, the taxi drew up outside the block of flats where Timothy had lived.

'I haven't got a key,' Melanie exclaimed.

'Don't worry. I'm sure the porter will recognize you and let you in.'

Luckily Anton was proved right, and using his pass key, the porter escorted them up to the third floor and into the flat at the end of the corridor.

It was the first time Melanie had been here since her wedding day and as she entered the narrow hall tears gushed into her eyes, and with a muttered exclamation, she ran across to the bedroom and closed the door behind her.

It did not matter whether she had loved Timothy deeply or not. All she could think of at the moment was that he had died needlessly and too young and the tragedy of it was so overwhelming that it was several moments before she was able to compose herself sufficiently to go into the living-room.

As she came through the door Anton turned from the small bureau, a bundle of letters in his hand.

'Are these what you want?' he asked.

'Yes. Where did you find them?'

'In the desk. I hope you didn't mind my looking for them? I thought it would save wear and tear on your nerves.'

Gratefully she accepted the packet of envelopes, thrust them into her bag and followed him quickly from the flat. As they reached the front door he stopped and looked at her.

'Are you sure there's nothing else you'd like to get?' he asked.

'Nothing,' she said firmly. 'It was never my home – I never even thought of it as *his*.'

'You were upset enough when we first got here,' he replied, and closed the door shut.

'Only because it brought back memories of Timothy. Made

me realize the tragedy of his death.'

Without answering he pressed for the lift and in silence they waited for it and in silence went down to the ground floor. Only as they reached the foyer did they see the rain pouring down like a torrent.

'You'd better hang on here,' Anton said, 'while I get a taxi.'

'You'll get soaked. Can't the porter phone for one?'

'In the middle of his lunch!' Anton joked, and with a wave of his hand disappeared through the swing doors.

Melanie sat on one of the settees near the wall and waited, forcing herself not to think that this place could – indeed would have been her home – if some unhappy fate had not intervened and changed the course of her own life at the same time as it had ended Timothy's. Nervously she stood up, conscious of the weight of letters in her handbag, and wishing she were back home so that she could hide them and never see them again. Or perhaps it would be better to destroy them? But even as she thought of this, she dismissed it; no matter what her emotions were today, the feeling she had once felt for Timothy was still too near to allow her to do such a thing. So deep was she in her thoughts that she did not notice the tall figure of a man crossing the carpet until he was by her side.

'This is an unexpected encounter,' a deep voice drawled.

Startled, she looked up and saw Gregory. As always he was perfectly groomed – no rain would dare touch him, she thought – and his expression as he watched her held more than a hint of curiosity.

'If I'd known you were coming here,' he continued, 'I'd have brought you.'

Feeling illogically guilty, she blushed. 'I didn't know – I only decided this morning. There were some things I had to collect. Personal things.' Even as she said the words she turned pinker, hoping he wouldn't read a deeper meaning in them.

'I understand.' His voice was cool and he half looked away from her.

'You don't understand at all.' Without knowing why, she was suddenly desperately anxious that he did not get the wrong impression. 'I'd written letters to Timothy. . . . I wanted to get them.'

He stared at her fully again. 'You don't owe me an explanation. I'm not your keeper, you know.'

'I just didn't want you to get the wrong idea. You've already got far too many about me.'

'I'll accept the fact that your relationship with my cousin was platonic until your marriage,' he replied without expression.

'It was never consummated at all!'

The words were out before she could stop them, and seeing the look on his face she would have given anything in the world to have been able to retract them. But it was too late now and she was forced to continue.

'I was never – never his wife in the real sense of the word. The Company was – we were flying to Australia the morning afterwards and there was . . . there were so many things to do . . . the packing and the . . .' It was impossible to say any more, and she stopped again, hoping that this time he would say something. But the silence continued, and she suddenly realized the iniquitous position she had put him in. 'I must have been mad,' she thought miserably, and looked at him from beneath her lashes. To her surprise there was a faint smile on his face, but it was not the smile of contempt with which she had come to associate him; this smile was soft and tinged with compassion.

'I suppose that explains your attitude to Timothy,' he said slowly. 'I often wondered what caused it.'

'My attitude?' she queried. 'What do you mean?'

'It's changeable. One moment I have the feeling that – that you genuinely loved Timothy and then I get the impression that you never cared for him at all.'

She longed to tell him the truth, but knew that this was not the time nor the place. Anton would be back with the taxi at any moment and she was suddenly anxious for Gregory not to know that she had come to the flat with anyone.

'I must get back to the theatre,' she said quickly. 'We're rehearsing and I'll be late.'

'If you could wait a few moments until I've been up to the flat I can drive you back.'

'I haven't time. Anyway, you might be longer than you think.' Before he could reply she rushed out into the rain, running down the street in the direction Anton had taken. Almost immediately she heard her name called and she glanced up as a taxi drew into the curb, splashing her ankles with mud.

'Why on earth didn't you wait inside?' Anton said irritably, opening the door for her.

Without answering, she jumped into the cab and slammed the door, drawing a breath of relief as the taxi swung round in a circle and took them back into the West End.

A couple of days later Gregory telephoned her at the flat to say he had not found anything of interest among Timothy's papers.

'I went through everything in the desk and I even spoke to Timothy's lawyers, but as far as I can make out he sold his shares willingly.'

'Then there's nothing you can do.'

'No.'

'How long will you be able to stop Mr. Fenwick from making the changes that he wants?'

'I'm not sure.' He hesitated as if about to say something else. 'It's tricky,' he said slowly, 'very tricky.'

Again she felt that he was keeping something back and the knowledge made her sarcastic. 'What about your charm? Aren't you still using that on him?'

'You can see for yourself if you like. Fenwick's dining with my aunt on Sunday and she hopes you'll come along.'

The idea of a formal dinner terrified her. 'I'm not sure I'm free.'

'That's a better excuse than saying you've nothing to wear! Make yourself free – it's the least you can do for your mother-in-law.'

He rang off abruptly and Melanie went into her bedroom to look through her wardrobe. If she did decide to accept the invitation it would be the first time she had met Gregory socially, for he had deliberately kept out of her way whenever she had gone to the house in Belgrave Square. But there had been a friendlier tone in his voice and though she could not have described it as warm, it at least had the merit of not holding its usual sharpness.

Idly she looked through her clothes. Several of her prettier dresses had been bought for her by Timothy – gifts which he had lavished on her despite her protests, but somehow she felt she wanted to wear something that she herself had chosen, a dress that held no memories of the past. She shrugged. Why shouldn't she buy herself something new? Since she had been given larger roles to dance she was now earning more money. It was ridiculous not to spend some of it.

The next day, still in the same unusual mood of extravagance, she went shopping and spent far more than she had intended on a chiffon dress the same deep aquamarine as her eyes. It was a more sophisticated style than she had ever worn before, with a completely bare back and the shoulders cut low to display the curve of her breasts. Used as she was to wearing theatrical costume with its dramatic accentuation of the physical, she was unaware of how beautiful and provocative it made her look, and it was not until Verenskaya came into her bedroom on Sunday night and threw her hands heavenwards that Melanie began to wonder whether she had chosen wisely.

'Am I too dressed up?' she asked.

'Too undressed, you mean!'

'Oh!' Melanie's hands flew to her throat. 'I'll change into something else. My black—'

'Rubbish! I was teasing you! You look beautiful.' Verenskaya held out her hand and on the palm lay a pair of aquamarine earrings set in silver. Melanie had never seen them before and she gave an exclamation of delight.

'Wear them,' Verenskaya said. 'They were given to me by a young officer in the Polish Army; the one man I might have married had he lived.'

'Are you sure you want me to wear them?'

'I would give them to no one else except you.'

Melanie put them on and the glittering jewels, dangling provocatively on either side of her face, gave added sparkle to her appearance, added confidence too, as she slipped into her coat and left the flat.

It was with some trepidation that she entered the drawing-room of the Ransome house a half-hour later, her heart pounding so heavily that she could barely hear her mother-in-law introducing her to Herbert Fenwick, a grey-haired, stocky man with a bluff Yorkshire voice. It was only when the introduction was over and she turned to accept a drink from the butler that she realized Gregory Ransome was not in the room. Only then did her pulse steady, and she was able to listen to the conversation with a semblance of calm.

'I thought Lydia was coming with you,' Mrs. Ransome was saying to her guest.

'Gregory's bringing her. She was spending the week-end with some friends near his place in the country and he said he'd drive her into Town.'

'He might get held up driving at this time of night,' Mrs.

Ransome said, and glanced round for the butler.

'I've sent him to get me some more ice,' Herbert Fenwick said, interpreting her look.

'Then I'd better tell Cook myself to hold back dinner. I'd rather Lydia and Gregory waited for the soufflé than the other way round!'

Left alone, Melanie did not know what to say to the man in front of her and there was an uncomfortable silence, broken finally by the Yorkshireman.

'I suppose you know I was your late father-in-law's partner?'

'Yes.'

'We started together. John was the brains on the engineering side, but I was the one who took care of the money.'

'Very successfully, I'm sure,' Melanie said diplomatically.

'It was,' he said heavily, 'until the last couple of years when I wanted us to expand. John was dead set against it and—'

'Do you think you should be telling me all this?' she interrupted.

'Why not? You're one of the family.' He leaned forward. 'Tell me, do you know exactly how ill your mother-in-law is?'

'I should think you'd know more about that than I would.'

'I only know what Gregory's told me. He said her heart was very bad, but I didn't know if he was exaggerating.'

Finding the conversation becoming more distasteful the more it progressed, Melanie stood up, but the man was either thick-skinned or determined, for he took no notice of her movements and went on speaking.

'There's something Gregory doesn't want me to do – concerned with the business, I mean – and I asked you about Mrs. Ransome because I wanted to make sure he isn't taking me for a ride.'

'I doubt if anyone could do that,' she said coldly.

'You'd be surprised.' He stopped and rubbed his chin. 'I don't want to upset anyone, but there's a limit to how long I can wait. Business is business, you know.'

'I don't. But I'm sure *you* do!'

'You've a pretty sharp tongue in your head!'

'I thought you'd appreciate plain speaking.'

'I do when there's a reason.' He gave her what he obviously hoped she would take to be a broad smile. 'But what have *you* got against me?'

'Nothing' she lied, and was relieved that her mother-in-law's return forced the man to change the subject.

'Were you in time to stop the soufflé going in?' he asked.

Mrs. Ransome smiled. 'Luckily I was. Lydia was never punctual at the best of times and if she's coming back from the country. . . .'

'You're right there.' Fenwick drained his glass and set it on the table beside him. 'Mind you, she's better than she was. Trouble is she doesn't work.' Gloomily he stared down into his sherry glass. 'It's bad for a girl to have too much time on her hands. I'd get a sight more peace of mind if she settled down.'

'I always thought she would have been married years ago.' Mrs. Ransome looked across at Melanie. 'Lydia is so pretty and gay,' she explained.

'She's had lots of offers,' Fenwick said, 'but too many of them came from fortune-hunters. Luckily I found out in time, but one day I'm afraid—'

He stopped as the door opened and Gregory and a titian-haired girl came into the room. It was the thick glossy mass of auburn waves which Melanie noticed first, but almost at once came the realization that she had seen the girl before. Could it be possible? Was her imagination playing tricks? She watched as Lydia Fenwick came forward to be introduced, a smile of welcome on the wide full mouth and no look of recognition in the dark brown eyes.

'So you're Timothy's widow,' the girl said in a husky voice, and then without more ado turned to kiss Mrs. Ransome.

It was the voice which finally dispelled all Melanie's doubts, for never could she have mistaken that low, arrogant sound. As if turned to stone she remained seated in the corner of the settee, wondering how she would be able to get through the evening without giving herself away, and wondering too if there were any possible excuses she could think of in order to leave at once. She half stood up, but even as she made the movement she saw Gregory watching her, and knew it would be impossible to leave without having him demand an explanation later on. Miserably she settled back, turning to watch Lydia Fenwick with a fascination born of bitterness and horror.

What a difference a change in the colour of hair could make in one's appearance! Indeed, if Lydia had not possessed such an unusually beautiful voice, Melanie would have had some doubt as to whether or not it was the same girl she had met on the night of her wedding, for then the auburn hair had been blonde and the pet name of Bibsie had been used. She closed her eyes as agonizing memories washed over her and the bitterness she had thought forgotten welled up in her again.

No wonder Timothy had known Lydia Fenwick since they were in their prams! No wonder the girl had been angry and jealous that he had married someone else! With their fathers being partners in business it was obvious that a marriage between them would have been welcomed by both families.

Looking at the finely chiselled profile in front of her, as Lydia Fenwick turned her face upwards for Gregory to light her cigarette, Melanie was amazed that the girl had been so skilful in hiding the fact that they had met before. At least she herself had come here tonight not knowing who Lydia was, but she could not believe that Gregory had not told the girl that Timothy's widow would be here tonight and she wondered whether the forewarning had helped her to carry off a situation which must, even for a most sophisticated person, be an embarrassing one. Yet looking at Lydia's confident manner as she laughed and talked with Gregory and Mrs. Ransome, Melanie knew that any embarrassment was entirely on her own side, and that whatever feelings Lydia might have, guilt or remorse had no part in it.

During dinner Melanie still found it impossible to participate in the conversation and was aware that her mother-in-law was looking at her with concern. But no matter how much she tried, she could not speak and longed only for the evening to be over so that she could return to the peace of her own room and think things out. Yet what was there to think about? She could never tell Mrs. Ransome the truth about Timothy and Lydia, and there was no point in telling Gregory. Indeed, from the relationship that appeared to exist between him and Lydia, she doubted if he would wish to hear anything about her that might be considered unflattering. Watching the way the auburn head kept bending close to the dark one, Melanie felt Herbert Fenwick had no need to worry that his daughter might fall in love with a fortune-hunter. Lydia wanted Gregory. It was obvious in the way she spoke to him, the way she looked at him, and the way she stayed close to his side even when they left the table.

It was the first time Melanie had seen Gregory in anyone's presence except his aunt's, and she was surprised by the ease with which he bantered Lydia's outrageous flirting yet at the same time managed to include both Fenwick and his aunt in the conversation. Any doubts she might have had as to his worldliness disappeared as she watched the way he took command of everyone, and she could understand why her mother-in-law found it so easy to turn to him when she wanted comfort or advice. Dislike him though she might, Melanie had to admit that Gregory was a man on whom one could lean and she could not blame Lydia for wanting him. Indeed, Gregory deserved a girl like Lydia, she thought bitterly, a girl who thought only of herself and who had the callous ability to look at Melanie with innocent, guiltless eyes.

'Who's the vendetta against?' a voice said quietly in her ear, and with a start that set her coffee cup clattering in her saucer she looked round to see Gregory by her side.

'You startled me,' she said, avoiding the question.

'I'm sorry.' He took the cup and saucer from her hand. 'You've finished your coffee. Would you like some more?'

She shook her head and he placed the empty cup on the trolley. Then to her surprise he came back and sat down beside her.

'That's a new dress, isn't it,' he stated.

'Yes.'

'In my honour?'

'In the family honour.'

'I hope you'll always be concerned about family honour.' His glance rested momentarily on Herbert Fenwick and then turned back to her. Guessing what he meant, she nodded.

'Mr. Fenwick asked me if it was true that my mother-in-law had a bad heart.'

'Trust him to check up!' Gregory said tartly.

'He's a clever business man like yourself. He wouldn't take anyone on trust!'

'Do you think *I* don't take people on trust?'

'I don't *think* – I know!'

'I grew up in a hard school.'

'Is that why you judge everyone harshly?'

'I've tried to be fair to you,' he answered.

'If you call your behaviour fair . . . !'

'When I first met you I believed you to be the girl who had

86

callously left my cousin on his wedding day. It wasn't until Madame Verenskaya told my aunt the truth that I learned Timothy had agreed to let you go on the tour.'

Hearing him repeat the statement that had come from Verenskaya's vivid imagination reminded Melanie forcibly of how little Gregory really knew of her. Yet what was the point of telling him the truth? He might not believe her – might even think she was lying in order to gain his interest. The very thought of it made her move back instinctively from him, and as she did so her handbag slid to the carpet. She bent to retrieve it and Gregory did the same, their hands meeting over the clasp, hers fragile and white, his large and tanned. For an instant neither of them moved and his eyes travelled up her slender arms until they rested on the creamy skin of her shoulders. She straightened quickly, instinctively holding the bodice of her dress.

'I'm glad to see your curves belong to nature,' he commented. 'Most ballet dancers are too thin.'

Blushing, she took her compact from her bag and dabbed some powder unnecessarily on her nose. Why had Gregory come to sit beside her? Was it only to do his duty or had it been to see if he could embarrass her into a *faux pas*? She glanced at him and seeing that he was still watching her, busied herself again with her compact.

'You don't need to gild the lily,' he said. 'You look lovely as you are.'

'That's the first nice thing you've ever said to me.'

'Is it?' He thought for a moment. 'I suppose it is. Still, I doubt if you need *my* compliments. I should have thought you got plenty in your profession.'

She laughed, 'You shouldn't think of ballet dancers in terms of Toulouse-Lautrec. Think of Dégas!'

'Talking about painting?' Lydia Fenwick's husky voice interrupted them as she sauntered over to the settee.

'Only indirectly,' Gregory answered. 'I was being told off about my ignorance of the ballet.'

Lydia gave Melanie a sweet smile, but looking at the dark eyes this time Melanie knew that Lydia was aware that she had been recognized. For an instant the smile hardened and the girl glanced over her shoulder to where Mrs. Ransome was talking to Herbert Fenwick. Melanie recognized the gesture for the warning it was meant to be and awarded Lydia full marks for quick thinking.

'It's funny how some men can't stand ballet,' Lydia said with amusement. 'But then it's a form of art about which people are so extreme.'

'On what extremity are you?' Melanie asked.

'A devotée, my dear.' Slim fingers with red-tipped nails rested on Gregory's arm. 'We must go and see the Verenskaya Company when their season opens.'

'You might find the tickets difficult to get,' Melanie said.

'Surely you'll send some to the family,' Lydia said sweetly. 'We'd like four, wouldn't we, Gregory? Then we can take Mrs. Ransome and Daddy.'

'I'll buy them from the box office,' Gregory said. 'You can't stop the Company making a proper profit!'

Lydia laughed and, putting her other hand on Gregory's arm, drew him gently but insistently to his feet. 'Come over and talk to Daddy. I can't let the family monopolize you any longer.'

With a half smile, Gregory allowed himself to be led away, and Melanie marvelled at the subtle way Lydia had relegated her to being one of the family. She half stood up, anxious to leave, yet once again settled back. If she walked out now Lydia would misconstrue it as pique, believing her to be angry at having Gregory Ransome taken away.

'As if I cared whether I spoke to him or not,' she thought angrily. 'Anton's right; I'm becoming obsessed with the Ransomes.' She sighed. Dislike seemed to be as strong an emotion as love! Out of the corner of her eye she saw her mother-in-law beckon her and, grateful for someone to talk to, crossed over to her side.

'You've been so quiet all evening, Melanie,' Mrs. Ransome said. 'I hope Lydia didn't say anything to upset you?'

'Of course not. What made you think she had?'

'Experience. I've known her since she was a baby and even in her pram she hated competition!'

The words were an ugly reminder of something one of Timothy's friends had said to her, and Melanie replied with unexpected force, 'I'd never compete with Lydia. Never!'

'*She* thinks you are.'

Melanie did not pretend to misunderstand. 'I think she and your nephew are well suited to each other.'

'They've both got pretty forceful characters,' Mrs. Ransome

admitted with a chuckle. 'But I think Gregory's the stronger.'

'Would you like them to get married?' The moment the question was out Melanie wished she could draw it back, but it was too late and she hoped it would not be seen as anything other than curiosity.

'I think it's time Gregory had a wife,' Mrs. Ransome said, 'and Lydia's a sweet girl even though she's been spoiled.'

The answer made Melanie realize how blind people could be; and though in this particular case she was also irritated by it, she could see that in some instances it had its merits. At least as far as Mrs. Ransome was concerned it had prevented her from recognizing Timothy's real character. How *could* he have sold those controlling shares to Herbert Fenwick?

She jumped to her feet, suddenly unable to remain in this flower-filled, overheated room any longer. 'I must go,' she said jerkily. 'We've an early call tomorrow.'

'If you wait, I'm sure Gregory will take you home.'

'I don't want to break up the evening.'

Hardly aware of saying good-bye, she left the house, and driving back in the taxi which had been called for her, she wished that in leaving she had also been able to leave behind her memories. But they were with her tonight as strongly as they had been on the day of Timothy's accident, and they remained tormenting her throughout the long night.

She had always known that one day she would meet the girl who had turned her wedding day into a sham, but never had she thought that the meeting would take place under such ironical circumstances. Lydia had already destroyed the happiness she might have had with Timothy and now it seemed as though she might destroy the happiness she could have found with. . . .

But even before she could bring herself to utter the name she cried aloud with horror. No, it couldn't be true! It *wasn't* true. Any emotion she might feel towards Gregory, any desire to make him think well of her, stemmed only from a determination to prove herself as a human being and not to prove herself to him as a woman. 'I don't care what he thinks about me,' she said aloud. 'If he wants to marry Lydia, he can do so. He means nothing to me. Nothing!'

CHAPTER SEVEN

ONCE again – as it had done in Australia – ballet became Melanie's escape.

With little more than a week to the opening night, the Company were rehearsing eight to ten hours a day, but long after everyone else had dragged themselves home, she and Anton remained behind to perfect the role that he had created for her in his own new ballet, with which Verenskaya had daringly chosen to open their London season.

Because it was only in work that she could find peace of mind, Melanie stayed in the rehearsal room even after Anton had gone home, fabricating excuses to remain behind and pretending that it would only be for a short while. But finally Anton, returning late one evening to collect a score, found her practising at the barre and after a moment of astonishment lost his temper.

'What on earth are you still practising for? You'll crack up if you keep on at this pace.'

'I'll crack up if I don't! I keep remembering that début I made in Australia.' She gave a shudder. 'I never want to go through anything like that again.'

'You'd hardly had any rehearsals for the part,' he retorted. 'This one's quite different.' He strode over to her. 'For heaven's sake, Melanie, give it a rest.'

'But the more I practise the more confidence I get.'

'You've years ahead of you,' he said softly. 'Don't try and beat Fonteyn in your first season as a ballerina!'

Aware that he was still angry, she tried to leaven the conversation. 'There's nothing to stop me from trying!'

He still did not smile at her teasing reply and, if anything, looked even more serious. 'Success never used to be so important to you, Melanie. What's got into you?'

She hesitated, wondering what he would say if he knew that her determination to be successful in her career was spurred on by a desire to prove to Gregory Ransome that she could attain everything she wanted by her own efforts. Yet to say this would only increase Anton's already strong dislike of the man, and unwilling to do so, she prevaricated.

'Perhaps I've become more ambitious,' she said lightly. 'After all, it's what you've been preaching at me for ages.'

'I never said you should work yourself to death! Practice won't make you any better than you are now. That will only come with experience and time.'

She smiled crookedly, too tired to argue. 'All right, Anton, you're the Master.'

His face underwent an abrupt change. 'Master! Must you always see me in terms of work? Can't you see me as a man?'

Before she realized his intention, he pulled her into his arms and pressed his mouth hard on hers. Her first instinct was to draw back, but she forced herself to remain passive, knowing that if she showed any distaste he would never forgive her. But her pretence was wasted, for almost at once he pushed her away angrily.

'You don't feel a thing for me, do you?'

'I'm sorry.' She gestured helplessly. 'Maybe I – perhaps I'm frightened of being hurt again.'

'You can't avoid emotion for the rest of your life. One day you'll fall in love again.'

She turned away, wondering what he would say if he knew that this had already happened. 'Please, Anton, let's go home. I'm too tired to argue.'

As the opening night drew nearer, Melanie was able to plead work as the reason for not going to see her mother-in-law. But even staying away from the house in Belgrave Square could not dim her memory of Gregory, nor the bitterness which she felt towards Lydia Fenwick.

Madame Verenskaya, more than usually preoccupied with the Company, did not notice Melanie's tension or, if she did, put it down to pressure of work. And Melanie was glad that she did not have to put up a pretence in her own home. Not that she and Verenskaya spent much time there; by day they were at the theatre and at night they returned home too exhausted to do anything except have a simple meal and fall into bed.

Melanie knew she was working at a pace she could not maintain, yet she refused to look beyond the next few weeks and hoped that as time passed she would gain more control over emotions which, at the moment, were destroying her peace of mind.

How unsuspectingly she had fallen under Gregory Ransome's spell! The thought tormented her, and she wondered whether it was a weakness or shallowness in her character that had made it possible for a man like him to capture her heart. Yet deep inside her she knew that had she only been searching for strength, she would have fallen in love with Anton in Australia.

No, her feelings for Gregory were more than just a desire for a man on whom she could lean, and she admitted wearily that he was everything she had been searching for throughout her life: a man of strength yet also kindness – as she had witnessed in his attitude towards his aunt; a man of intelligence – as indicated by his successful career – and a man of wit and charm. But neither his kindness nor charm had been directed towards her, and apart from the fleeting compassion he had shown her when they had met outside Timothy's flat and the few teasing remarks he had made to her on the night of the dinner party, his attitude had been mainly one of implacable dislike.

At last the Company's first night arrived, and Melanie locked herself in the tiny dressing-room she had been given and remained there until the callboy came to tell her she was wanted on stage. Nervously she sped down the corridor to the wings. The curtain was still lowered and she stepped on to the stage and peeped at the audience through a chink in the velvet.

She had sent her mother-in-law four tickets and she stared up at the third box on the left, anxious to see whom Mrs. Ransome had invited. Herbert Fenwick and his daughter were seated on either side of her, while on Lydia's left sat another man, his face in shadow. Melanie strained her eyes, but she could not make out who it was.

'It's Ransome all right,' Anton said behind her.

Startled, she swung round. 'What makes you think I—'

'Your mind's an open book to me,' he interrupted, 'and as far as I can see, Ransome's name is on every page of it!'

Silently she returned to the wings, and a moment later the overture to the new ballet began. Melanie closed her eyes, letting her emotions drift with the music. The violins grew louder, Anton's hand tapped her elbow and with a lift of her head she danced on to the stage.

From that moment on she forgot everything except the present, swept up in the simple story of first love and first disillusion that comprised Anton's new one-act ballet.

As a partner he was ideal, guiding her expertly through her most difficult steps, yet making everything appear effortless to the audience. Although off-stage she had never felt completely at ease with him since he had kissed her so passionately and unexpectedly a few days ago, dancing with him as his partner made her forget everything except the part of the gentle, love-sick girl she was portraying. All the emotions she had deliberately held in check now came to the fore, giving her every movement a subtlety it had never held until now, helping her to evoke the very spirit of new love and, finally, lost hopes.

As they came to the final steps and the last chords of the orchestra faded away there was a long silence – the most supreme tribute an audience could pay – before a storm of applause broke around them.

In a daze she and Anton took curtain call after curtain call until the front of the stage was turned into a bower of flowers.

'Still worried about your success?' he murmured as they took their final call.

She shook her head, too overwhelmed to speak. She had received great ovations during their Australian tour, but it was nothing compared with the applause tonight.

The sound of it was still ringing in her ears as she returned to her dressing-room. No longer buoyed by excitement, she was so exhausted that every movement was an effort, and lethargically she took off her costume, put on a silk dressing-gown and proceeded to cream off her make-up.

She was interrupted by a knock on the door and heard Mrs. Ransome's voice asking if she could come in.

Trembling, Melanie turned to greet her, her excitement dying as she saw that her mother-in-law was alone.

'You were wonderful, Melanie! I had to come backstage and tell you. I hope you don't mind?'

'I'm delighted.' Melanie forced a smile. 'As you can see, I'm not being inundated with visitors!'

'You will be after tonight. You've a great future ahead of you – I never realized it until now.' The woman looked round the room. 'You should have a bigger room than this.'

Melanie laughed. 'I'm lucky to have a room of my own at all. Until tonight I was sharing it with someone else.' She cleared a chair of stockings. 'Do sit down. I won't be long.' Determined not to ask what Gregory had thought of her dancing, she faced the mirror again and continued to wipe off her make-up, aware that her mother-in-law was still standing by the chair.

'I can't stay, Melanie. I only came to ask if you'd like to join Mr. Fenwick and myself for dinner.'

Melanie met the blue eyes reflected above hers in the mirror, but the thought of seeing Gregory made her heart beat so fast she could not speak. However Mrs. Ransome's next words destroyed all her excitement.

'I can promise it won't be very tiring for you,' the woman went on. 'There'll just be the three of us. Gregory and Lydia have gone on to a party with some friends.'

'That's a relief,' Melanie lied, 'I'd prefer it to be quiet.'

'Good. Then I'll leave you to get dressed.'

Left alone, Melanie dabbed more cream on her face, but her hands were shaking so much that she could not wipe it off. How stupid she had been to have expected Gregory to come backstage and congratulate her when, on his own admission, he had said he despised people who regarded ballet with the fervour of a religious fanatic; to have hoped he would come and see her now was like expecting an atheist to kneel in front of an altar!

Yet though she was able to use logic to excuse him for not coming with his aunt, she could not use logic to excuse his lack of a telephone call or flowers on the following day – a gesture of courtesy which she had expected of him. More than ever she accepted the fact that they came from different worlds and had nothing in common, and more than ever she forced herself to think only of her work.

Melanie's London début did not go unnoticed in the press and for several weeks she was interviewed and written about. But the only real difference it made to her life was a further increase in salary and a dressing-room permanently her own.

With the season successfully launched, Anton immediately began work on a full-length ballet and told Melanie he wanted her to dance the female lead.

'Tanya will never stand for it,' she said. 'She's our principal dancer and—'

'You can't build a company on one dancer alone,' he said. 'Tanya's jealousy of you is personal. It has nothing to do with the fact that you're now dancing bigger roles.'

Recognizing the truth of what Anton had said, Melanie did her best to ignore Tanya's jealousy, which manifested itself in irritating ways during rehearsals.

As always when in the grip of a new work, Anton spared no one. He no longer talked to Melanie of slowing down and instead pushed her to such extremes of effort in his desire to have the new ballet ready to include in the current repertoire that one afternoon Verenskaya was forced to intervene.

Coming into the practice room she took one look at Melanie's white, exhausted face and ordered her home to rest before the evening performance.

'Melanie's always pale,' Anton scowled. 'It means nothing.'

'Rehearse her at this pace and her dancing tonight will mean nothing either!'

'I'm not a bit tired,' Melanie intervened, but Verenskaya ignored her.

'Come with me, Anton, I have some contracts I'd like you to look at.'

They went out and Melanie, grateful for the chance of a rest, changed from her practice clothes into a full-skirted white dress and set out for home.

Away from the dusty confines of the theatre she paused to enjoy the blue sky and the feel of the sun on her face. How wonderful it was to have a few hours of freedom. Only now did she admit how badly she needed it. Savouring thoughts of a cool bath, she sauntered to the bus stop and had joined the queue when a voice called her name. Thinking it was someone from the company, she turned, the blood draining from her face as she saw Gregory.

He was wearing a grey suit and a pale blue shirt which gave unexpected warmth to eyes she had always thought of as icy grey. There was a smile on his face too, though when he spoke his voice was as cool as she had always known it.

'On the loose in the middle of the day? I thought you were always rehearsing?'

'Verenskaya sent me home to rest.'

'I'm not surprised. You look as pale as a ghost.'

Immediately she was conscious of how she must appear to him: her skin waxy, shadows of fatigue marking her cheekbones and lying dark beneath her eyes. As he continued to stare at her she became even more uncomfortable, and aware that her low-heeled pumps made her look absurdly small she defiantly tilted her head, knowing even as she did so that she did not reach higher than his heart.

'You don't only look as if you need a rest,' he said abruptly. 'You look as if you need some food.' Without giving her time to protest, he raised his hand to a passing taxi, peremptorily said

'Dorchester' and pushed her into its dim interior.

'I'm not dressed for the Dorchester,' she protested.

'Nonsense! You look fine.'

His assurance did little to appease her and she settled into the corner of the seat and wondered what had prompted his invitation. She glanced at him, but his expression was so stern that she knew that whatever had caused his gesture it was certainly not liking. Duty perhaps? Maybe even pity. Well, even pity was better than hate. She looked down at her hands and sighed. Perhaps in time she could make him realize she was not the heartless girl he thought her to be. She toyed with the idea of telling him the whole truth about herself and Timothy, but even as her lips parted she realized she could not do so without disclosing the part that Lydia Fenwick had played, and Lydia's father now held a controlling interest in Ransome Engineering. There was no knowing what he would do if Gregory attacked his daughter – as he very well might if he learnt that Lydia had been responsible for Melanie going to Australia: an act which had finally resulted in Timothy's death.

All these thoughts flashed through Melanie's mind, but she was still undecided what to do when the decision was made for her by the taxi drawing to a stop outside the hotel.

Diffidently she followed Gregory through the busy foyer and into the large lounge. They sat down on a settee backing on to a peach mirror and she watched silently as Gregory conferred with the waiter. Even when the man had gone he seemed in no hurry to talk and, with his usual deliberation, took out a cigar and lit it, smoking it in silence until the waiter returned with what appeared to Melanie to be an enormous amount of food. She watched as various plates of assorted sandwiches and cakes were set before them, followed by a pot of coffee and one of tea.

'I hope you've got a big appetite,' she said quickly. 'You don't think *I'm* going to eat all this, do you?'

'Only half of it,' he answered. 'I intend to eat the other half myself.'

'I never thought of you as the sort of man who ate cream cakes.'

'Did you assume I lived on lemons?' She turned scarlet, and he smiled, 'I'm sorry. I shouldn't tease you.'

'You've never done so before.' She reached for a sandwich. 'But then we've never been on teasing terms.' He did not answer and, made bolder by her surroundings, she said: 'Why did you invite me here?'

'As a slight repayment for the wonderful evening you gave me a few weeks ago. I never knew until then what a beautiful dancer you are.' He hesitated and she saw his hand clench and unclench on his cigar. Then, as if suddenly aware of what he was doing, he stubbed it out in the ashtray, uncaring that he had smoked barely a quarter of it.

'I wanted to come backstage with my aunt that night,' he went on, 'but I couldn't leave Lydia. And somehow I didn't think you'd appreciate having *her* come round to see you as well!'

'Whatever gave you that idea?' Melanie asked in an innocent voice.

'I don't profess to have a great understanding of women, but I know enough about them to recognize when they don't like each other!'

'I never expected you to come,' she said, ignoring the remark. 'But I'm glad to know you liked the ballet.'

'I liked *you*,' he corrected. and his emphasis of the pronoun brought the colour to her face. 'I never thought of you as being ungainly, but it wasn't until I saw you on the stage that I realized what a fragile little thing you are.'

'I only look fragile,' she said. 'You have to be strong to be a ballet dancer.'

'It's a lovely strength,' he said softly, and his voice was so gentle that she was horrified to feel tears well into her eyes.

Quickly she glanced down at her lap, afraid that he might see them. This was the first occasion she had seen Gregory since she had admitted to herself that she loved him and until now she had half hoped – had in fact almost convinced herself – that what she felt for him was only a figment of her imagination. Yet now, sitting so close to him, smelling the tobacco he smoked and enveloped by the aura of his personality, she knew that the emotion he aroused in her was no schoolgirl crush nor a Jezebel desire to provoke him.

She loved him. Deeply, passionately and irrevocably she loved him.

'You're not eating.' His voice broke into her thoughts and confusedly she looked up.

'Neither are you,' she said.

'Let's both eat together!'

Simultaneously their hands reached out for a sandwich and their fingers met. She drew back as though she had touched a flame and concentrated furiously on chewing food which, at that moment, tasted exactly like sawdust. But as their tea progressed she began to relax, soothed by the warmth, the smell of perfume and flowers and the general air of luxury.

'I've never been to the Dorchester before,' she admitted as she dug her fork into an éclair.

'Didn't Timothy bring you here?'

'We never went out during the day, and I was dancing every night. By the time I'd finished and changed, the only places that were open were night clubs.'

'I can't imagine Timothy leading a quiet life for long.'

'It wasn't for long,' she said artlessly. 'We only knew each other a few months. Though in the last few weeks he *did* suddenly splash out.' She stopped abruptly, remembering where the money to do so must have come from.

A strange expression crossed Gregory's face too, and expecting him to make a comment on Timothy's sale of his shares, she was taken aback by the question he did ask.

'And who were you in love with before Timothy?'

'No one. He was my first boy-friend.' Deciding she had better go before his questions became dangerous, she stood up.

He signalled the waiter for the bill. 'Where to now?' he asked.

She looked at her watch. 'It isn't worth while going back to the flat. I might as well stroll around in the fresh air and do some window shopping.'

'Every woman's favourite occupation! Where shall it be – Bond Street or Regent Street?'

Uncertain whether he meant to accompany her, she hesitated, and he decided for her.

'Let's make it Bond Street,' he said, and led her out of the hotel.

It gave Melanie a strange feeling to walk along the pavement beside him. Somehow it seemed much more intimate than when she had dined with him at her mother-in-law's house. Perhaps that was because their previous meetings had been forced on him, whereas this one had been of his own making.

'Is there anything you like here?' he asked, bringing her to a stop outside the window of a jewellery shop.

She gazed at the display and nodded. 'There certainly is.'

'I thought so.' He stared at the elaborate ruby and sapphire bracelet given pride of place in the centre of the window. 'Personally I think emeralds would be more flattering for your eyes.'

She looked at him puzzled, then suddenly laughed. 'Good heavens, I wasn't looking at that thing. No one would possibly want *that* except as an investment!'

'Then what's your choice – the diamond necklace?'

'Too showy.' She pointed to an unusual baroque gold bracelet in the corner. 'That's much more my style. I'm not very tall, but that type of jewellery suits me.'

'That's the cheapest thing in the window.'

'Then I'm lucky I haven't got expensive tastes!' Too late she remembered the jewellery Timothy had given her, but if Gregory remembered it too he gave no sign, and they continued to walk. Most of the shops had already closed and people were hurrying home. Quite a few of the girls gave Gregory an appraising look and Melanie could not help a feeling of pride in his tallness and strength.

Once more he stopped, this time outside an art gallery. Only one picture was on display: a pastel study of a ballet dancer.

'Is that your taste too?' he asked.

'Certainly not. If that girl tried an entrechat she'd fall flat on her face! Just look at her legs! I do wish painters would study their subjects.'

'This little sketch costs more than you earn in a year,' he said dryly. 'It's the sort of thing that fits ideally into a stockbroker's drawing-room!'

'I'd rather have my Dégas prints. At least he knew what dancers looked like.'

He shrugged. '*I'd* rather have nothing on my walls than a reproduction. I'm afraid I'm a purist.'

The words chilled her, emphasizing their difference in standards and outlook and making her realize more than ever how unbridgeable these differences were.

'I'm sure you *don't* have bare walls,' she retorted. 'You'd be surprised how quickly you'd change your ideas about repros if you couldn't afford the real thing.'

He was quick to sense the hurt in her reply. 'I suppose you think I'm pompous?'

'Yes, I do. Pompous and stupid.'

'Because I hate anything tawdry and cheap?'

'Expensive things can be nasty too!'

There was an unusual twinkle in his eyes. 'You *are* sharp this afternoon.'

'I'm sorry.'

'Don't apologize. I like it.'

He took her arm to cross the street and she felt a stab of quick, unexpected joy at his touch. It was something she had never known before, not even with Timothy.

Timothy. . . . She had loved him with the painful intensity of a schoolgirl, and not until she had experienced sorrow and bitterness had she changed from a child into a woman. She glanced at Gregory. Surely he wouldn't have asked her to have tea with him unless he had really wanted to be with her? He was not the sort of man to waste his time with someone he did not like. The thought filled her with joy, dispelling her earlier despondency and making her give a little laugh of pure happiness.

'What's the joke?' he asked.

'Everything and nothing!' She turned. 'I just feel it's good to be alive.'

He grinned at her, looking years younger. 'I'm beginning to think so myself.'

They laughed again, and at that moment a taxi swept past them and turned into Maddox Street. It was moving fast, but Melanie was almost certain Lydia Fenwick had been the occupant, certain too that the beautiful face had twisted with temper as she had seen them.

She pushed the thought of Lydia away, determined not to let anything spoil these wonderful moments as they slowly strolled the length of Bond Street. But as they reached the top Gregory glanced at his watch and gave an exclamation. 'Good lord, I'd no idea it was so late. I'm meeting someone at my club.'

'Is it far?'

'A few minutes' drive. I'll get you a taxi and—'

'Don't bother,' she said quickly. 'It's the rush hour and it's difficult. I'll go by tube.'

He looked at her doubtfully. 'Are you sure?'

She nodded, hoping he would ignore her gesture. But to her chagrin he accepted it with alacrity and, with a preoccupied smile – as though he were already mentally keeping his rendezvous – he hurried away.

It was not until he had disappeared from sight that she realized he had said nothing about seeing her again, and the joy that had filled her ebbed away, leaving her as desolate as she had been before their meeting. How stupid she was to have believed that this afternoon might have presaged the beginning of a new relationship between them. Gregory had merely been polite, using their casual encounter as a chance to say thank you for the evening of pleasure she had given him at the ballet.

It was not until later that night, when the applause of the audience had helped to ease her bruised feelings, that she was able to come to terms with her disappointment, seeing her encounter with Gregory as a sign that he at least no longer hated her! Perhaps in time he might even come to like her; to think further than that was unwise.

She ran down the corridor to her dressing-room and was just at the door when one of the callboys came up to her and handed her a small parcel.

'For you,' he said brightly. 'From the Rajah of Ping Pong!'

Laughing, she took the package and turned it over. There was no name on it other than her own and, puzzled, she went into her room, perched on a chair and undid the wrapping to disclose a little leather box. Quickly she lifted the lid, giving a gasp of pleasure and astonishment as she saw the baroque gold bracelet which she had admired earlier that day.

Happiness went to her head like wine and she jumped to her feet and danced round the room. Then, heedless of the fact that she only had a few moments in which to change into her next costume, she ran to the stage doorkeeper's small office and searched in the telephone book until she found Gregory's number. With shaking hands she dialled it, waiting nervously till she heard the ringing stop and then Gregory's deep voice. She was filled with such an intensity of longing for him that it was a few seconds before she could speak, and when she finally managed to do so, all she could blurt out was a gasping 'Thank you.'

'So you got it?' he said in reply.

'Just now. It was such a surprise. I never thought – I never expected. . . .'

'That's why I left you so abruptly before,' he answered.

'You mean you didn't have an appointment?'

'No. I just wanted to get back to that jeweller's shop before it closed. Do you really like it, Melanie?'

'I adore it.' Out of the corner of her eye she saw the callboy beckoning her. 'I can't talk any more. I'm on stage in a minute.'

'Then I won't keep you. But if you're free I'll pick you up afterwards and take you out to supper.'

'Tonight?'

'Yes. Just a quiet meal somewhere. If you'd like to come, of course.'

'I'd love to come,' she gasped, throwing discretion to the winds.

'What time shall I make it?'

'I'm only on in this first act and I'll change straight afterwards.'

'Will an hour give you enough time?'

'Plenty,' she replied, and replaced the receiver with trembling hands.

It was not until she had done so that she remembered she had nothing to wear except the white dress in which he had seen her that afternoon, and she picked up the telephone to call him back. If he collected her at the flat half an hour later than they had agreed, she would have time to go home and change. But even as she dialled his number, she stopped. Somehow it smacked too much of the obvious if she told him this; might make it appear as though she were reading too much in his offer to take her out. After all, he had said they would just have a quiet meal somewhere, and if she told him she wanted to go home and change first, he might think she was asking to be taken out more elaborately.

She clattered the receiver back into place and ran back to her dressing-room to have a final look at her make-up. If only there were not so many undercurrents to mar her relationship with Gregory, so many bitter accusations that she could remember him hurling at her. It was making her too sensitive to him, too afraid to behave normally. Yet behave normally she must. For if their evening was awkward or embarrassing together it would be a disaster he would be unlikely to repeat.

At exactly ten o'clock she left the theatre and found him waiting for her at the stage door, a position which, in her wildest dreams, she had never imagined him occupying.

He must have felt the incongruity of it too, for he gave a faint smile as he spoke. 'I feel I should be wearing an opera cloak and carrying a bouquet of roses!'

'That sort of stage door johnnie went out with King Edward!' she laughed, and held up her arm for him to see she was wearing the bracelet. 'It's beautiful, Gregory, but I don't feel I should have accepted it.'

'Why not? You accepted things from Timothy.'

The words hit her with such force that she stopped walking, but he was half-way to the car before he realized it and turned to look at her. The light from a street lamp shone directly on her head, turning her hair into a black cloud and heightening the anguish on her face.

With an exclamation, he strode back to her side. 'I'm sorry, Melanie, I don't know what made me say that.'

'I do,' she said in a cold, tight voice. 'No matter how much you might pretend – try to forget what you know – you keep remembering the past.'

'I'm sorry,' he repeated.

She continued to speak as though she had not heard him. 'I was already engaged to Timothy before I accepted *anything* from him – and even then I never asked him for presents. *Never!*'

Gregory caught her hand in a tight grasp and almost pulled her over to the car. But not until he was seated beside her did he speak, his voice vehement and determined. 'You've got to forgive me. I didn't mean to hurt you. I only meant that as you had accepted things from one man I didn't see why you couldn't accept things from another.'

'I don't accept things from men!' she said angrily. 'I was Timothy's fiancée. Can't you see the difference?'

'Of course I can.'

Gregory rubbed his hand across his forehead and even though she was still furious with him she was aware of being surprised to see that his hand was shaking.

'I wish I could make you understand what I mean, Melanie.' His voice was low and so jerky that she had to concentrate in order to hear him. 'Everything I say to you seems to have a double meaning – makes you think I'm trying to hurt you. But I'm not. I never want to hurt you.' He turned and faced her directly. 'I was waiting outside the stage door tonight for nearly an hour, and all the time I was remembering the things I'd said to you when we first met.'

'I was thinking about them too.'

'I'm not surprised.' He put his hand on her arm. 'If there was any way I could unsay those words – if I could turn back the clock so that we could start again. . . . What I'm trying to say is that no matter what Timothy did or how extravagant he was, I'm certain in my own mind that you had nothing to do with it.'

It was an admission she had never expected to hear from him, and if anger had made her speechless before, happiness now had the same effect.

'Do you believe me?' he asked anxiously.

'Yes,' she said slowly. 'And I'm glad you said it. All I ever wanted was Timothy. At least the Timothy I thought he was.'

'Don't judge him too harshly,' Gregory said. 'Because he sold his shares doesn't—'

'I wasn't only thinking of the shares.' She spoke without thinking, and only when she saw his look of puzzlement did she realize her stupidity. Happiness at being with Gregory had made her forget that there were still many things he did not know of her relationship with his cousin.

'You speak as though Timothy hurt you,' Gregory said.

'I think we – I think we hurt each other.' She paused, longing to tell him the truth, yet still held back by loyalty.

As though aware she did not intend to say any more, Gregory set the car in motion, but he did not speak until they were driving along the Strand. 'I know you didn't have time to go home and change, so I'm taking you to a little place in Soho. It's quiet and simple, but I can guarantee you'll enjoy the food.'

It was not until they were sipping their coffee after a superb meal served on plain white china with a minimum of fuss that he told her he had seen Herbert Fenwick the day before.

'He's determined to bring in automation, and I'm not sure how much longer I can make him hold off.'

'He can't!' Melanie exclaimed. 'It would kill Mrs. Ransome if she found out Timothy had. . . .'

Gregory pushed aside his cup. 'It's taken all my efforts to get him to do nothing for the past three months. I don't see how I can keep stopping him.' Seeing her pinched face, he sighed. 'I'm sorry, Melanie. I shouldn't burden you with my problems.'

'It's my problem too. After all, I'm responsible.'

'For Timothy's selling the shares?' There was an un-fathomable expression in Gregory's eyes. 'You can't take the blame for that. Timothy was always short of money, always trying to borrow from me or his friends. If he hadn't had you as a reason there would have been something else.'

Seeing this as another apology for his earlier remarks to her, she sat quietly, and after a moment he gave another deep sigh. 'It's this Fenwick business that's really worrying me.'

'Is there anything I can do to help?'

He shook his head. 'This is one problem only *I* can deal with.'

'I should imagine you like to deal with all your problems yourself.'

'I've never had anyone with whom I'd want to share them – even if I could.' He was looking down at the tablecloth as he spoke and she noticed how thick his lashes were and knew an intense desire to cradle his head against her breast.

'I suppose I've been luckier than you,' she said softly.

'Why? You were orphaned young too, weren't you?'

'Yes. But I was adopted by the whole company and there was never any shortage of listeners! My problem was the opposite, in fact! Every one was *too* interested in what I did and thought!'

He laughed and the mood of sadness vanished, so that when he spoke again it was to question her about her work and the way she prepared for each role.

It was inevitable that in answering him, Anton's name kept recurring, but Gregory gave no sign of any particular feeling, and after a few moments she was able to talk without any artifice, telling him exactly how the company rehearsed and how the choreography was planned. Indeed, it was some while before she stopped hastily, afraid that she had lost his attention by being too technical.

'It's so difficult to explain ballet in simple terms,' she apolo-gized. 'I'm sorry if I've bored you.'

'I never allow myself to be bored! As a matter of fact I'm finding it very interesting.'

'You'll be turning into a ballet fanatic if you're not careful,' she laughed.

'Not of the ballet,' he grinned, 'more likely of you!'

She blushed, but he went on sipping his coffee and she forced herself to see his words as a meaningless compliment with no hidden significance.

It was well past midnight when they left the restaurant and drove silently through the lamplit streets. The car purred to a stop outside the shabby house in Bayswater and she put her hand on the car door.

'It's been a lovely evening, Gregory. Thank you.'

'I hope you'll let me repeat it.'

'Any time,' she whispered, and ran quickly from the car.

It was only as she closed the front door and stood leaning against it while she listened to the sound of his departing engine that she realized he had fixed no time or place for another meeting. But this time there was no fear in her heart, for she was certain she would see him again soon.

CHAPTER EIGHT

THE rest of the week passed without a word from him, and the week-end came with its quiet Sunday, that gave her too much time to think. She made an effort to push him from her mind and forced herself to walk across Hyde Park, but the expanse of green grass made her wonder if Gregory had gone down to his home in the country, made her wonder too if he was spending the week-end alone or perhaps with Lydia Fenwick. She dug her hands more deeply into the pockets of her jacket and walked quicker, but she could not walk away from her thoughts, and they accompanied her back to the flat and filled her mind for the rest of the evening.

It was a relief when Monday came and she could occupy herself with work again. That night she and Anton were once more dancing his one-act ballet, and the ovation she received from the audience afterwards was a forcible reminder that even though she did not possess the man she loved, she was lucky to have such an absorbing compensation.

But applause did not last for ever, and alone in her dressing-room she changed despondently into her outdoor things. Usually she waited to return home with Verenskaya, but to-night she could not face the post-mortem on the performance that would inevitably comprise their conversation, and she slipped into her coat and decided to go home by herself. The corridor leading to the exit was empty and she walked slowly down its length, waved goodnight to the stage doorkeeper and walked outside. A chill breeze had sprung up and she pulled her coat more tightly round her and shivered.

'You really should have a fur,' a deep voice said.

With a startled exclamation she looked up to see Gregory moving forward from the shadows. Her sadness and tiredness disappeared as though by magic and she gave a laugh of pure joy and held out her hands to him.

He took them and pulled her closer. 'Pleased to see me?' Not waiting for her answer, he continued, 'I had to go abroad unexpectedly for a few days. That's why I haven't been in touch with you.'

'I thought you'd forgotten me.'

He stared down at her, then saw by her expression that her remark was not a flirtatious one. 'You really mean that, don't you?' he said softly.

'Yes.'

'I couldn't forget you, Melanie. I've been thinking about you the whole time.' He took her arm beneath his and they walked along to where he had parked the silver-grey Rolls.

Once again he took her to a quiet restaurant, a different one from the previous time, but where the food and service were equally good. She did not know of what they spoke, but only knew that the time passed as though on wings. Yet she was aware that he was enjoying himself, for he laughed frequently and spoke frankly of his childhood and schooldays and his early years in business.

This second evening set the pattern for the many others that followed, and they met so frequently that on the evenings when he did not see her she felt as though a part of herself were missing.

'And what is going to be the outcome of all this?' Verenskaya asked one evening as Melanie let herself into the flat.

'Outcome of what?' Melanie said, deliberately avoiding the question.

'You know very well what I mean. You and Gregory. It's three weeks since he first took you out and this is the tenth – twenty – time you have seen him!'

'Not as many as that,' Melanie smiled, 'so don't go all dramatic on me. Gregory and I are just friends.'

'There's no such thing as friendship between a young man

and woman. Not if they are both normal!'

'Gregory is quite normal,' Melanie retorted.

'Has he kissed you?'

'Of course not,' she said hastily. 'Why should he?'

Verenskaya snorted. 'What nonsense you talk. Why should he kiss you?' The claw-like hands lifted in a wide gesture. 'Because you are pretty and desirable, that's why.'

'I'm sure he knows women far more desirable than I am.'

'Then why doesn't he take them out?'

'Perhaps he does. I don't see him every night, you know.'

'I'd be surprised if he is seeing someone else.' The humour had gone from Verenskaya's voice. 'Be careful, Melanie. This man can be dangerous. I don't want you breaking your heart again.'

'You're making something out of nothing,' Melanie retorted. 'We're just friends.'

'Is that how you really feel about him – as if he is a friend? Don't your pulses race when you see him? Don't you want to throw yourself into his arms and—'

'Stop it!' Melanie burst out. 'Must you question everything I do?'

'I don't want you to be hurt again,' Verenskaya said remorselessly, 'and the way you are going on, you will.'

Melanie sighed and sat down in the chair opposite Verenskaya. 'You're always right,' she said wearily. 'Of course I want to throw myself into his arms when I see him, but what good would it do?'

'You don't know until you try.'

'Gregory isn't the sort of man with whom you try. *He* has to make the first move.'

'And he hasn't?'

'No.'

'I am surprised.' Verenskaya's voice was more guttural than usual, a sure indication of her concern. 'I would not have thought he was slow. From the first moment I saw him he struck me as a man of deep feeling.'

'Perhaps that's why he's being careful. After all, I was married to his cousin. . . .'

'You have never told him the full truth about that, have you?'

Melanie shook her head. 'I can't. It seems so disloyal. Perhaps if Gregory said something to me – if I knew what he felt about me. . . .'

'One day you will have to tell him the truth,' Verenskaya said ponderously. 'You owe it to him and yourself.'

'At the moment I can't. We're still only friends.'

'Then don't see him so often. Perhaps if you refuse him a few times he might say something to you.'

'He might equally decide that I don't want to see him.'

'If he loves you and you refuse to go out with him, he'll demand an explanation. If he doesn't, you will know he does not love you.'

'I don't want to know,' Melanie said slowly.

'You would rather live in a fool's paradise?'

'There's no point in discussing it. I'm already in love with him. Whether or not he loves *me* doesn't make any difference.'

But these were words uttered out of pride, and the next night she made a determined effort to arouse him, wearing her aqua-marine dress and setting her hair away from her face, a style which emphasized her slanting eyes. Yet Gregory made no comment throughout the evening, and only as he said good-night did he give any indication that he had noticed her more glamorous appearance.

'If I'd known you were going to dress up, I'd have worn a dinner jacket and taken you to the Savoy'

She shrugged. 'I just thought you might be tired of seeing me in cotton dresses all the time!'

'I wouldn't get tired of you if you wore a sack!' He leaned closer and she tilted her face upwards, convinced that he was going to kiss her. But though his lips met hers it was a fleeting touch, over almost before it had begun.

'I won't be able to see you during the week-end, Melanie, Fenwick's invited me down to his country place.'

Disappointment made her catch her breath, but it gave way to anxiety as she absorbed what he had said. 'He's not going to do anything with the factory, is he?'

'I'm not sure. That's one of the reasons I've accepted his invitation. I'll see you as soon as I get back.'

He was at the car when she spoke his name aloud, and he swung round to look at her. 'Did you call me?'

'Yes. I wanted to know if – if you liked my dress.'

Even in the moonlight she could see the smile playing at the corners of his mouth. 'Not the dress,' he said gravely, 'as much as the girl who's filling it.'

During the week-end Melanie hugged his words to herself, saying them over and over again, and each time reading a different meaning into them. Even the knowledge that Lydia would certainly be spending every moment with him could not mar her happiness, and she counted the hours until she would be seeing him again.

On Monday morning she awoke with a feeling of pleasurable anticipation, and every time the telephone rang she expected it to be Gregory. But there was no word from him during the entire day, and by Tuesday she was irritable with worry and fear. Why hadn't he called her as promised? Was he staying in the country longer than he had anticipated or had the few days spent in Lydia's company made him realize how unsuitable she herself was?

On Tuesday afternoon, unable to bear the anxiety, she telephoned his office and asked the switchboard operator if he was away.

'He's in conference,' came the reply. 'Would you like to speak to his secretary?'

'No, thank you.' She replaced the telephone and faced the unpalatable fact that he might have decided not to see her again or – at best – to see her less frequently. The knowledge filled her with depression and, as always, her dancing was affected, causing acid comment from Anton as she left the stage that night.

'I suppose you've quarrelled with Gregory again?'

'Do I always dance badly because I'm upset by a man?'

'That's generally your reason.'

'Well, you're wrong,' she retorted. 'I happen to be feeling off colour, and it's got nothing to do with Gregory or anyone else!'

'Then get changed and I'll take you home.'

'I'm not dying,' she answered, still irritated. 'I'd prefer to be by myself.'

In her dressing-room she listlessly changed and, with her coat over her arm, went downstairs and out into the alleyway. As the stage door shut behind her a man stepped forward, and seeing his face she gave an exclamation of joy.

'Gregory!' She held out her hands. 'I wasn't expecting you.'

Not touching her, he walked slightly ahead of her to the car, and with an undefinable feeling of anxiety she followed him and took her place beside him. To her surprise he did not make for Soho where they usually dined, but headed the car towards Hyde Park.

'Did you have a nice week-end?' she asked.

'The usual. Too much food and not enough exercise.'

His answer was so unforthcoming that she did not question him further, and sat in silence as he skirted the dark, gleaming Serpentine, and finally came to a stop beside it.

He twisted round in his seat. 'I managed to get a ticket for tonight's performance,' he said abruptly. 'You were wonderful.'

She warmed to the compliment, feeling her unease lift. 'Thank you. Anton's a marvellous partner.'

'Is he a good lover too?'

The question was so brutal and crude that she was speechless.

'Well,' Gregory said harshly, 'you haven't answered me.'

'I'd rather pretend you hadn't asked.'

'Why? Are you afraid to answer?'

'No!' she burst out. 'Only afraid that if I do, I might say something I'll regret. Now, if you don't mind,' she continued in a tight voice, 'I'd like you to take me home.'

He made no move to do so and she edged into the far corner of her seat, fighting back the tears and wishing she were a million miles away. The silence lengthened and the darkness around them seemed to increase, though it might have been born from the darkness of despair that engulfed her. Gradually her anger faded and, unwilling for things to end this way, she forced herself to ask the question uppermost in her mind.

'Why did you ask me that about Anton? I know you don't like him, but why should you suddenly think that he – that I. ...' Her voice died away and she waited for his answer. But none came, and after the silence had continued for what seemed an unbearable length of time, her anger returned. 'You've no right to accuse me of something and then not give me a chance to defend myself.'

'I *have* given you a chance. I asked if Anton was your lover and you refused to answer.'

'Would you believe me if I said no? Even the way you asked the question was an accusation! What have you heard about me, Gregory? What am I supposed to have done?'

'Walked out on Timothy the day you married him and spent your wedding night in Anton's flat!'

Melanie gave a shuddering sigh and closed her eyes, hoping that by shutting out Gregory's face she could also shut out his words. But nothing could erase them, and each one burned in her brain like a wound. So this was how Lydia had spent the week-end; filling Gregory with lies that had aroused all his old, earlier dislike of her. Yet oddly enough she could not feel any anger towards the girl, only pity that she could have acted so cheaply.

'I suppose Lydia told you,' she murmured. 'Don't bother denying it,' she added as he made a disclamatory gesture. 'She's the only one Timothy might have told!'

'Tell me if it's true,' he asked.

'That Anton's my lover or that I stayed with him on my wedding night? I'll only answer one question, Gregory, you'll have to decide the other one for yourself.' She clenched her hands tightly together. 'I *did* stay with Anton the night I married Timothy! Does that help you to find the other answer?' Even in the dim light that came from the dashboard she saw him turn so pale that his eyes were like black sockets. 'You always believe the worst of everyone,' she said pityingly. 'You don't know the meaning of faith.'

Her words acted on him like a whiplash. 'What faith can I have in you if you spent your wedding night with another man?'

'Where did you expect me to spend it?' she cried, her control snapping. 'With a husband who'd been making love to another girl an hour before?'

'What?' Gregory shouted the word and caught her shoulders. 'What did you say?'

'You heard,' she said wearily, too exhausted and shocked to pretend any longer. 'That's why I went to Australia with the Company. I hadn't had any intention of going on the tour, but after I saw ... after I discovered. ...' Tears choked her and, unable to continue, she turned her face away and stared unseeingly through the window.

Behind her there was a slight movement and she felt a handkerchief placed into her hand. 'Wipe your eyes,' Gregory said gently, 'and tell me the whole story.'

For several moments she did not answer, though she was intensely aware of the man beside her. She heard the scrape of a match and saw his reflection briefly in the window as he lit a cigarette. Then there was no other sound except her own fast, shallow breathing.

'I'm waiting, Melanie,' he said at last. 'Tell me what happened.' His voice deepened. 'I beg you.'

It was the last sentence more than anything else which prompted her to answer him, but she still kept her head averted as she recounted as briefly as possible the ugly events of her wedding night, though she omitted the name of the girl she had seen in Timothy's arms.

'And now you know the whole sordid little story,' she concluded. 'I made it perfectly clear to Timothy that I never wanted to see him again, but he didn't take any notice. He decided to fly out – and the rest you know.'

'Why didn't you tell me this before?'

'I wanted to. . . . There were times when I tried, but it didn't seem right.'

'Such stupid loyalty,' he said roughly. 'You preferred to blacken your own name, rather than—'

'I didn't prefer it,' she interrupted, 'but if I'd tried to tell you the truth when we first met you wouldn't have believed me. And afterwards—'

She did not continue, and he said curiously: 'And afterwards? Why didn't you tell me then? When we first started to go out together.'

'I wanted to know if you could see for yourself that I wasn't – that I wasn't the sort of girl who'd run away from marriage.'

'I told you I believed in you,' he said quietly. 'I told you that only a few days ago. Why didn't you tell me the whole story then?'

'Because it didn't seem important any more.' She still kept her head averted. 'I hadn't realized your belief in me was so ephemeral; that it could change so quickly.'

There was the sound of a window gliding down and his movement told her that he had thrown his cigarette away.

'You've every right to be angry,' Gregory's voice held an unusual shakiness. 'I've no excuse to offer except that – except that jealousy can make a man blind.' There was a pause and when he spoke again his voice was harder. 'Who was the girl?'

Melanie did not reply.

'Was it Lydia?'

She said nothing, but the way her body stiffened at the mention of the name must have given him his answer, for he gave an exclamation of anger. 'She must have been mad! What could she have hoped to gain by it?'

'I suppose she was just furious at being turned down by someone she considered inferior. . . . Or perhaps she was just as drunk as Timothy was. It was just bad luck I came in and saw them.' Melanie turned her face away from the window but still did not look directly at Gregory. 'If the same thing happened today, I'd probably behave differently, but at the time I was so naïve I couldn't face the fact that my Prince Charming only existed in my imagination.'

All at once she began to cry, the relief of telling him breaking the control of months. She put his handkerchief to her eyes and the aroma of after-shave lotion which he used was strong in her nostrils, making him seem even closer than he already was and reminding her how easily his belief in her had been shattered by Lydia's ugly accusation. The tears fell faster and her breath came in gasping little jerks which made him move across his seat and pull her into his arms.

'Don't cry, Melanie. It's all over.' He smoothed the hair away from her damp cheeks and, taking the handkerchief from her hand, gently wiped her eyes. 'You've no reason to cry any more. You've got so much happiness ahead of you. You are a successful dancer and one day you'll be famous.'

'I don't want fame,' she gulped. 'It isn't enough.'

'I thought it was what you wanted most of all.'

She shook her head. 'If I'd only been interested in my career I'd never have married Timothy. It was only when things went wrong that I concentrated on my dancing. If it hadn't been for that, I don't know how I'd have got through those awful months.'

'And I haven't helped by reminding you of them.' His hand stopped stroking her hair but remained on her head, making it difficult for her to move away. 'Poor Melanie! The Ransomes seem to have an aptitude for hurting you!'

'You haven't hurt me,' she said quickly.

'I did when we first met,' he said gravely, 'and I did so again tonight.' She did not answer, and he put his other hand on her head and lowered them both to cup her face. 'I never want to hurt you, Melanie. I love you too much to cause you a moment's unhappiness.'

Incredulous, she stared at him, unable to believe she had heard him correctly yet frightened to ask him to repeat it. But he could see from the look in her eyes how she felt and he gave a slight, imperceptible nod. 'Yes, Melanie, it's true. I love you.'

Still she found it impossible to speak and mistaking her reaction, he dropped his hands away from her and moved back into his seat. 'I wasn't going to tell you yet.' He spoke swiftly and jerkily. 'I wanted to give you a chance to get to know me properly – to forget the way I behaved when we first met.' He gave a short, unamused laugh. 'I must say I've done pretty well tonight.' He swung round to look at her again. 'Can you forgive me, Melanie? Is there a chance that—'

'Gregory!' she put her hand against his lips. 'Darling, don't be so stupid.'

At the tone in her voice he bent closer, and the look on her face this time made any more words between them unnecessary. With an exclamation he pulled her close and for the first time placed his mouth firmly and directly on hers. It was a kiss of control, yet she sensed the passion and, knowing an undreamed-of joy, an ecstasy never before experienced, her lips trembled and parted beneath his. The movement was enough to break his guard, and his grip became tighter as his control disappeared in a tide of passion that obliterated time and coherent thought.

At last he pushed her away from him with shaking hands. 'No, Melanie! There's a limit even to *my* self-control!'

Echoing the sentiments though she did not say them, she smoothed down her ruffled hair, aware that though he was keeping his distance he was watching her every movement.

'How beautiful you are!' he said softly. 'The way you turn your head ... your arms ... your grace.' He reached out and caught her hand, his grip so tight that she winced with pain but said nothing, unwilling for him to let go his hold.

'It would have saved so much unhappiness if you'd kissed me before,' she whispered.

'Were you very unhappy, my darling?'

She nodded. 'I loved you so much I couldn't think of anything else.'

'You once loved Timothy that way too.'

The words were uttered without expression, but the jealousy

in them was too obvious to be ignored and she knew that unless she could dispel it now it would always be there to haunt him and spoil their relationship.

'Don't begrudge what I felt for Timothy,' she said quietly. 'He was my first love – a romantic ideal that didn't really exist except in my imagination. It was a dream, Gregory, that had no basis in reality, no foundation of friendship or understanding or even mutual interests. We were both children playing at love.'

'But you married him. You were his wife. If you hadn't seen Lydia that night you'd . . . .'

'I suppose I would,' Melanie answered the unspoken question, but then followed it with another one. 'How long do you think it would have lasted? You knew Timothy better than I did, Gregory. From what you know of me now, do you think my marriage to him would ever have been successful?'

'It isn't fair to ask me that.'

'Everything's fair if you're fighting for your happiness,' she retorted passionately. 'And I'm fighting for you!'

This time she was the one to pull him close, cradling his head in her arms and stroking the crisp dark hair. 'I'll never love anyone else, Gregory. Only you. You must believe that.'

His answer was to raise his head and draw her face down to his, the touch of his lips making words unnecessary.

CHAPTER NINE

AT breakfast the next morning Melanie told Verenskaya that Gregory had told her he loved her and the old woman threw her hands up in the air and let flood a torrent of Russian.

'In English!' Melanie protested. 'I can't understand a word you're saying!'

Verenskaya stopped abruptly and spooned sugar into her coffee. 'All I said was that you do not look as happy as you should.'

'What a thing to say!'

'But I have said it!'

'That still doesn't mean it's true!'

'But it is.' The dark eyes were shrewd. 'You are unhappy

because you think you will have to give up your dancing.'

Melanie sighed. 'Can't you ever leave anything unsaid?'

'No. That is an Anglo-Saxon habit which is alien to me. Besides, I do not agree with it! Hidden feelings rarely die; they build up and explode or they magnify and distort.'

'It's too early for Chekhov,' Melanie expostulated.

'I was not quoting anyone,' came the dignified reply. 'The sentiments were my own.'

Despite herself Melanie could not help smiling, and seeing it Verenskaya pounced. 'It is true what I said, no?'

'Yes,' Melanie agreed. 'It is true. I've been thinking of my dancing.'

'He has asked you to stop when you become his wife?'

'He hasn't proposed to me yet,' Melanie said with care.

'It was an unspoken proposal,' Verenskaya said with certainty. 'I have no great belief in a man's honour, but he is not the kind to want anything from you without marriage.' Absentmindedly the woman put additional sugar into her coffee. 'But the dancing: he will want you to give it up?'

'I'm sure of it. He runs a large company and he must do a lot of entertaining. Once we – if we marry he'll expect me to be with him. He won't want to come home to an empty house night after night.'

'You would not be dancing night after night as a ballerina. There will be many occasions when you will be free.'

'My life still wouldn't be my own.'

Verenskaya sipped her coffee, made a face and then put it down. 'So once again you will give it up?'

'No.'

It was a quiet sound but spoken with such force that a broad smile marked Verenskaya's face. 'So at last you realize what dancing can mean.'

'Yes. It took me a long time, but I know it now. It's part of my life.' She stopped, bewildered. 'But it doesn't make sense. I gave it up for Timothy, yet for Gregory – whom I love much more – I can't do it.'

'But you are a different person now. And a different dancer too. You have a chance of greatness ahead of you and that is something one cannot give up lightly.'

'Even for love?'

'Real love would not demand it.'

Melanie remembered these words later that morning when

the bell rang and she opened the door of the flat to see Gregory on the threshold.

'I know I should have rung you to say I was coming,' he said, stepping in and gathering her into his arms, 'but I wasn't really intending to. I was on my way to the office and the car made a detour all by itself!'

She returned his kiss with fervour and then drew him into the living-room. 'I love surprises like this,' she exclaimed, and pushed him down into a chair, enjoying the sight of him, so tall and large and incongruous among the knick-knacks and the gilded ikons.

'Why I really came,' he said slowly, 'was to make sure last night wasn't a dream.' He held out his arms as he spoke and she sat down in his lap and rested against him.

'Does this make it seem real?' she whispered.

For answer he nuzzled against her throat and for a long while they did not speak.

It was Gregory finally who sensed there was something troubling her, for he pushed her into a sitting position and, keeping his arms firmly round her waist, asked her what was wrong.

'Don't bother saying it's nothing,' he said. 'I can tell when you're upset. Is it the damn stupid things I said to you last night?'

She shook her head. 'No.'

'Then what is it? I know it's something important or it wouldn't affect you like this.'

She looked down at her hands and, surprised to see they were clutched together, knew how deeply she subconsciously felt. Verenskaya was right. It would be impossible to live a lie with Gregory.

'It's my dancing,' she said carefully. 'It will be difficult – very difficult for me to give it up again.'

'I see.' He leaned back in the chair, the tilt of his head giving his features an arrogance she had not seen on them for a long time. 'What makes you think I'd *want* you to give it up?'

She stared at him. 'But I thought . . . I assumed. . . .'

'You assumed too much, my darling. I don't only love you, Melanie, I *understand* you.' He moved his head and she saw that his mouth was curved in a tender smile. 'And understanding you, I know that your work is a part of you, and that to ask you – or expect you – to give to up, would be selfish and wrong.'

Relief welled up in her, but she pressed it down, determined to make him see exactly what his words meant. 'If I do go on with my dancing, it won't be easy for you. You'll spend many evenings alone and—'

'I'll come and watch you.'

'Even when you're giving business dinners?'

'There'll be problems,' he agreed, 'but we'll overcome them.' His grip tightened. 'You've got more than talent; you have a rare gift that I'd be crazy to try and destroy. Of course there'll be times when I'll resent not having you at home with me – when I'll want to come into the dining-room and see you facing me across the table instead of watching you on the stage. But there'll be compensations too. Our time alone together will be sweeter, more meaningful.' He pulled her back against him. But even with his heart beating close beneath hers, she still felt uneasy.

'Are you absolutely sure?' she asked.

'Positive.' He pushed her up into a sitting position. 'Do you think I want a fool of a girl who spends her mornings shopping, her afternoons gossiping, and her evenings sitting in front of a television set? I don't only love your body, Melanie, I love your mind and the spirit that's given you the talent which you stupidly believe I want to stop. If I loved a painter do you think I'd ask her not to paint? If you were a pianist would I ask you to give up your music?'

'But ballet demands so much more. There may be times when it will even take me away from you.'

'If I asked you to give up your dancing in order to marry me,' he said quietly, 'I believe *that* would take you away from me even more.'

She looked him fully in the face, for his answer told her clearly how well he understood her feelings. 'I'm so lucky to have found you,' she said huskily.

'We're lucky to have found each other.' He picked up her hand and, turning the palm upwards, kissed it. 'We must go shopping,' he said in a completely different tone of voice. 'The finger on your left hand looks much too bare. Put on your coat.'

She gave an exclamation of disappointment. 'Oh, darling, I can't go shopping now. I have a matinée today and I'm already late for rehearsal.'

'I'm learning quicker than I realized,' he said ruefully. 'Never mind, though, I'll drive you to the theatre just to show there's no hard feelings!'

'Will you pick me up tonight?'

'Nothing will keep me away.'

Buoyant with happiness Melanie arrived at the theatre, and had just changed into her practice tights when Anton strode into her dressing-room without knocking, his face livid with anger.

'What's this rubbish Verenskaya's just told me about you and Gregory Ransome?' he demanded. 'You can't be crazy enough to marry him!'

'I'd be crazy if I didn't! I love him.'

'Wasn't one marriage enough? Do you have to ruin your life again – and end your career just when–'

'I'm not giving up my dancing this time,' she retorted swiftly. 'Gregory's agreed that I can–'

'*Agreed!*' Anton spat out the word. 'Did you have to have his agreement before deciding the most important thing in your life?'

'Yes,' she said quietly, 'I did. And it's childish for you to make a scene for nothing. Gregory never even expected me to stop dancing. He *wants* me to have a career.'

'That's what he says now. But wait till you're his wife. It'll be a different story then!' With an oath Anton stormed out, banging the door so hard that the pots of greasepaint on the dressing table rattled.

Trembling, Melanie bent to lace up her pumps, wishing she knew how much of Anton's fury stemmed from hurt pride that she had not fallen in love with him, and how much from genuine fear that she might give up the ballet. But either way there was nothing she could do to appease him.

She walked over to the mirror to powder her flushed cheeks, and looking into her eyes knew that despite the vehemence with which she had assured Anton – and Verenskaya too – that her dancing was something she would not be able to give up – knew that one day in the future she would give it up willingly in order to have Gregory's children.

Gregory's children. The thought filled her with such intense emotion that she sank on to a chair, lost in a happy dream from which she was only aroused by the callboy's voice reminding her that she was wanted on stage.

By the time the rehearsal was over there was only an hour left before the matinée, and Melanie decided to rest in her dressing-room, savouring the joy of all that lay before her. How different it would be tonight when Gregory called for her; no longer would she need to hide what she felt for him, and she could run into his arms and let him see all the love that was his for the taking.

Counting the hours until she could be with him, it came as an unpleasant shock when he telephoned during the interval to say he would be unable to see her that night.

'Something's cropped up that I must deal with,' he explained, his voice so weary and strained that she intuitively felt it was more of a personal reason than a business one.

'The second performance doesn't begin till seven-thirty,' she said. 'Can't we meet for a few minutes then?'

'I'm afraid not.'

'Is there anything wrong, Gregory?'

'I can always see you dance another night.'

His answer to her question was so ridiculous that for an instant she was puzzled.

'Someone's with you, isn't there?' she said softly.

'That's right.' His voice was noncommittal.

'Then I won't keep you. Telephone me later if you get the chance. I won't go to bed before midnight.'

'I'll try.'

Abruptly he hung up, and still disturbed she put down the receiver and returned to the wings. But though she tried not to worry she kept thinking of him throughout the evening, glancing at the clock frequently in the hope that he would call her before she left the theatre. But no word came from him and she went back to the flat, where she drank tea she did not want until the chiming of the clock told her he would not be telephoning her that night.

Despondently she went to bed, but though she fell asleep at once, anxious dreams disturbed her rest, filling her with a nameless terror that several times woke her up in startled, inexplicable fear. She was in the middle of another haunting nightmare when Verenskaya's voice brought her fully awake, and she sat up quickly, anxiety restoring her to full consciousness.

'What is it, Madame? Is anything wrong?'

'No, child. But Mrs. Ransome's on the telephone. She seemed anxious to talk to you.'

'I bet Gregory's told her we're engaged.' Melanie jumped out of bed and, without stopping to put on dressing gown or slippers, ran into the hall and picked up the receiver.

'I'm so sorry if I woke you up, dear,' Mrs. Ransome's voice was warm and friendly. 'But I wasn't sure what time you start rehearsing, and I wanted to catch you. I thought it would be nicer to tell you first, rather than have you read it in the papers.'

'Read what in the papers?'

'The engagement.'

'Do you mean it's already leaked out?' Melanie asked incredulously.

'Yes. And it's on the front page too, with a big picture of Gregory and a lot of nonsense about all the money he's made.' The woman chuckled. 'I bet he's furious at the publicity.'

'I can imagine,' Melanie said ruefully. 'I wonder how they heard.'

'Lydia must have told them.'

'Lydia? Why on earth should *she* do so?'

'To show off, I suppose. She's been in love with him for months.'

Melanie clutched at the hall table, unwilling to believe what she was hearing, yet knowing it was not a figment of her imagination nor a nightmare from which she would awaken. But it could not be true. It was impossible.

'What exactly does it say in the papers?' she asked huskily.

'Just that he and Lydia are engaged to be married.'

Though Melanie was not conscious of speaking she must have made some sound, for Mrs. Ransome stopped abruptly. 'Is anything wrong, dear?'

'No – no. I just – it's only that—' she caught her breath – 'it's cold out here.'

'How naughty of me to keep you talking. Go back to bed and I'll speak to you later. It's just that I wanted to tell you the news before you read it. You're one of the family, you know.'

'Yes . . . thank you.' Melanie spoke slowly, enunciating the words carefully for fear she would not be able to say them at all.

Then with the same care she put the receiver on its rest and went into her bedroom.

Verenskaya took one look at her face and hurried forward. 'What is it, Melanie? Has something happened to Gregory?'

'Yes,' she said quietly. 'His engagement's been announced – to Lydia Fenwick.'

It was only on rare occasions that Verenskaya was robbed of speech, but the news that Gregory had become engaged to Lydia Fenwick was one of them, and hearing it from Melanie the old woman sat down in a chair speechless, her body bending forward so that her black dress fell around her like a shroud.

Frightened by the yellow tinge on the wrinkled face, Melanie forgot her own misery and hurried into the kitchen to make coffee. Her mind was a blank and she did the task automatically, filling the kettle with water, waiting for it to boil, setting out the cups and returning to the bedroom with the coffee brewed.

Verenskaya was still sitting in the same humped position, but she accepted the coffee gratefully and by the time she had sipped it, the colour had returned to her face and, with it, speech to her tongue.

'You are well rid of him, my child. Never would I have thought it possible! I have met some strange men in my time, but none as difficult to understand as this one.'

'I can't understand why he did it.' Melanie still spoke without emotion, as if she were discussing the affairs of a stranger, and though she knew that she was merely experiencing the calm before the storm, she was at least grateful that she was able to talk about it with some rationality. 'Why did he do it?' she repeated. 'He didn't need to say he loved me. He needn't have said anything.'

'Perhaps he was carried away by the moonlight!'

'There was no moonlight when he came here yesterday morning. The whole thing doesn't make sense. We didn't just go out for a few days, Madame – he's been taking me out for weeks.'

'Perhaps he found it difficult to extricate himself.'

'Gregory?' Melanie shook her head. 'If he wanted to say good-bye he'd have done so without any feeling of guilt. Anyway, he had nothing to feel guilty about. It wasn't until he – he told me he loved me that he even kissed me.' She jumped to her feet. 'I don't believe the whole thing was a lie. I'm sure the story in the newspaper is a mistake.'

'Then why hasn't he rung to say so?'

'Perhaps he hasn't seen it yet.' Melanie hurried to the wardrobe and pulled out the first dress that came to hand.

'You are not going to see him,' Verenskaya said behind her.

'That's exactly what I am going to do!'

'You are crazy! Where is your pride?'

'I haven't got any with Gregory. I love him and I'm going to see him.' Melanie swung round to face Verenskaya. 'If he was lying when he implied that he wanted to marry me – if it was just a game for him – he'll have to tell me so to my face.'

The outrage on Verenskaya's face gave way to unwilling admiration. 'You are growing up, little one. Once you ran from love like a frightened child, but now you are prepared to go out and fight for it. You are truly a woman.'

But a half hour later, as she waited in the elegantly appointed offices of Ransome Properties, she did not feel like a grown-up woman but a gauche and totally inadequate child, conscious of her wan cheeks and swollen eyes, the shabbiness of her three-year-old suit and the unaccountable run she had just seen in her stocking. What sort of woman was she when she did not even have a woman's instinct for making the best of herself? Instead, she had grabbed the first thing in her wardrobe and rushed to see Gregory before her resolution faded.

A buzzer sounded on the desk of the sophisticated blonde girl at the switchboard, and a discreet murmur was heard before the girl looked over at Melanie and nodded. As she did so, a door at the other end of the room opened and a thin young man in a dark suit came towards her.

'Mr. Ransome will see you now. If you'd follow me . . .'

Melanie did as he asked, walking beside him down a long thick-carpeted corridor lined on either side with offices. At the very end, double doors faced her and it was here that the young man stopped.

Melanie braced herself, turned the handle and walked in. She was vaguely aware of the room being extremely large, with parquet floor. a Persian carpet and panelled walls lined with many books. In front of her loomed a large desk and behind it, remote in the depths of a black leather armchair, was Gregory. Pale-faced, dark-suited and impeccably groomed, he was the Gregory she had first met so many months ago. Although it was so early in the morning, she saw a cigar stub already in his ashtray and saw too that he was smoking another one, noticing with something near despair that the hand that held it was perfectly steady.

He stood up, made as if to come towards her and then stopped and pointed to a chair. 'I was going to come and see you,' he said. 'You shouldn't have come here.'

'I had to. When Mrs. Ransome told me I—'

'I'm sorry you had to learn it from my aunt,' he said swiftly, his voice showing the first sign of emotion. 'Believe me, Melanie, it was the last thing I thought she'd do. If I hadn't had a board meeting, I'd have been round to your flat first thing this morning.'

'And when were you planning to come and tell me of your engagement?' she asked shakily.

'Immediately afterwards. It was only when my aunt rang me – after she'd spoken to you – that I knew what had happened.'

Melanie's composure fled and she leaned forward, her hands outstretched. 'Tell me it isn't true! Tell me it was a mistake – that Lydia did it for spite.'

'No, I can't say that. It's perfectly true.'

'But why? Why did you speak of marriage? Why did you say you loved me? You couldn't have been lying! What's gone wrong, Gregory?'

If anything he became even paler, but when he spoke his voice was still controlled. 'I'm afraid I allowed my emotions to get the better of me. You were very sweet the other night and I—'

'But what about yesterday?' she interrupted. 'You came to the flat yesterday morning. You weren't carried away by emotion then. You're not telling me the truth, Gregory. There's something else behind it.' Uncaring that she was pleading, that her hands were still outstretched and tears were pouring down her face, she continued to speak. 'I love you and I know you love me. You weren't pretending when you said so. But something's happened to make you change your mind and I must know what it is.'

There was a long silence and he stared at a point beyond her shoulder, his face devoid of expression, so that it was impossible to know what he was thinking. But at last he spoke, leaning back in his chair and tilting it slightly so that he was facing the window behind him, giving her a view of his profile, stern and implacable against the clear light shining in on him.

'It would be much better if you hadn't asked for an explanation, Melanie. Trying to give a reason for what I said –

for what I did – can only result in giving you more pain.'

'I'm used to pain,' she said bitterly.

He ignored the interruption. 'We come from different worlds – different backgrounds. I tried to ignore it – to make myself believe that the differences wouldn't matter – that once we were married everything would work out. But the more I thought about it the more I realized I was looking at a mirage and not the reality of the situation.'

'Many people from different classes and backgrounds have happy marriages.'

'Not as many as you think; and even then, you'll find that one or other of them has had to sacrifice something – either giving up their family or trying to change their whole pattern of existence.'

'You speak as though we come from different countries; as though I was a foreigner.'

'In many ways you *are* foreign to me. You've been brought up in a milieu where dancing is all-important, where everything, in fact, is subservient to ballet.'

'You said you didn't want me to give it up.'

He half turned in his chair and glanced at her briefly before turning away again. 'Would you have done so if I'd asked you?'

'No,' she admitted, 'at least not right away.' She stood up and came forward so that only the desk separated them. 'But if you'd made it a condition, if you'd said I had to choose between you and my career, I'd have chosen you.'

'And hated me ever after. No, Melanie, you're not being truthful to yourself.'

'Are you being truthful?' she retorted. 'Do you expect me to believe what you've just said?'

'I'm afraid you'll have to. I mean every word. I should never have mentioned marriage. I did so because I found you—' he hesitated, and then faced her squarely. 'Because I found you extremely desirable.'

'Don't tell me you were so carried away by passion that you lost all your reasoning powers!'

'That's exactly what I *am* trying to tell you.' He was standing now, his whole body outlined by the light from the window, so that he appeared taller and broader. 'The night before last – when we were together – I allowed myself to believe that we could be happy together. But when I thought about it afterwards I realized it wasn't true. To have gone on pretending would have been wrong for both of us.'

'Then why did you pretend yesterday when you came to the flat?'

For the first time he did not have an answer ready and it was a moment before he spoke. 'I don't know,' he said at last.

'When *did* you decide that you knew? Was it last night when you rang me at the theatre?'

Again he took time before replying. 'It was becoming clearer to me then,' he admitted.

'Clearer that we were too different to be happy, or that you loved Lydia Fenwick?'

Colour came into his face, and a strange expression passed over it, leaving his mouth narrow and unexpectedly tight with anger. 'Must we go on with this catechism? What the hell do you hope to get out of it? I've changed my mind about marrying you. I'm bitterly sorry you had to hear about it from my aunt, but coming here and holding an inquest won't make me change my mind.'

Melanie moved back from the desk, longing to run from the room yet knowing that her trembling limbs would not take her that far. She stared across at him, trying to see in the icy grey eyes staring back at her the loving and responsive man who had held her in his arms yesterday. It was incredible that his feelings for her could have changed so quickly; and not only changed, but turned towards another woman. It was this more that anything else that she found unacceptable.

'All right, Gregory,' she said huskily. 'I'll accept the fact that you've changed your mind – that you realize you mistook desire for love. What I can't accept – what I can't understand – is your engagement to Lydia. Or are you asking me to believe that you fell in love with *her* as quickly as you fell out of love with *me*?'

Carefully he tapped the ash from his cigar into the ashtray in front of him. 'What I feel for Lydia is not the same emotion I felt for you.'

'Then why marry her?'

'Because it's time I had a wife. That's one thing you did make me realize.'

'Don't!' she gasped.

'I'm not going to pretend that my – that what I feel for Lydia compares with my – with what I feel – what I *felt* for you,' he admitted. 'But one can't base a marriage on passion.' Even as he spoke he turned away from her again and stared intently out of the window at the blank blue sky.

Looking at his rigid back, the faint hope that had brought her here to plead with him died its final death.

'What you mean,' she said carefully, 'is that you would rather have a loveless marriage with a girl from your own background than have real happiness with me.'

'It wouldn't be a lasting happiness. I've given you my reasons for thinking that.'

'But they're wrong!'

'You're entitled to your opinion, Melanie, and I'm entitled to mine. I'm going to marry Lydia. I should never have mentioned marriage to you, and once I admitted it was a mistake, the only way of making you accept it – or so I felt – was for me to marry someone else.'

'To stop me from pestering you, I suppose!' she burst out.

His shoulders lifted in a shrug and, hearing her give a gasp of pain, he turned to face her again. 'My biggest regret is that you had to learn about it from my aunt. As I told you when you came in, I had every intention of seeing you myself, but I had an early morning meeting and it wasn't until half-way through it that I found out that Lydia had already announced our engagement to the newspapers. I never wanted you to learn of it the way you did. If you believe nothing else, you must at least believe that.'

'Why do you care what I believe?' Melanie said scornfully. 'Don't tell me you've got a conscience.'

A spasm of pain crossed his face. 'Despite what you believe at the moment, I'm not heartless. If I could turn back the clock – take back what I said . . .'

'Don't bother,' she said wearily. 'Suffering is supposed to be good for the soul, so you've at least assured me of a happy after-life!'

She was at the door when he called her name, and she stopped and, still clutching at the doorknob, looked back at him. 'Yes?'

'What are you going to do now?' he asked. 'Where are you going?'

'To the theatre. Or did you think I was going to throw myself under a bus?'

'I hate it when you talk so bitterly.'

'Whatever makes you think I'm bitter?' she asked scornfully. 'I'm only thankful that I found out the sort of person you are. I never thought I'd have to thank Lydia Fenwick for anything, but at least she's made me see how despicable you are!'

'I deserved that,' he said quietly.

'You deserve much more,' she answered, 'but I can't give it to you. I'll leave that to your new fiancée.'

CHAPTER TEN

MELANIE went straight from Gregory to the theatre, for only there would she be forced to control her emotions. Quickly she changed into practice tights and went to the rehearsal room, but she had only been practising at the barre for a few moments when Anton came up to her.

'So you finally decided to put in an appearance,' he said by way of greeting. 'I suppose now you're going to be Mrs. Gregory Ransome you think you can afford to skip rehearsals!'

Momentarily she closed her eyes. Obviously Verenskaya had not told him the happenings of this morning – an unusual feat of diplomacy which she desperately wished had not been the case. When Anton chose to be unpleasant his tongue had a cutting edge that she was in no state to take.

'I'm sorry, Anton. I didn't mean to be late.'

'Apologies won't make up for lost time. Either you work with the rest of us or get out!'

'Don't!' she cried, and averted her head, praying he would go away.

But instead he came closer, his body shielding her from the other dancers. 'What's wrong, Melanie? Had a quarrel with Ransome?'

She nodded, too weary to dissemble.

'I assume he wants you to give up the ballet?'

She shook her head. 'He wants to give up *me* ... he already has.'

Anton's slanting brows rose in perplexity, making him look even more puckish than ever. 'I don't follow you.'

'It's quite simple. I've been jilted. Thrown over.'

'If this is some sort of joke I—'

'The joke's on me,' she interrupted. 'Gregory's going to

marry Lydia Fenwick.'

With the truth brought out into the open, clearly stated to the one person who – above all others – would be delighted at the news, Melanie braced herself for what Anton would say.

'You poor kid. You shouldn't have come in at all.'

The reply, briskly spoken, yet so obviously sympathetic, brought tears to her eyes, and she fumbled helplessly for her handkerchief.

'Use this,' he said, and gave her his own. 'We'll be breaking for lunch in half an hour. If you like, I'll take you home.'

'I'd rather stay here.' She wiped her eyes and held out the handkerchief, resolutely meeting his gaze. 'It's not the end of the world, Anton. I've a brilliant career ahead of me. You said so yourself!'

'So I did,' he said slowly. 'And now there's nothing to stand in your way.'

Not until later that evening, as they waited together in the wings, did he refer to their earlier conversation, asking with unusual diffidence if there was anything he could do to help.

'If you'd like to tell me about it. . . . It might help if you got it out of your system.'

'Ballet's the only thing that will help me,' she said, keeping her eyes fixed on the dancers on stage. 'Anyway, there isn't much to tell. He just – just decided it wouldn't work out . . . that we were too different.'

'*We're* not different,' Anton said. 'Remember that.'

The music changed and, glad it was their cue, she poised ready to make her entrance with him.

'I love you,' he whispered as they moved forward. 'I'll always be here when you want me.'

In the weeks that followed Melanie found herself taking advantage of Anton's offer, and most of her spare time was spent with him. It was a long, unusually warm summer, but because they had been away from London for six months on their Australian tour Verenskaya had decided not to take the company round the provinces, which had been their normal procedure. Instead they remained at their London theatre and, with an influx of foreign visitors, were dancing night after night to packed houses.

But every Sunday Anton drove Melanie to the country, each time choosing a different venue, a new restaurant, another beauty spot from which she returned mentally refreshed and better able to cope with the arduous week that lay ahead. Yet always she had to be on guard not to mention Gregory, to keep her mind fixed firmly in the present, with no thought of her own bleak, loveless future.

But try though she did, there were painful occasions when the sight of a tall, commanding figure or crisp dark hair would bring him forcibly to mind, and it was then that gaiety became feverish and her conversation brittle and excited.

It was at times like these that she appreciated Anton's sympathy most, for though he was always warm and understanding, he refused to let her give way to self-pity, and would tease her until she was forced to defend herself and, in so doing, to forget her heartache. Indeed, their relationship was slowly becoming a repetition of what it had been in Australia, and one night as he drove her home from the theatre and parked outside the flat she remarked on it.

'I always turn to you when I'm in trouble. You shouldn't let me, Anton. It isn't good for me.'

'It's good for me, though. I want you to rely on me, Melanie. I love you.'

In the light cast by the street lamp she noticed the lines of weariness at the corners of his eyes and, moved by tenderness, she reached for his hand. 'Dear Anton,' she murmured.

He slid across the seat, the tiredness vanishing from his face. 'Can't you think of me as more than just a friend? I wouldn't ask for much.'

'It would be wrong. I've so little to give.'

'Whatever you give is better than nothing.' Gently he drew her close and with a sigh she surrendered to his kiss.

Yet though she wanted desperately to respond to him, it was impossible to think of him as anything but her friend and dancing partner and she remained passively in his arms, unable to show any answering response. But if he was aware of it he gave no sign and when he drew back there was satisfaction on his face and a more proprietorial air in the way he helped her out of the car, took the key from her handbag and let her into the flat.

From that moment on, there began a new phase in their relationship, and more than ever she looked to him as her guide and mentor, not only in matters of dancing but in her personal life too, accepting his advice before she bought any clothes – an act which an increase in salary made possible, and taking his opinion on make-up and how she should wear her hair. Anton revelled at playing Pygmalion, obviously seeing it as an extension of their working relationship, and enjoying the knowledge that not only was he helping to mould her career but also her life.

He made few physical demands on her and, anticipating that he would ask to be her lover, she was surprised that he seemed satisfied with their gentle good night kiss. She knew him too well to believe it was a role he would be content to play for long, but she was glad that for the moment he accepted the little she could offer and wondered whether – when the time came and he asked for more – she would be able to give it. The knowledge that she might not be able to do so frequently filled her with guilt, a guilt which increased whenever she went to see Mrs. Ransome, for her visits to the Belgravia house always brought Gregory so forcibly back into her mind that she doubted if she would ever be free of him.

Frequently she toyed with the idea of not going to see Mrs. Ransome at all. But to do this would have caused the woman pain and all she could do was to make her visits as brief and infrequent as possible.

It was on one such occasion, a Monday afternoon in late autumn, when Melanie was unexpectedly free of rehearsals and was spending an hour with Mrs. Ransome, that the question of Gregory's marriage was discussed.

'Lydia would like to get married soon, but Gregory keeps putting it off. He said he wouldn't have time for a honeymoon and he's determined not to get married until he can go away for at least six weeks.'

Melanie's brief flare of hope at hearing Gregory was not anxious to get married died as she heard the rest of what Mrs. Ransome said, and the depression that always enveloped her when she was here now became intolerable.

'If Lydia nags long enough,' she said carefully, 'I'm sure she'll get what she wants.'

'With Gregory?' Mrs. Ransome smiled. 'You know how obstinate he is. Mind you, he's wonderful with Lydia. He's never been much of a person for parties, but they seem to be out every night.' Mrs. Ransome leaned forward and lightly touched Melanie's hand. 'But what about you?'

'Me?' Melanie asked, startled.

'Yes. What about *your* future? You surely don't want to end up like Verenskaya, do you?'

'She's very happy.'

'Without a home and children?'

'The Company's her home and her children.'

'But that wouldn't satisfy you,' Mrs. Ransome said firmly. 'You should be married, Melanie, and have a home and children of your own.'

'Dancing is all I need.' Unable to face Mrs. Ransome's direct gaze, Melanie jumped up and walked over to the window. 'I love the trees in autumn,' she said. 'The colours are so beautiful.'

'You won't always be able to go on with your dancing,' Mrs. Ransome continued, blithely ignoring Melanie's determined effort to change the conversation, 'and then what will happen to you?'

'That's looking too far ahead,' Melanie said, and glanced surreptitiously at her watch, wondering how soon she could leave; much more of this conversation and she would start to scream.

'Come back and sit next to me,' Mrs. Ransome said suddenly. 'I want to talk to you and it's tiring if I have to shout.'

'I don't want to talk about my future any more,' Melanie said, keeping her voice light with an effort. 'Just because – just because Gregory's getting married there's no reason for you to try and marry me off too.'

'I wouldn't dream of doing any such thing. Old women who give orders are never appreciated and you might stop coming here if you felt I was trying to do *that*!'

'I'd never stop coming to see you,' Melanie said quickly.

The older woman acknowledged the remark with a contented sigh, but Melanie felt a vague sense of unease as she looked at her, wondering whether it was imagination that made her think Mrs. Ransome looked frailer than usual.

'Are you keeping all right?' she asked with sudden concern. 'You look tired.'

'I've been overdoing it this week. Gregory's been abroad and I've taken advantage of his absence. When he's here he always checks up to make sure what time I go to bed at night.'

'Then I'll have to do the checking in future.'

'You needn't bother now,' Mrs. Ransome smiled. 'My running around is over for the time being. Everything's arranged.'

She gave a smile of satisfaction. 'I'm giving a party for Gregory and Lydia,' she explained, 'and I wanted to get it all settled without Gregory knowing.'

'He won't like that.'

Mrs. Ransome chuckled. 'I'm having it a fortnight on Saturday and I hope you'll be able to come.'

'I'm dancing that night,' Melanie replied, thankful that she had a genuine excuse for refusing the invitation.

'You can come straight on from the theatre. We won't be beginning until nine o'clock anyway. I'm putting up a marquee in the garden and I've arranged for an orchestra and ...' She waved her hands. 'It's going to be like old times – the last time I gave a party like that was for Timothy's twenty-first birthday.'

'Are you sure you should be doing it – I mean without telling Gregory? I'm sure the excitement will be bad for you.'

'Excitement is only relative, Melanie, and I *want* to give him this party.'

She looked so happy that Melanie did not feel she had the right to criticize, besides, doing so would prolong this conversation and she could not bear it. She pushed back her chair and stood up.

'Going so soon?' Mrs. Ransome asked.

'I'm on stage in an hour and a half and I always like to have a rest before the performance.' She leaned forward to kiss her mother-in-law's cheek and as she did so noticed a tension in the frail body. 'Are you sure you're all right?' she asked anxiously.

'Perfectly. I'm just a bit on edge. I want to ask you a favour and yet I don't feel I should.'

'You can ask me for anything. Surely you know I'll help you if I can.'

'That's the trouble. I don't want you to think I'm taking advantage of you.'

Melanie smiled, 'Ask me and I'll let you know.'

Mrs. Ransome did not reply at once. She looked down at her hands, fidgeted with a tassel on the cushion beside her and then picked at the lace on the handkerchief lying in her lap. 'It's about the party. I'd like you and Anton to dance for me.'

'Dance for you?' The request took Melanie by surprise. 'Do a ballet here?'

'Just an excerpt. Something simple.' The sad blue eyes were

eager. 'You've never met any of my friends, Melanie, and I've never had the chance of showing you off. The party would be such a wonderful occasion for me to do so.'

'Why on earth should you show me off?' Melanie said quickly.

'Because you were Timothy's wife. Please, Melanie, say you'll do it for me.'

The thought of dancing at a party given for Gregory and Lydia was intolerable, yet to refuse her mother-in-law was equally impossible. Desperately she searched round for an excuse that would allow her to say no with grace. But nothing came to mind and she knew she was trapped.

'Please, Melanie,' Mrs. Ransome said again. 'Won't you and Anton dance as a favour to me?'

Accepting the inevitable, Melanie let out her breath on a sigh. 'Of course we will.'

'I'm so glad. I'll tell the caterers to put up a stage.'

'Put up a stage?' Anton echoed the words later that night when Melanie told him the news. 'You don't mean you actually agreed to dance?'

'She would have been terribly hurt if I'd refused.'

'How about your own feelings for a change? Or do you expect me to believe you'll enjoy dancing for Gregory and Lydia?'

'I'm doing it for Mrs. Ransome.'

'I appreciate that,' he said dryly.

'Then you'll dance with me?'

'You don't think I'll let you go to the party alone, do you?' He caught her hand and squeezed it. 'You're a sucker for punishment, Melanie.' He dropped her hand, and when he spoke again his voice was so casual that it rang false. 'Have you ever seen Gregory since you—'

'No,' she interrupted. 'Never.'

'So the party will be the first time?'

'Yes.'

He made no comment and neither did she, though she was well aware that for the rest of the evening he watched her with unusual keenness.

As the night of the party drew nearer, Melanie's nervousness at the prospect of seeing Gregory increased to such magnitude that she doubted whether – when the time actually came – she would be able to dance at all. If only she had not allowed sentiment to sway her into making Mrs. Ransome such a ridiculous promise! A promise she had given and to which she was bound. Indeed, even if she wanted to draw back, Anton would not let her, for he regarded their dancing at the party as though it were a gauntlet personally flung in her face by Gregory.

So it was that, inwardly trembling but outwardly composed, she arrived at the house in Belgravia on the last Saturday in September. Lights blazed from every window and the gentle strains of music filtered out into the square. The main reception rooms were filled with people and the entire garden had been closed by canvas to provide a marquee of enormous size and splendour. Seeing it her resolution faltered, and only the pressure of Anton's hand on her arm forced her through the crowd of people to where Mrs. Ransome was standing with Gregory and Lydia.

What a striking couple they made, she thought involuntarily, both so tall and assured, so obviously from the same background and social position. How could she ever have believed that she might have had a future with him? That he would have been prepared to share the splendours of his life with a girl who – because of the demands of her work – could at best only have been a part-time wife. It was ironical that she should be dancing at this party tonight, for by exhibiting herself professionally she was showing him how right he had been to say they came from different worlds, and proving once and for all how great was the gulf between them.

But then there was no more time for thought, for Gregory was smiling at her coolly and Lydia's hand, thin and sharp, was clutching at her with false warmth. Greetings were exchanged and she must have uttered the right congratulations, though she was unaware of what she said, and then Anton was propelling her away into the blissful anonymity of strangers who did not give them more than a passing glance.

'A glass of champagne for you,' he murmured, and produced it as if by magic.

Gladly she took it from him and drank it at a gulp.

'Steady on,' he cautioned. 'We're dancing, remember.'

'I'm trying to forget.'

'Think of it as cathartic medicine!'

'I'm afraid it's difficult to swallow,' she said bitterly. 'I must be like one of Pavlov's dogs! I think the sight of Gregory will always affect me.' Abruptly she turned away and stared at the satin-draped walls of the marquee, but it was Lydia who filled her mind's eye, her beautiful figure enhanced by deep green velvet, her magnificent titian hair elaborately sculptured around an emerald and diamond parure that matched the emerald and diamond ring that blazed so conspicuously on the third finger of her left hand.

A little before midnight Mrs. Ransome took Melanie and Anton upstairs to change, showing Anton into a guest room but taking Melanie into her own bedroom. Intrigued, the woman watched as Melanie unpacked a small suitcase and shook out her costume, leaving it on the bed while she began to alter the style of her hair.

'I didn't realize you'd have to go to quite such bother,' Mrs. Ransome apologized.

'It's no bother. Changing into costume is pretty automatic for me.'

'But having to redo your hair and your make-up . . .'

'I'm a professional,' Melanie said with masochistic delight. 'Please don't worry about it.' With relief she looked up as Anton came in, resplendent in tights and glittering jacket.

'You do look splendid,' Mrs. Ransome observed. 'Who are you meant to be?'

'Romeo.' He glanced at Melanie. 'How long will you be?'

'A few minutes.'

'I'll take you downstairs,' Mrs. Ransome volunteered, 'then you can see if the stage and lighting are all right.'

Anton followed his hostess out of the room and, glad to be alone, Melanie took off her evening dress, did her warming-up exercises and put on her costume. The soft white skirts fell gracefully around her, the simplicity of the design making her seem thinner and younger. Carefully she fixed a pearl net cap on to her dark hair and then bent to adjust her ballet shoes. Behind her the door opened and, thinking it was Mrs. Ransome again, she did not look up. 'I'm nearly ready. How do I look?'

'Absurdly pre-Raphaelite.' The deep familiar voice made her straighten abruptly and the colour drained from her face as she saw Gregory leaning against the door.

'What do *you* want?'

'I came to fetch a pill for my aunt. Unfortunately she didn't tell me you were changing here.' He walked over to the dressing-table, picked up a bottle of capsules, extracted one and slipped it into his pocket. Then, still standing where he was, he looked at her. 'I didn't know until tonight that you were dancing here. My aunt had wanted it to be a surprise for me.'

'I hope it was a pleasant one.'

'On the contrary.' His voice deepened. 'She should never have asked you. She wouldn't have done so, of course, if she had known about us. . . . I'm very sorry, Melanie.'

'There's no reason to be,' she answered, marvelling that she could keep her voice controlled. 'It's my job to entertain. Besides, it proves how right you were.'

He looked at her as though puzzled by her remark, and the knowledge that he seemed to have forgotten the reason he had given her for terminating their own engagement filled her with such fury that she longed to lash out at him, to hurt him as much as he had hurt her.

'Yes,' she repeated. 'How right you were in saying our marriage would have flopped. I could never have been happy in your world, it's pretentious and false.'

'Your world is false too,' he said, and pointed to her costume.

'At least we know we're pretending!'

He acknowledged the retort by a slight lift of one eyebrow. 'What are you dancing?'

'An excerpt from *Romeo and Juliet*.'

'The star-crossed lovers! Very romantic! I hope it's not an omen for my own future.'

'If I'd thought of that,' she said, 'Anton and I would have done something from *The Rake's Progress*!'

Gregory's mouth tightened. 'You're unusually sharp, Melanie.'

'I've had need to be lately.' She turned her back on him and fumbled in her handbag. Behind her she heard him move to the door and she swung round and called his name, at the same time holding out her hand: in it was the baroque gold bracelet he had given her. 'This is yours,' she said.

A spasm — almost of pain — passed across his face, but it was gone so quickly that she was not sure whether she had imagined it.

'I bought it for you,' he replied.

'You don't think I still want to keep it, do you? For heaven's sake, take it.'

Silently he did as she bid. 'You still hate me, don't you,

Melanie?'

'One can't hate what doesn't exist, and as far as I'm concerned you don't.'

He looked as though he were going to reply, but then, thinking better of it, he swung on his heel and left the room.

She sank on to a chair and buried her face in her hands. This unexpected meeting alone with Gregory had unnerved her completely, showing her more clearly than ever how difficult it was going to be for her to forget him. Even the hope that her love for him might have lessened had been denied by the pounding of her heart at the sight of him and by the intolerable longing she had felt to throw herself into his arms and beg him to take her on any terms he liked. Was this the sort of thing that love could do? she wondered. Destroy your pride, shatter your morals, make you willing to be a mistress if you could not be a wife?

There was a sound in front of her and she lifted her head quickly, hope dying as she saw it was Anton.

One look at her face and he was kneeling at her side. 'Get a hold on yourself, Melanie. You look like death.'

'I can't dance,' she gasped. 'You'll have to go down and tell them.'

'Never! You've *got* to dance. If you don't you'll be playing right into Gregory's hands.'

'He doesn't care whether I dance here tonight or not.'

'Of course he cares! The biggest blow you can ever give him is to show him you're a success.'

Unconvinced, she shook her head. 'Whatever I am doesn't matter to him.'

'Well, it does to Lydia. She'd crow like hell if I went downstairs and said you were too ill to dance.' He caught her roughly by the shoulders. 'Do you think she doesn't know you're in love with Gregory? She's cunning and astute and she was watching you tonight like a snake, waiting for you to give yourself away.'

'She can't know,' Melanie burst out. 'Gregory would never have told her.'

'I'm not saying he did,' Anton conceded, 'but there are some things that don't need telling. You've got to come down and dance, Melanie. If you don't, you'll give yourself away completely.'

The truth of Anton's words brought Melanie to her feet and

once more pride came to her rescue. In silence she powdered away the tear marks, smoothed her skirts and preceded him down the stairs to the marquee. The dance floor in the centre had been completely cleared and elevated slightly so that everyone present could have a full view of it. It was almost an exact replica of a theatre in the round and she knew that to dance here would not only call for more skill but would also show off her ability to its greatest advantage. With head high she climbed the two steps and took up her position with Anton. For a brief instant her eyes moved across the people in front of her and she saw Lydia and Gregory close together. For a second her composure failed, then the music started and the long arduous years of her training reasserted itself as it always miraculously did; the tired, disheartened little ballet dancer vanished and in her place stood the eager, vibrant young Juliet, satiated with her night of love with Romeo, yet pleading with him to remain. As always, Anton was a superb partner and tonight he excelled himself, as though he too knew that he was on test. It was as if neither of them were playing a part and that they really were star-crossed lovers taking what passion they could, while they could, as though realizing it was not to last.

As the final strains of the music died away the eloquent quiet of the audience was broken by tumultuous applause, and people surged forward to sweep them off the stage in triumph. So eager was everyone to offer their congratulations that they did not have a chance to go upstairs and change out of their costumes and, still in the simple white nightgown which she had worn for her portrayal of Juliet, Melanie found herself being escorted from one admiring group to another. She would not have been human had she not enjoyed the sensation she had caused, particularly as it had momentarily relegated Lydia to the sidelines.

'You've never danced better,' Anton said during a sudden lull when he was standing by her side. 'Once you're seen in my full-length ballet you'll be an international star.'

Excited though she already was, the excitement caused by his statement made her feel dizzy. 'You don't mean *I'm* going to dance it with you?'

'All the choreography's been done with you in mind,' he said quietly.

'Tanya won't let me do it.'

'She can't stop you. She's a wonderful dancer, I admit, but

she can't compare with you.'

'Perhaps there's something to be said for unhappiness, after all,' she said with sudden wryness.

'If it's helped to make you dance the way you did tonight, then don't regret it, Melanie. If you go on this way your name will be among the great stars of ballet.'

Elated by his words, she felt an outflowing of gratitude towards him which showed in her eyes and the curve of her body as she bent close to him. 'There's so much I owe you. If you hadn't helped me I'd still be in the corps de ballet.'

'Isn't that a slight exaggeration?' a mocking voice said, and Melanie turned to see that Gregory had come up to stand beside her. 'I'd have thought your success came from your own efforts more than from anyone else's.'

Heart pounding, Melanie moved closer to Anton. 'In ballet the teacher is all-important, and Anton taught me everything I know.'

Lydia, following close on Gregory's heels, caught the end of the remark. 'That could be a very misleading statement,' she said lightly. 'Are we to take it at its face value?'

'Do we have the same sort of values?' Melanie asked coolly.

For an instant Lydia lost her poise, and her eyes glittered, hard and angry. Then the mask was resumed and the face was once more calm and beautiful. 'I was just letting my curiosity get the better of me,' she said sweetly, 'but it's your own fault really. You and Anton danced so beautifully and realistically that we've all been wondering how much of it was acting.'

Melanie drew a deep breath, but a sudden sharp nip on her thigh from Anton's fingers served as a brake to her temper. 'I'm afraid everyone will have to go on being curious,' she replied.

'You mean you won't even tell *me*?' The husky voice was pleading. 'We'll keep it strictly in the family, won't we, Gregory darling?'

'Speak for yourself,' Gregory said. 'Personally I think Melanie's private life should remain private.'

'How man-like of you,' Lydia protested, and placed a possessive hand on his arm. 'I wasn't meaning to be nosey, it's just that I'm so happy I want to feel that everyone is the same.' She glanced at Melanie. 'I never knew what happiness was until I found Gregory, and I'd love to think that you had found the same sort of happiness with Anton.'

'Melanie finds her happiness in ballet,' Gregory said before

Melanie herself could answer. 'Now come along, Lydia, we must talk to our other guests.'

Together they moved away, and the moment they were out of earshot Anton swore fluently at Lydia's departing back. 'She'd be well worth hanging for,' he said grimly, and caught Melanie's hand. 'Don't take any notice of what she said. She's just jealous because you've captured everyone's heart here tonight.'

Everyone's heart except the one she most desperately wanted. But it was a thought that Melanie kept to herself, and as she and Anton continued to move among the guests, no one would have known that inside a part of her had died.

CHAPTER ELEVEN

It was Christmas when Anton's new ballet was performed and it met with the success that every choreographer dreams of but rarely achieves. A tragic story, it told of a soldier killed in war, whose young widow moved from one war-torn country to another, finding in every garrison of soldiers one who evoked the memory of her husband and to whom she gave herself in the vain hope that by doing so she could make her husband live again. But each giving ending in death, theirs in battle, hers in the realization that she had made love to a mirage and that her husband would never return. The music was as sombre as the theme, yet with long stretches of exquisite melody that accompanied every act of love.

Dancing the part of each soldier with whom the widow tried to find happiness, Anton gave the greatest performance of his career. But it was Melanie who received the highest accolade, for her performance not only received acclaim as a dancer but also as an actress. After the first night, queues wound their way round the theatre in a continual wait for tickets, and during the weeks that followed, the name of the Company – and Melanie – was featured in every magazine and newspaper.

Despite a determination to maintain her private life as private, Melanie found that everything she did was reported to the gossip columns, and could not even go to the hairdresser without finding it mentioned publicly the following day.

'What does it feel like to know you've reached the top?'

Anton asked one afternoon after a long session with the photographers.

'Tiring,' she answered. 'I seem to be working harder at publicity than I am at my dancing.'

'Then we'll have to work out a better routine.'

'Can't we just scrap the publicity?'

He grinned. 'It's worth too much money to the Company. Do you know the whole season's sold out?'

'You're joking!'

'Do I ever joke about money?'

'No,' she admitted, 'you don't.' She frowned. 'But it's rather scaring somehow. I almost wish it hadn't happened.'

'You mean you regret your success?'

She nodded. 'It's a strain to live up to it. You find yourself wanting to do better and yet you know that you can't, and that's when you become scared.'

'Every great artist gets scared. That's what keeps them great.' He put his hands on her shoulders. 'But they still go on, Melanie, and so will you. You'll be at the top of the tree!'

'You already said I was at the top of the tree,' she reminded him. 'The only place I can go from there is to fall right down to the bottom!'

'You'll remain at the top,' he assured her, 'but you'll strengthen the roots.'

Despite herself she laughed. 'You've got an answer for everything.'

'It's a good thing I have. You're looking for answers all the time.' His hands dropped from her shoulders and clasped her round the waist. 'But you're happy with the Company, aren't you?'

'Of course I am. Why do you ask?'

'Verenskaya's afraid you'll get a better offer from someone else.'

'And leave her? But this company's my home. Verenskaya has been like my mother. She can't think I'd leave.' Melanie looked at him aghast. 'Do *you* think that, Anton?'

'I'm not so sure. If you had an offer from New York you might see it as an escape from Gregory.' She averted her head but he went on inexorably, 'But you'd be crazy if you ran away. Distance won't help you to forget him. The only thing that can do that is—'

'Work,' she interrupted bitterly. 'If I work any harder I'll collapse.'

'I was going to say love,' Anton retorted.

'Not that,' Melanie replied. 'I couldn't go through that again.'

He opened his mouth to say something, stopped as though thinking better of it and then finally said: 'Then it will have to be work after all. If you don't want to have a love affair, then go all out for your career. It's the best salve to mend a broken heart.'

Many times in the succeeding months Melanie remembered Anton's words, for the adulation of the nightly audience and the appraisal of the critics inevitably began to leave its mark on her. She was now ranked with Tanya as one of the leading ballerinas of the company, and she enjoyed the respect she commanded and the many celebrities she met at the fashionable parties to which she was continuously being invited. No longer was it only Anton who gave her assurance, and the realization that other men found her desirable increased her confidence to a degree she would never have believed possible a few short months ago.

Gradually all trace of the bitter, disillusioned girl she had once been vanished, and by the end of the season she could even begin to think of Gregory with some semblance of equanimity. She had not seen him since the night of the engagement party, though she knew from Mrs. Ransome that he had gone to South America on business and had postponed his wedding until after Christmas.

'I was surprised he didn't marry Lydia in a register office and take her with him,' her mother-in-law admitted. She had come to see a matinée performance in which Melanie was dancing and was now having tea with her in the dressing-room. 'Lydia was dying to go with him, as you can imagine, but he absolutely refused to be rushed into the wedding.'

'Lydia shouldn't have let him know she was so anxious. That's one way to make sure Gregory doesn't do what you want!'

Melanie spoke with such vehemence that Mrs. Ransome sighed, 'I thought at one time you were beginning to like him, but it seems you still don't.'

'I'm sorry,' Melanie said stiffly. 'I've tried but – but we don't see things the same way.'

'He's very kind when you get to know him.'

'I'm sure he is. But somehow he always manages to rub me up the wrong way. Even *you* must admit he's not the soul of tact.'

'But he is. That's why his behaviour with you has always been so puzzling. I wanted you to have dinner with us before he went off to South America, but he wouldn't—' Mrs. Ransome stopped in confusion. 'But it was partly a business dinner – perhaps that was the reason. You see he wanted to talk to Herbert.'

Curiosity stirred in Melanie and carefully she phrased her next question. 'What is happening with the company? Is Mr. Fenwick doing any – making any alterations?'

'None at all. Gregory is watching it for me and he says Herbert is carrying on the company just the way my husband would have wanted.' Mrs. Ransome suddenly frowned. 'You *are* getting income from it, aren't you, dear?'

'Income?'

'Yes. Gregory has given Timothy's shares over to you, hasn't he?'

'Oh yes,' Melanie lied. 'I get my money regularly.'

After this conversation Melanie was always careful to avoid any mention of Gregory or Herbert Fenwick when she was with Mrs. Ransome. Indeed, she would have preferred not to have seen her mother-in-law at all – for even an hour at the Belgravia house brought Gregory achingly to mind – but the woman's growing frailty made Melanie's total absence impossible, and though she could genuinely plead work as an excuse for the infrequency of her visits, she did not have the heart to use it as an excuse to stop them completely.

However Verenskaya's decision to take the Company on a short European tour came as a particularly pleasurable escape, and Melanie desperately hoped that she would be out of the country when Gregory returned from South America and got married. No matter what Mrs. Ransome said, that was one invitation she had no intention of accepting.

The company's tour of the major cities in Western Europe was a series of unqualified triumphs and they were fêted to the point of exhaustion. Yet always – at some point – Melanie had to return to her luxurious but alien hotel bedroom, each one a twin of the one before it, and here she forgot the plaudits of the crowd and remembered only her loneliness and grief. As long as she lived no man would matter to her as Gregory had once done, and she did not know whether to laugh or cry when the critics wrote of the growing rapport that they were convinced existed between herself and Anton.

Yet that there *was* a rapport she could not deny, for though she had occasionally accepted invitations to dine with other men, they had only served to increase her sense of loneliness, so that she had returned more eagerly to Anton, knowing that with him there was no need to simulate a gaiety she did not feel. He was the only man with whom she was entirely at ease, and his casual acceptance of her company and the rare times when he kissed her lulled her into a feeling of tranquillity which, though she knew was false, she none the less accepted.

It was Verenskaya – as always– – who made Melanie face reality.

'You cannot go on like this with him, my child. He is a man, not a boy. One day he will demand more from you, and if you go on using him, you will not be able to refuse.'

'Does one always have to pay for friendship?' Melanie asked with unusual asperity.

'You are accepting more than friendship from him. You are taking up all his time and all his hopes and dreams – and that is cruel.'

It was a truth that could not be denied, and Melanie turned to the window and stared out at the incomparable loveliness of the Acropolis. In the clear Athenian air it stood outlined on its hillside, seemingly near enough to reach out and touch. From a nearby taverna the poignant music of bouzouki was borne up to them, and with a sudden knife thrust of pain she yearned to be sharing this moment with Gregory. She shut her eyes momentarily before turning back into the room.

'I'm afraid Gregory has spoiled me for any other man,' she said quietly. 'I can never love Anton in that way.'

'Then give him what you can.'

'It wouldn't be fair to him.'

'If he is happy to accept it, why should you worry? He needs you, Melanie. You are his inspiration. Surely you know that?'

'I do. But I still don't think it would be right of me to give him second best.'

Verenskaya threw up her hands. 'I will not discuss it any more. You are too obstinate to listen to reason.'

Tacitly agreeing to disagree, they changed the conversation, but Melanie could not forget all that had been said and she would not have been human if she had not been flattered by the knowledge that she was Anton's inspiration.

As if bearing out Verenskaya's statement, he continually discussed new themes with her, but it was not until they were sitting together on the aeroplane that was taking them back to London that he suddenly threw the words 'Theseus in the Cretan bullring' at her.

'What do you think of that for a ballet?' he asked.

'Is there a part in it for me?'

For an instant he stared at her and she realized this was a question she had never asked before; always she had waited to be told, and then to be assured that she was equal to it.

'Without you there wouldn't *be* a ballet,' he replied. 'You'll be the Athenian girl bull dancer who sacrifices her life for the young king. I'm going to commission special music, make the sets a reconstruction of the Palace of Minos and take the costume designs from Greek vase paintings.'

It was the most ambitious project he had yet attempted and her imagination began to race. 'What did girl bull dancers wear?' she asked.

'I'm not sure, but I see you in a simple white tunic and a short, fair wig.' He looked at her challengingly. 'The best bull dancers could vault right over the bull's horns on to its back. How high can you leap, Melanie?'

She took a deep breath and felt as if she was flying already. 'I'm beginning to believe the sky's the limit!'

He laughed. 'It's a pity we won't be able to give it its premiere in New York.'

'New York – don't tell me we're going there?'

He nodded. 'Verenskaya got a cable from the Director of the Lincoln Arts Centre this morning,' he explained. 'He's invited us to dance there.'

'But what about our London season?'

'We'll still be able to do that – all it means is delaying it for six weeks and renting the theatre while we're away.'

'Then we'll be in the States for the whole of January.'

'Will you mind?'

'Not at all.' Even as she spoke she realized it was the answer to her prayers, for it meant she would be out of England when Gregory got married. It had come as a bitter blow to her when

147

she had received a letter from Mrs. Ransome saying that he had been delayed in South America and would not be returning to England until the early part of January, for she had realized then that she would almost certainly be in London when he married Lydia. Ever since hearing the news she had been racking her brains to manufacture an excuse that would enable her not to go to the wedding, but now she had a genuine reason, for she would be thousands of miles away on the day he made Lydia his wife.

'You'll love New York.' Anton's voice broke into her thoughts, and she gave such a start that he realized she had been a long way from him. 'What were you thinking about?' he asked. 'The ballet or Gregory?'

'Both. He'll be marrying Lydia in January and I'm glad I'll be out of England.'

'You still care about him, don't you?'

'I'll never forget him,' she answered carefully.

'That wasn't what I asked you. I never kidded myself you would forget him completely. I've just been hoping that you'd forget him enough to try and make something of your life with me.'

As he said the final words he swung round and put his hand on her thigh and his action was so unexpected that she stiffened. Instantly he took his hand away, an unbecoming flush colouring his face.

'I'm sorry if my touch revolts you,' he said bitterly.

'Don't be silly,' she cried.

'Then why did you cringe like that? If it had been Gregory's hand you'd have—'

'Please, Anton,' she begged, 'don't keep nagging all the time.'

'I've never nagged you at all. Perhaps it would have been better if I had. Instead I've treated you as if you were my sister – as if you were a little girl and not a woman. But it's got to end soon,' he said quietly. 'I love you, Melanie, and I've got to know if there's a chance for me.'

'I can't pretend I love you when I don't.'

'I'm not asking you to pretend. I will be happy with whatever you give me.'

'And how long do you think *that* will satisfy you?' She tried to keep her voice from shaking, knowing that only by being as logical as possible was there any hope of making him see that he

148

was wrong. 'How long will you be content to love a statue; to hold a woman in your arms who doesn't respond to you?'

'When you love someone the way I love you, you'll take them on any terms. Let me love you, Melanie. That's the only way you'll get Gregory out of your mind.'

If only what Anton said were true. If she could believe that by allowing Anton to love her she would forget Gregory, then she would willingly have Anton as her lover tonight. But logic told her that what he said was not true. Perhaps later, it might be possible, but at the moment Gregory was too firmly entrenched in her heart for her to forget him in the arms of another man.

'Well,' Anton asked, 'will you let me prove I'm right?'

'Ask me again when we come back from America.' Though it was an effort she looked him fully in the eyes. 'By then Gregory will be married and perhaps when I know it's final . . . that it's all over . . .'

'Very well. I've waited so long, another couple of months won't matter.'

The company only stayed in London for two weeks before flying to the States and, with a special Command Performance given during this time, Melanie only had one free afternoon in which to go and see Mrs. Ransome.

To her dismay, she found the woman in bed looking tired and unusually pale.

'I was overdoing it again,' Mrs. Ransome said hastily before Melanie could say a word. 'But I'll be up and about again in a couple of days.' The blue-veined hand patted the coverlet. 'Come and sit beside me and tell me all about your tour.'

'The tour I've come back from, or the one I'm going on?' Melanie asked with a smile.

'Both.'

'There isn't much to tell. It was a whistle-stop journey through Europe and one theatre looks pretty much like another. The audiences are different, though. Some show their enjoyment more than others.'

'But *you* were a great success every time you danced,' Mrs. Ransome said contentedly. 'I read about it in the newspapers.'

'Then you don't need me to tell you,' Melanie said.

Mrs. Ransome smiled. 'I was just using it as an excuse to keep you here longer. I hardly seem to see you any more.'

'That's only because I've been away. But when I come back from the States you'll see much more of me.'

'You say that now, but I'm sure you'll find an excuse to stay away.'

'I promise I won't.' Noticing that Mrs. Ransome's breathing was quick and shallow and there was a blueness about the lips which even the skilfully applied make-up could not hide, Melanie got to her feet. 'I'm not going to stay and talk to you any more now,' she said firmly. 'You look far too tired to be bothering with visitors.'

'You're not a visitor, you're my family.'

'Then don't try and pretend you're feeling well.'

Quickly Melanie bent to kiss the rouged cheek, keeping a smile fixed on her face as she made her final good-byes.

Downstairs in the hall the butler was waiting with her coat, luxurious dark mink, and it reminded her forcibly of how far she had come since the first time she had set foot in this house.

'Mrs. Ransome doesn't look very well,' she said as she walked to the door.

'I'm afraid she isn't. Mr. Gregory's already brought two different specialists to see her and I understand she'll be starting some new treatment next week.'

Hearing Gregory's name mentioned made Melanie's heart race, but she fought to keep her voice normal and concentrated all her thoughts on the woman who was lying upstairs.

'I hope the new treatment works,' she said. 'I hate going to New York and leaving her like that.'

'I can well understand that, madam,' the butler said formally. 'It's in Mr. Gregory's mind too. That's the reason he's delayed his marriage.'

Half-way through the door Melanie stopped. 'Don't tell me it's been put off again!' she said with an attempt at casualness.

'Only for a couple of weeks. Mrs. Ransome wanted it to be held here, but Mr. Gregory wouldn't allow it. I understand it's going to be a very quiet, family affair.'

'That's the best thing,' Melanie said through lips so stiff that she could hardly form the words. 'I'm sure any excitement would be very bad for my mother-in-law.' The butler nodded, and followed Melanie down the steps to open the door of the taxi that was waiting for her.

Thankfully she settled back in its dark interior, the pretence of calm leaving her now that she was alone. A quiet family affair! The butler's words echoed in her brain making all other thought impossible. The desire to feel Gregory's arms around her and the warmth of his lips on her own was so intense that it required all her willpower not to tell the taxi-driver to take her to his office. She must find a way of ending his hold over her – of making a life of her own. Hard on this thought came the memory of her last conversation with Anton. Was he right when he had said that only in another man's arms would she be able to find oblivion? Was it only with another man's touch that she would be able to forget Gregory? Wildly she stared out of the window. The road was familiar and with a shock she recognized that they were just driving past Anton's flat. Was this an omen? Should she stop the taxi and get out – go to Anton and give herself to him? Yes, came the logical answer, it's the only way. But her emotions would not let her give in to this sudden weakness of spirit, and she remained huddled back in the seat, her body wrapped in mink, her heart wrapped in ice.

It was only as she was finishing her final packing that night that she wondered whether she should ring Gregory to find out exactly how ill her mother-in-law was. But fear that he would construe her concern as merely being a desire to talk to him made her dismiss the idea almost as it entered her head. Besides, to talk to him could only upset her at a time when she needed all her confidence to face her American debut.

The first few days of her arrival in New York were filled with interviews for the press and television, but after the first rush of publicity had abated she found that Gregory was constantly in her mind. Perhaps it was the knowledge that he would soon be getting married that made her keep thinking of him, and she had only to close her eyes to see him in front of her, only to be alone in a silent room to hear his voice.

Indeed on one such occasion his presence seemed so real that she feared for her sanity, and went rushing down the hotel corridor to Anton's room.

'You're very easy to take advantage of right now,' he said as she clung to him, her body trembling. 'But I promised I'd leave you alone until we left New York and I intend to keep my word.'

'Why the scruples?' she asked, keeping her face hidden against his shoulder.

'Because I want your respect even if I can't have your love.'
He tilted her chin and looked deep into her eyes. 'If only you weren't so innocent, Melanie, it would be much easier for me.'

'Innocent?' she said bitterly. 'How laughable that I should have suffered so much and yet still be innocent.'

'Six weeks from now I'll remedy the innocence!' he promised, and pushed her firmly away from him. 'Now go back to your room and stop trying to seduce me. I'll need my strength for tomorrow.'

Thinking of the premiere, she shivered. 'Suppose we flop?'

'Supposing the moon falls out of the sky,' he retorted, and with a lithe movement opened the door and pushed her out. 'A glass of milk and a sleeping pill,' he called after her as she went down the corridor. 'It's important you have a good night's rest.'

But though Melanie followed Anton's advice she only slept fitfully, and at dawn she was so wide awake that she sat by the window and watched the sky lighten. The central heating was overpowering and the double glazing kept the window-panes warm, yet even so she knew that outside it was bitterly cold with that special biting wind that was so much a part of New York. The tall steel and glass skyscrapers made it difficult to see the sun, but she was able to watch the changing colour of the sky, and was absorbed by the way the buildings seemed to come to life as light and shadow moved across their surfaces, giving a sudden sheen to a plate-glass window or depth to a smooth surface of steel. Far below came a faint drone that grew steadily louder as the traffic, like a living beast, stirred into wakefulness and writhed and moved its way through the sharp-angled intersections of the city.

She decided to dress and go down for breakfast, unable to bear the confines of her room, and she was half-way through the door when she went back for her coat, deciding to do as most other members of the company did and have breakfast in the drugstore opposite the hotel.

A little later, perched on a stool in the warm, brightly lighted drugstore, she felt happier than she had done for a long time. It was still too early for any other members of the company to be here and she was surrounded instead by young girls gulping down a cup of coffee before going to their offices, and harassed-looking businessmen either doing the same or ploughing their way through a concoction of bacon, pancakes, eggs and maple syrup.

By the time she had finished her own breakfast – a much more modest affair of bacon and eggs – the places at the counter were beginning to be filled by members from the company, and conversation was entirely restricted to the première that lay ahead of them tonight.

For the first time in several weeks Melanie had an opportunity to talk to Anna, but it was a stilted conversation and bore no relation to the easy comradeship that had once been theirs.

'What's the matter with you?' Melanie asked bluntly. 'At one time you used to drop into my room and see me, but now unless I go out of my way to talk to you . . .'

Anna looked uncomfortable. 'It's difficult now you're so famous.'

'What difference does that make?' Melanie asked in astonishment.

'The other girls would think I'm sucking up to you.'

'Don't be crazy, they know we've been friends for years.'

'It's still difficult,' Anna said. 'Anyway, most of your free time is spent with Anton.'

'I've never refused to see you. For heaven's sake, Anna, ballet's the one profession where everybody's equal.'

'Except those that are more equal than others!' Anna retorted. 'You can't turn back the clock, Melanie. You're a ballerina now. We don't mix in the same league, and after tonight we certainly won't.'

'What do you mean?'

'You'll be lionized – sought after by every hostess in New York.'

'You're exaggerating.'

'I'm not. You just don't know what's in store for you.'

They were words that Melanie remembered as, later that evening, she waited nervously in the wings while the audience settled in their seats.

'It's a full house,' Anton said, coming up to her. 'Take a look through the curtain. You've never seen so many diamonds!'

Melanie shook her head. 'I don't want to see them.' Her hands clutched him nervously. 'I'm scared.'

'You're always scared on a first night.'

'But this is worse. I've heard New York audiences can be the cruellest in the world.'

'The most cruel and the most generous. Give them your best and they'll take you to their hearts as no other audience in the world.'

Behind him the first, piercing flute notes flooded the hushed auditorium and the curtain rose. Melanie's fears vanished, leaving only the reality of the music, the intricate movements of the choreography and Anton's arms waiting to lift her to the pinnacle of success. With a deep breath she moved forward.

Three hours and twelve curtain calls later, Melanie returned exhausted to her hotel. The rest of the cast had gone on to a champagne supper given in their honour by a prominent socialite, but she had adamantly refused the invitation, declaring that all she could face at the moment was a hot bath and bed.

'That is ridiculous,' Verenskaya said crossly. 'You will not be able to avoid the parties all the time. You are famous and you belong to your public.'

'They pay to see me dance,' Melanie retorted, 'not to share my private life.'

'A celebrity does not have a private life,' Verenskaya said sweepingly.

'Meet one celebrity who intends to change the rule – not that I consider myself a celebrity anyway.'

'You are, my child, and you cannot deny it. Tonight you achieved your greatest success and there is no going back for you.' The snapping black eyes regarded her appraisingly. 'You have still not made up your mind about Anton?'

'I talked to him before we came to New York.'

'But you are still just friends?'

Melanie nodded. 'It will probably be different when we return to England.'

'I do not understand the young these days.' Verenskaya waved her arms in one of her dramatic gestures. 'How can you plan a thing like that? You are dealing with emotions, not making a carefully-timed soufflé!'

'The trouble is I've got no emotions,' Melanie said bitterly.

'You have, my child, but you have buried them. Tomorrow you must remember that you are part of the company and that I will not allow you to run away and hide.' The guttural voice softened. 'I know it is hard for you, but I am doing it for your own good.'

'I realize that.'

The rest of Melanie's words were drowned as the door of her dressing-room burst open and a group of photographers and pressmen surged in.

It was the first time Melanie had been besieged by a determined assault by American reporters who, though not as demanding and rude as their Italian counterparts, were far more aggressive than the British pressmen to whom she was accustomed. Questions were fired at her, seemingly hundreds of flashlight photographs were taken, and it was more than an hour before she at last found herself alone and able to change into her street clothes.

But even outside the theatre she still had to face the ordeal of autograph-hunters, and it was only the concerted efforts of Anton and some of the young men from the corps de ballet, who acted as a living barricade, that enabled her to push her way into a waiting taxi.

Breathless she sank back in the seat, and looked at Anton in surprise as he climbed in after her, slammed the door and gave the driver the name of their hotel.

'Don't tell me you're not going to the party either?' she asked.

'I'll see you safely to the hotel first.'

'That wasn't necessary. I'm perfectly all right – just tired.'

'I hope that isn't going to be your permanent excuse! It's important for you to mix with people, Melanie, not only for the publicity but for your own development.'

'I know,' she said wearily, 'and I've promised Verenskaya that I'll do it. But not tonight, Anton. Tonight I've got to be alone.'

Appearing satisfied with her reply, he sat in silence until they reached the hotel, but as he went to climb out of the taxi she stopped him.

'Please don't come in, Anton. I'm perfectly all right.'

'If you do change your mind and want to come on to the party afterwards, do you know where it is?'

'Yes,' she said with a slight smile, 'but I won't be coming. I'm going straight up to bed.'

She leaned forward and kissed him lightly on the cheek. 'Try and find some tobacco heiress, Anton. You deserve much more than I can give you.'

'In money, yes,' he said puckishly, 'but there are other things you can give me that don't come with tobacco millions!'

She gave a soft laugh and entered the hotel. But once in the lobby, the smile left her face, although she was forced to put it back on again as several of the desk clerks called out to her in greeting. News of success evidently travelled fast in this city, for already several other people in the lobby – still crowded although it was well past eleven o'clock – turned to point her out as she moved swiftly and gracefully to the lift.

It was not until she was alone in her room that she was able to give way to her weariness. Though normally always tired after a strenuous performance, what she felt now was more of a mental enervation, and as such went deeper. Too tired to switch on the lights, too tired even to undress, she merely kicked off her shoes and lay down on the bed. But no sooner had her body relaxed than her mind took over. Midway between sleep and waking the darkness filled with faces; Mrs. Ransome's pale against the whiteness of pillows, Timothy's flushed with drink, and beyond him Lydia Fenwick in Gregory's arms, the pale, scarlet-tipped fingers caressing the dark hair.

With a cry she sat up and switched on the bedside lamp. Only the light could end the nightmares that were haunting her. But this time the light was not able to save her, for the nightmare was still going on and Gregory was staring at her across the room, his tall body blocking the doorway, a faint smile on his face.

With a moan she put her hands to her head, afraid that at last the strain of the past few months had taken their toll of her. She closed her eyes and prayed for her sanity to return, but when she opened her eyes again Gregory's figure was still in front of her, but coming nearer this time, nearer and nearer until he was directly in front of her.

'You're not dreaming, Melanie,' he said, almost as if he had known what was in her mind. 'I'm really here.'

CHAPTER TWELVE

MELANIE stared at Gregory incredulously, still unable to credit that he was not a figment of her imagination but a living, vital presence, standing in her bedroom only a few feet away from her.

She shrank further back against the pillows. 'Who let you in?'

'The bell-boy. When I gave my name at the desk the clerk sent me straight up. I suppose he took me for your husband.'

The unthinking cruelty of his remark jerked her to her feet. She swayed unsteadily, but when he put out a hand to steady her she thrust it aside in panic. 'How dare you come here! Get out!'

He closed his lids in a gesture of sheer weariness and she noticed, without wanting to, the fine lines at the corners of his eyes, lines which had not been there at their last meeting. Then he opened his eyes and stared at her.

'I don't blame you for feeling so bitter about me,' he said quietly, 'but I came here because I wanted to see you – because I wanted to talk to you.'

'We've nothing to say to each other.'

'I've got some bad news.'

At once she knew what he meant. 'Is it Timothy's mother?'

'Yes. She died in her sleep two days ago.'

Tears flooded into Melanie's eyes and she sank down on the bed. 'Why didn't you telephone me?'

'What was the point? It happened suddenly and you couldn't have flown back in time to see her.'

'I still wish I'd been there. It's awful to think of her dying like that . . . so alone.'

'She was alone from the time Timothy died; she never wanted to live after he was killed.' Gregory bent forward and, afraid that he was going to touch her, she moved over to the dressing-table where she sat down on the stool and made a pretence of combing her hair.

'I still don't know why you bothered to fly out and tell me the news – or did you have to come to America anyway—'

'I came only to see you.'

'It was an unnecessary waste of time.' Although her voice

was cool her hands were shaking so much that she put down the comb. 'I'm very tired, Gregory. If you could see yourself out . . .'

She kept her eyes lowered, refusing to look in the mirror because she knew she would see his reflection there and was afraid that the sight of him would make her lose her composure. But there was no sound or movement behind her and she realized that he was still in the room.

'Please go,' she said huskily.

'I want to talk to you.'

'We've nothing to say to each other.'

'I love you, Melanie.'

Her head jerked up and through the mirror their eyes met. Had she imagined his words? Had they been conjured up out of her own intense longing to hear him say them? But the tenderness on his face, the glitter – could it be of tears? – in his eyes told her that it was no figment of her imagination but the strange, incredible truth.

'I love you,' he said again and coming close, put his hands on her shoulder. 'Now that my aunt has died I can tell you the truth.' She still went on staring at him wordlessly and he pulled her up and swung her round to face her. 'Don't you understand?' he said with a touch of his old impatience. 'I'm free. I don't need to marry Lydia.'

Melanie put a shaking hand to her face. 'I still don't understand.'

'It was because of Herbert Fenwick. He knew Lydia wanted to marry me and that was part of our bargain; he wouldn't tell my aunt that Timothy had sold him his shares, provided I agreed to become his son-in-law.' The hands on Melanie's shoulders were now gripping her so tightly that the fingers seemed to be digging into her flesh. 'You don't know what agony it's been – the tightrope I've been walking on. Each time Lydia set the date for our wedding I had to find a way of postponing it – of playing for time.' His voice lowered on a sigh. 'But that's all in the past, thank heavens. It's over and I'm free.'

Hearing his explanation, so much that Melanie had not understood before became clear, and the jigsaw-puzzle of his idiosyncratic behaviour fell into a comprehensive pattern. 'Why didn't you tell me? Why did you let me believe you didn't love me?'

'I was afraid if you knew I was being forced to marry Lydia you would have insisted on staying with me; of living in the shadows . . .'

'You were right,' she said soberly. 'If I had known you loved me, I would never have left you. Never!' Her voice broke. 'You made me suffer so much, Gregory. There were times when I didn't even want to live.'

'What about me?' he said huskily. 'I was playing a waiting game, stalling Lydia in the hope that I could work something out with Fenwick. I even offered to buy him out completely, but he wouldn't hear of it.'

'And if your aunt hadn't died,' Melanie forced herself to ask the question, 'would you have gone ahead and married Lydia?'

'I doubt it. I tried to make myself believe I would, but if it had really come to the crunch, I don't think I could ever have gone through with it.'

'You took a big gamble,' she said softly. 'What would have happened if I had married Anton?'

'That was the one fear that always haunted me. I know he loves you – that he's always wanted you—' Gregory stopped speaking and pulled her close. 'Is he your lover?' he asked harshly. 'Tell me the truth, Melanie. I won't blame you if you were, but I've got to know the truth.'

He saw the answer in her eyes and with a groan, like a wounded animal returning to the comfort of its home, he rested his face against hers, the trembling of his body telling her how close to breaking-point he was. It was a moment entirely devoid of passion, when all that mattered was the need to be close to each other, to be unified and strengthened.

It was a long while later that they drew apart and sat together on the settee. There were so many things they had to say to each other, yet most of it seemed unnecessary; all that mattered was that they were together, now and for the future.

Yet the thought of Lydia remained with Melanie like a dark cloud, and an irrational fear made her voice her thoughts aloud. 'I don't believe she'll give you up as easily as you think. If she wanted you enough to have her father blackmail you into marrying her, she'll still put up a fight to keep you.'

Gregory shook his head. 'Lydia never knew the real reason why I proposed to her. She believed I loved her. That was another part of Fenwick's bargain. He swore me to secrecy.'

Jealousy cut through Melanie like a knife. 'I suppose that included playing the part to the full.'

For an instant Gregory looked uncomprehending, then he burst out laughing.

'There's nothing funny about it,' Melanie said angrily.

'I'm sorry, darling.' Instantly he was contrite. 'But I was just remembering all the damn stupid excuses I used to dream up to avoid having to see her – let alone kiss her. I even took sneezing powder to make her think I had a chronic cold!'

'And you fooled her?'

'I like to think I did.'

More than ever Melanie was certain that Lydia had known of her father's hold over Gregory. For that reason alone she would have pretended to have been fooled by his excuses of a cold, realizing that to have forced him into a show of love which he did not feel might have precipitated him into rejecting the whole thing.

'Forget Lydia,' Gregory said. 'It's all in the past, now. My aunt's death has set me free. From now on Fenwick can do what he likes with the company. I couldn't care less. All I care about is making you my wife.'

She echoed the words on a sigh and he caught her close. But this time there was no tenderness in his hold, only a deep and urgent passion that communicated itself to her like fire.

'When will you marry me?' he asked, breathing the words against her lips.

'Marry you?' she said the words in a sigh of ecstasy. 'I can't believe it's ever going to happen.'

'It won't take me long to prove it,' he said with a slight laugh, and then there was no laughter any more, for his mouth was hard on hers and the heartache and longing of the past months disappeared, as she gave him back kiss for kiss, revelling in his strength, in the delicacy of his touch which seemed to melt her very bones.

With unusual abandonment she clung to him, desire overcoming all reticence. 'Gregory,' she pleaded. *'Darling . . .'*

'No!' The word was loud and sudden, and he pushed her away from him and stood up. In the rose glow that came from the bedside lamp he stared at her and then, without a word, walked over to the window.

'You're a temptress,' he said thickly, 'but I'm damned if I'll make you mine in front of the whole Verenskaya Company!'

She laughed softly and came over to stand by his side. 'I'm committed to this tour, darling, but I'm sure Verenskaya will free me for a month as soon as we get home.'

'How much longer will you be here?'

'Four weeks.'

'That's a lifetime!'

'For me too.' She rested against him, giving a little shiver of pleasure which he mistook for the tremor of fatigue, because he instantly drew back and looked anxiously into her face.

'What a selfish fool I am. You've had a strenuous first night and here I am keeping you up till all hours. You must rest!'

'When will I see you again?'

'For breakfast. My room is on the floor above. I just hope there's no fire escape or I might not be able to resist the temptation!'

She giggled, the mood of passion dissolving in laughter as they parted at the door.

Waking next morning, happy in the knowledge that Gregory was only a few yards away, the one flaw in Melanie's happiness was the anger and hurt she would have to face from Anton. She toyed with the idea of not telling him but knew it would be futile: one look at her face and he would know the truth.

But Melanie had not reckoned with the grapevine, and entering Verenskaya's bedroom at mid-morning, after a blissful hour with Gregory, she took one look at the old lady and Anton and realized that they both knew what had happened.

'So it's a fairy-tale ending after all,' Verenskaya said. 'Anton has just told me that Gregory arrived last night.'

Melanie looked at Anton quickly, but there was no anger or reproach on his face, only a strange calm that bespoke enormous self-control.

As though realizing what her fears had been he suddenly smiled. 'I knew I wouldn't stand a chance with you if Ransome came back, but at least if *he* has the woman *I* still have the dancer. And that's the most important part of you.'

Wisely she did not disagree with him, though she knew already that the assertion was untrue, for if it had done nothing else, the bitter parting from Gregory had made her realize that no careeer, however successful, could ever be sufficient compensation for a life without him.

'I suppose you have come here to ask for the day off?' Verenskaya said abruptly.

'I hadn't, as a matter of fact,' Melanie replied, 'but it sounds an awfully good idea.'

'Don't be late at the theatre,' Anton said, and watched unsmiling as she gave Verenskaya a quick kiss of gratitude and ran out.

She and Gregory spent an enchanted day together. He had visited New York many times before and took delight in taking her to many of the well-known and accepted tourist sights: the Statue of Liberty, the Empire State Building, Times Square, and an hour of part delight and part horrified amusement in the Guggenheim Museum.

'But there's so much more for you to see here,' he said in the taxi that was taking them to the theatre later that evening. 'Once we've got the obvious things out of the way, I'm going to show you *my* New York, and then there's Long Island. You'll love that, darling. Even in winter, without any leaves on the trees, it's one of the most beautiful places I know. And we can spend a week-end in Connecticut with some friends of mine. They have a beautiful farmhouse there and—'

'I'm here to dance,' she interrupted, laughing. 'I'll never get a whole free day again, and a week-end's right out of the question.'

'Well, Sunday then. Verenskaya can't make you dance on Sunday.'

She caught his hand. 'How long can you stay?'

'Until the middle of next week.'

She gave a sigh of happiness. 'That's a lifetime away.'

But all too soon the lifetime came to an end, and with an unutterable sense of depression she drove with him to Kennedy Airport and watched as he boarded the aircraft. She waited till the doors closed and the giant plane taxied out of sight to the runway, then with heavy heart she returned to the city, wondering how she would be able to bear the three long weeks until she saw him again.

Though she had known she was going to miss him, she had not realized to what depths her loneliness would take her, and neither her name up in lights nor one celebrity-packed party after another could assuage her need of him.

Slowly one day dragged after the other, with triumphant performance following triumphant performance, until at last the morning of their departure dawned. Never had Melanie been so pleased to see the back of a city as she was of New York and, as they winged their way across the Atlantic, she counted the hours until she would be in Gregory's arms.

Although she had cabled him the time of her arrival, she had asked him not to meet her at the airport, knowing that they would be besieged by photographers and not wanting him to feel he was being ignored. It would be so much better for them to meet alone at the flat, where she could rush straight into his arms and assure herself again that the few magic days in New York had not been a dream.

Their arrival at London Airport had the hysterical acclaim normally given to victorious World Cup footballers, and they were all feeling battered and exhausted when they were at last free to drive into London. Diplomatically Verenskaya announced that she would go the theatre first and Melanie was glad that she would be able to see Gregory on her own.

It was dusk when she stepped out of the taxi in front of the Bayswater flat and she looked anxiously round for Gregory's car. It was parked directly under a lamp-post and she saw him at the wheel.

'Darling!' she called excitedly, and ran towards him.

He got out of the car but made no move towards her and there was something so strange in his expression that fear gripped her throat, and her outstretched arms dropped to her side. 'Darling, what's wrong?'

'Can't you guess?'

Her fear grew. 'Don't talk in riddles. Tell me what's happened.' She ran to his side and clung to him. 'What is it, Gregory? Don't you love me – is that what you're trying to say?'

'I wish to heaven I could!' Their eyes met, hers full of shock, his full of bitterness. 'But even finding out what you are – what you did – can't make me stop loving you.'

CHAPTER THIRTEEN

THE shock that Melanie felt at Gregory's words robbed her of any anger and she remained staring at him in bewilderment. It was unbelievable that the man who had left her only three weeks ago – eager and adoring – should have now become this white-faced stranger with the eyes of a man in torment.

'We can't talk here,' she said haltingly. 'Come inside.'

On legs that were trembling so much she could barely walk, she led him into the flat. A vast pile of welcome home telegrams from unknown admirers was stacked in a heap on the hall table, while every occasional table in the living-room was covered with vases of flowers, each bouquet bearing a card. How willingly she would have forgone every single bloom for just one kind word from Gregory! She dropped her coat over a chair and turned and looked at him.

'What's happened, Gregory? Why are you looking at me with such hatred?'

Silently he handed her an envelope and as she saw the front of it she started to tremble. It was from Timothy. She had received too many letters from him during their brief courtship not to recognize his handwriting. But the envelope was addressed to his mother at a hotel in Jamaica, though she noticed that the stamps on it were uncancelled and that the flap had never been sealed.

'Read it,' Gregory said. 'It will give you your answer.'

Reluctantly she took out the letter and, as she saw the date on top of the page, her heart missed a beat; it had been written on the day she and Timothy had been married.

'I don't think I can bear to read it,' she said tremulously, and went to give it back. 'Can't you tell me what it says?'

'I'd rather you read it for yourself – again.'

'What do you mean by saying "again"? I've never read it at all!'

'Don't pretend any more,' he said scornfully, 'it's too late for that!'

Cheeks burning, she bent her head to the familiar scrawl and hoped that by reading it she would get a clue as to the reason for Gregory's attitude. However the first page only contained fulsome praise about herself and it was not until she came to the second page that she began to have some understanding of what Gregory had meant.

'I hate having to tell you this,' Timothy had written, 'but I'm afraid I've overspent my allowance again, and as you are so far away I asked Gregory to help me out. As usual all he gave me was a pious sermon – which didn't do me much good, as there was a jeweller breathing down my neck – and I didn't fancy ending up in a debtor's prison! So I decided to ask old Herbert for a loan instead. To my surprise he coughed up like a lamb. The only odd thing is that when he learned I was spending my honeymoon skiing in the Dolomites, he asked me to give him some security till I repaid him – in case I broke my neck, I suppose! Anyway, I gave him my shares in the firm to hold – that extra ten per cent that Dad left me when he died – and I'll reclaim them as soon as my new allowance comes through and I can pay him back.

'I really am sorry that I overspent my money this quarter, but at least I can assure you I didn't lose it at the gaming-tables, which I know is your one big fear. Since meeting Melanie I haven't even had the urge to bet on anything – all my time has been spent in trying to persuade her to marry me. She's a wonderful girl, Mother, and when you meet her I'm sure you'll love her . . .'

Melanie stopped reading. 'Poor Timothy . . . borrowing money to give me jewellery I never wanted.' All at once she realized the purport of the letter. 'But this is the evidence you want! It proves Timothy *didn't* sell those controlling shares! Fenwick has no right to them after all.'

'Exactly.'

'If only you'd found it before,' she said. 'Then you wouldn't have had to get engaged to Lydia.' She looked at the letter still in her hand. 'Where did you find it?'

'I didn't. Lydia found it. Apparently it was among her father's papers. She was looking for something in his desk and she saw it. She gave it to me at once.'

'No doubt hoping you'd think I gave it to him.' Melanie had spoken with irony, but as she saw the expression on Gregory's face, she realized that he believed it to be true. Shock made the blood drain from her head. It was impossible! He could not believe she had given Timothy's letter to Herbert Fenwick. But everything about his behaviour since they had met tonight indicated that he did.

'So you're acting true to form,' she said scornfully.

'I don't know what you mean.'

'I mean that you've judged me guilty without listening to anything I might say. Just the way you've always done!'

'That's not true!' He was angry now.

'It's perfectly true. When Lydia gave you that letter, did you even think for one single minute that her father might have got it some other way, or did you immediately jump to the conclusion that *I* had given it to him?'

'How else could he have got hold of it if you hadn't sold it to him?'

'*Sold* it to him!' Nausea welled up in Melanie as she re-echoed his words, and she dropped the letter on to the table. 'How dare you say a thing like that to me!' she whispered. 'I've never seen this letter before. Never!'

'You mean you didn't find it at Timothy's flat?' A pulse was beating at the side of Gregory's forehead. 'Be careful how you answer me, Melanie. Don't forget I saw you in the lobby the day I went to the flat myself. You told me you'd been there to collect some of your things.' His finger pointed at her accusingly. 'One of the things you found was that letter.'

'You're out of your mind! I didn't even know it existed.'

'I'll concede that point. But once you did find it you realized what it meant.'

She looked down at the letter, frowning slightly as she absorbed what Gregory had just said and trying to formulate an answer. 'If I *had* found this letter, it doesn't make sense that I'd have given it to Mr. Fenwick. After all, if what Timothy writes here is true, then the shares were still his, and as his widow they would have been mine.' She swung round and looked at Gregory. 'And they were worth money. So why should I give the letter to Mr. Fenwick?'

'Because Fenwick was holding those shares until his loan had been repaid. Don't forget Timothy borrowed fifteen thousand pounds from him. And you'd have had to repay that money before the shares reverted to you. And the one thing you couldn't do was to pay back the money in order to get the shares. So you went to Fenwick and made a bargain with him.'

'Go on,' she said tremulously. 'What sort of bargain?'

'I'm not sure. Perhaps he paid you to forget you'd ever found the letter.'

'You can't believe that! It doesn't make sense!'

'Not if you look at the position the way it is now,' he admitted. 'But at the time it would have been quite logical to have sold him the letter. After all, you had no idea I was going to fall in love with you, so there were only two things you could have done: repaid Fenwick the fifteen thousand pounds Timothy had borrowed from him and got back the shares, or try to get extra money from him by promising to forget you'd ever seen the letter at all!'

'You've worked everything out,' Melanie stated in a tired, flat

166

voice. 'But you've forgotten one thing: I'd already sold my jewellery, so Verenskaya didn't need any more money.'

'A ballet company can always use more money.'

For a moment she was silent. Pride told her that if Gregory loved her he should never have believed her capable of such behaviour, never have put her in the position of having to defend herself like this. Yet he did believe it; and fear of what it would do to their relationship if she could not make him see that he was wrong forced her to try and prove her innocence.

'You're the one who's not being logical now,' she said, forcing her voice to remain calm. 'From the moment we met you've always found it difficult to give me the benefit of the doubt. But at least you've always credited me with having had some feeling for Mrs. Ransome.'

'I won't deny that,' he said.

'Then don't you think my affection for her would have prevented me from giving or selling this letter to Herbert Fenwick? Do you think I'd have run the risk – for all the money in the world – of giving him control of the business?'

'I've thought of it from that angle too,' came the reply. 'But perhaps Fenwick promised that he wouldn't do anything while my aunt was alive. Anyway, from his point of view the letter gave him sufficient power to force me into proposing to Lydia.'

'And I suppose you think I knew that was going to happen too!' Melanie flung at him.

'No, I don't think that,' Gregory said. 'The one thing I do happen to believe is that you love me.' He took a step towards her. 'From the moment Lydia gave me this letter, I haven't been able to think about anything else. I've gone mad trying to work out what was in your mind.'

'And what conclusions have you come to?'

'I don't believe you realized the full implication of what you were doing when you gave the letter to Fenwick. I think you believed it would just give him more shares and a greater percentage of the profit – as well as giving you a little extra cash in hand in case Verenskaya needed it.'

Listening to him Melanie felt as though there was nothing more he could say to hurt her. If it were possible to reach rock-bottom in one's life, she had reached it at this moment. 'Thank you for trying to find some excuse for my behaviour,' she said in a voice from which all life had gone, 'but as I didn't find the letter and I didn't sell it to Herbert Fenwick, all your suppositions are wrong.' She tilted her head and stared him fully in the face. 'But if I *had* found this letter, I would have given it to you.'

'So you're still pretending you're innocent?'

'I'm not pretending! I'm telling you the truth.' Seeing his expression of disbelief, her apathy was replaced once more by anger, an anger so strong that all her inhibitions fled. 'But don't take any notice of me – listen to Lydia – the way you always do! But don't delude yourself that she brought you this letter because she cared about clearing Timothy's name. All she cared about was destroying mine! She knew her father had the letter the whole time, and the only reason she decided to show it to you now was because she knew how you'd react. And she's been proved right!'

Gregory reddened angrily, but his voice was calm when he answered. 'Even if Lydia knew about the letter – and I am not saying she did – why would her father have given it to her? He puts business above everything else, and bringing this letter out into the open has cost him Timothy's shares.'

'On the contrary,' Melanie retorted, 'unless I can pay him back the fifteen thousand pounds, those shares still belong to him. And he knows very well that I haven't got that sort of money.'

'You will have soon,' Gregory replied. 'You'll have considerably more, in fact.'

'What do you mean?'

'Apparently my aunt left instructions that on her death the Trustees were to sell her entire stock to Fenwick and that the money from the sale should be divided between you and myself.'

Melanie stared at him incredulously. 'You mean I get half?'

'Yes. So paying Fenwick back his loan is something you'll be able to do quite easily. You're a rich woman now.'

Melanie shrugged away his words, only able to think of the letter lying on the table. 'So Fenwick and Lydia win either way. He has control of the business – even if I don't sell him these shares – and Lydia has managed to destroy me as far as you're concerned.'

Outside the front door slammed and Verenskaya's guttural voice could be heard and then Anton's softer, quicker one. Steps crossed the floor, the door opened and Anton came in.

Seeing Gregory he hesitated, then smiled slightly and came forward. 'Sorry to butt in, but Verenskaya and I hung around till we thought the lovers' greetings were over!' Suddenly aware that neither Gregory nor Melanie looked particularly lover-like, the smile left his face and he looked from one to the other, one eyebrow raised inquiringly.

Answering the implicit question in his look, Melanie picked up Timothy's letter and gave it to Anton. At the sight of it, his face – normally sallow – became ashen, and she stared at him in perplexity.

But Gregory had no doubts as to what it meant, for he took an angry step towards Anton and then swung around violently to Melanie. 'So he's in it too! I might have known Anton would be involved in it somewhere along the line!'

'I don't know what you mean,' she faltered.

'Save your lies! There's no point pretending any more. You put the Company above everything else and you're prepared to lie and cheat in order to keep it going. Well, this is the last time you've lied and cheated to me. I'm finished with you!'

He strode to the door, but Anton stepped in his path. 'Don't be so quick off the mark, Ransome. Melanie knew nothing about that letter. *I* was the one who found it and *I* was the one who took it to Fenwick.'

'Save your breath,' Gregory said. 'I expected you to try and take the blame.'

'I'm telling you the truth.'

'You wouldn't even know the meaning of the word!' Gregory's voice was icy with contempt. 'You were both in it together and you both deserve each other!'

Melanie watched the two men as though she were looking at a scene in a nightmare. Pride urged her to let Gregory go, but as he stepped past Anton and moved to the door, she ran after him and caught his arm.

'Gregory, don't! Try and believe me! Try and think clearly!'

'I've had plenty of time to think,' he replied. 'But it's no use.'

'You mean you don't love me?'

A look of pain crossed his face and his voice was weary when he spoke. 'I'll love you for the rest of my life, but I could never trust you. And without trust, there is nothing.' Suddenly, as though losing his control, his hands came out and gripped her arm like a vice. 'If you'd only admit what you did – admit that you were wrong – then maybe we could—'

'No!' She wrenched away from his hold. 'I won't admit something that isn't true. Believe what you like. I don't care any more.'

Tears flooded into her eyes and his figure seemed to expand and then fade into a watery ghost. She put her hands to her head, and when next she lifted her eyes, only Anton was there to watch her.

For a long moment they stared at one another and it was he who turned away first, pacing the room like a caged animal.

She watched him without any sense of anger; perhaps that would come later when her present anguish abated and she would be able to feel some other emotion.

'You must hate me very much,' Anton muttered.

'Why did you do it?' she whispered.

'I don't know. But when I found that letter in Timothy's desk, it was such a shock . . . such a temptation . . .'

'To get money,' she asked, 'or to make mischief?'

'Not money,' he answered quickly.

'Then why?' she asked again. 'Why didn't you give *me* the letter?'

For several moments he did not reply, but she knew instinctively that it was not because he was searching for an answer, but because he was afraid that when he gave one, it would damage him irreparably in her eyes.

'I did it because of you,' he said at last. 'I didn't give Fenwick the letter until you told me you were going to marry Gregory. I thought Fenwick could use it to keep you apart.'

She swayed and caught hold of the back of a chair. 'That was the most vicious thing you could have done.'

'I see that now.' His voice was slurred and he came over and touched her shoulder. 'Forgive me, Melanie . . . I was so crazy with jealousy I couldn't think straight. And by the time I realized what I had done, it was too late.'

'It would never have been too late to have told me the truth!'

'What good would it have done you?'

'It might have made me realize that Gregory had been black-mailed into his engagement to Lydia.'

For the first time the remorse on Anton's face was replaced by a sneer. 'Do you think your knowing that would have made any difference? As long as Mrs. Ransome was alive, Gregory would have been tied to Lydia. He put his aunt's happiness before yours.'

'He also put it before his own! Do you think he *wanted* to marry Lydia? His love for his aunt forced him to act the way he did. But *you* acted out of spite. Everything *you* did was guaranteed to destroy my happiness!'

'I wanted to keep you with the Company,' he muttered. 'Ballet is your life ... I thought Gregory would make you give it up.'

'That still didn't give you the right to play God,' she said remorselessly. 'Or perhaps it would be better if I said devil.'

With a groan, he sank down in a chair. 'You've every right to hate me. If only you knew how I've hated myself ...' He looked up at her, his eyes dark with grief. 'When Gregory got engaged to Lydia, I was convinced that you'd forget him. That in time you'd turn to me – the way you had in Australia.'

'I was a different person then.'

'I found that out in New York,' he admitted. 'Once Gregory came over and I saw you together, I knew I didn't stand a chance with you; that if you couldn't have *him*, you'd have no one.'

'I could have told you that a long time ago,' she said, 'but you wouldn't have believed me.'

Anton's body curved in dejection and slowly, like an old man, he stood up. 'I am going to tell him the truth.'

'He won't believe you. He'll still think I knew about it.'

'I'll *make* him believe me.'

'No!' she said sharply. 'He should have taken *my* word – believed what *I* told him. But if he has so little trust that he can believe I would have done such a despicable thing as – as—'

'As *I* did?' Anton said.

She nodded and turned away, too full of bitterness to speak. Behind her she heard him move, and though she still did not turn, she was aware that he had come to stand beside her.

'Gregory judged you harshly because he loved you,' he said softly. 'When he hears the truth from me, he'll—'

'No! You're not to go and see him. I will never forgive him for not taking *my* word.'

'You're only saying that because you're hurt. You'll feel differently later on. Let me tell him the truth.'

Even as he spoke he walked to the door, but her voice, quiet

171

and firm as she called his name, made him stop. 'I don't want you to go and see him, Anton. I could never be Gregory's wife knowing he did not trust me.'

'And you can never be a dancer without him either,' Anton replied.

'Yes, I can,' she said firmly. 'I'll prove it if it takes me the rest of my life.'

'You won't succeed.'

'I will.' She moved over to the fireplace. 'But there's one thing you must promise me.'

'Anything,' Anton said, his voice suddenly vibrant again. 'I'll do anything you say, Melanie.'

'Then don't ever speak to me of love. I'm a dancer, and on the stage I will be your partner. But there can be nothing more between us – ever.'

'I understand.' The words were soft as a sigh, and the closing of the door was their final echo.

Forced for a second time to put Gregory out of her life, ballet once again became Melanie's chief comfort. Within a week of their return from New York they opened their new season, and from then on she was allowed little time for idleness, for when she was not dancing, she was rehearsing, and when she was doing neither she was surrounded by interviewers and reporters.

No longer could Verenskaya complain that she was not helping the company get publicity, Melanie thought one night as, exhausted from a performance of *Giselle* followed by a hectic party at the Savoy, she collapsed on her bed. Indeed if she continued at this pace she might even have Verenskaya ordering her to rest! The idea of this happening was so uncharacteristic of the woman that Melanie laughed, and the laughter grew louder and louder until her entire body was shaken with hysterical mirth.

By the time she had gained control of herself she was shivering with fright and, huddled against the pillows, she realized how near to breaking point she was, and wondered how much longer she would be able to stand the pace she was setting herself.

Next morning at the theatre Anton came into the rehearsal room with a large folder of drawings and swatches of material: suggestions from the costume designer for the new ballet

Theseus in the Cretan Bullring to which Anton was now putting the final touches.

'I'd like you to look at these when we break for coffee,' he said to Melanie.

'I can look at them now,' she replied, and followed him over to a corner of the room.

He spread out the designs on a chair and draped the samples of fabric over the back. 'Don't bother with all the drawings,' he said. 'Just concentrate on yours and mine. I want to make sure you like them.'

There was a deference in his voice to which, by now, she should have grown accustomed. Yet it reminded her of the guilt he felt towards her, and she knew that if she herself could not forget Gregory, Anton would never be able to forget that he had been the one to part them.

'If *you* like the costumes,' she said quickly, 'I'm sure they'll be all right.'

'But at least look at them!' He lifted up one drawing and held it in front of her.

'No, not now. I'm too tired.'

The Anton of old would have argued with her, but the new Anton merely nodded and watched in silence as she walked away from him to the far side of the room.

But even at the barre Melanie did not have peace for long, for within a few moments the familiar sound of Verenskaya's cane announced the woman's approach.

'What do you think of the designs?' the familiar, heavy accented voice asked.

'I didn't look at them. I was too tired.'

'I am not surprised. It was four o'clock this morning before you came home.'

Melanie looked up from the barre, startled. 'Did you hear me?'

'Not when you come in; but only afterwards . . .'

With colour flooding her cheeks, Melanie turned her head away. 'I haven't cried for weeks,' she said defensively.

'Not aloud,' came the answer. 'But inside you have been crying since Gregory left you.'

'Can we change the subject?'

'Only if you can change the way you are living. You cannot go on like this any longer, my child. There are dark circles under your eyes and the dressmaker has told me this is the third

173

time this month that she has had to take in your costumes.'

'The material keeps stretching.'

'In *all* your clothes? Rubbish!' A bony hand caught Melanie's arm. 'You are not to do any more morning rehearsals. The afternoon practice will be quite enough for you.'

'But I'm rehearsing for the Gala,' Melanie protested.

Verenskaya rubbed her hands across the top of her cane. 'I was forgetting the Royal Gala. Very well. You may rehearse all day – but only until the Gala is over. After that, you must take a holiday.'

'I don't need one. I'm perfectly all right.'

'No one who turns down a holiday is perfectly all right!' came the majestic reply. 'No, child, you will listen to me. After the Command Performance you must go away. I will let Anna go with you if you wish.'

'You're very kind,' Melanie said tremulously, and then fearing she would burst into tears if the conversation were prolonged, concentrated on her exercises.

As the night of the Gala drew near, Verenskaya became as ruthless as Anton in her demands on the Company, and the suggestion that Melanie should not work so hard seemed totally forgotten.

Yet though Melanie's thoughts were occupied with the coming show, at night sleep still continued to elude her, and daily she grew thinner, her eyes becoming larger and more deeply shadowed, until she began to wonder where she would find the strength to keep her going. Yet she could not give up now. When the Gala was over, she would accept Verenskaya's offer and go away on a holiday with Anna. Suddenly the thought of long, idle days on a sun-washed beach became her idea of heaven and, with sweat pouring down her body as she rehearsed and practised and rehearsed again, she counted the days until she would be free.

On the day before the Gala, Verenskaya ordered a full-scale dress rehearsal and, because of it, said there would be no morning practice for anyone. With her mind now resolutely fixed on a holiday, Melanie decided to use the unexpected free time to replenish her wardrobe and she spent several hours in Fortnum's indulging in an unusual spending spree, not only ordering beachwear for herself but also for Anna.

She had just given her name and account number to the assistant when a waft of perfume made her stiffen like a dog smelling an unexpected and frightening odour, and even as she turned she braced herself for the sight of Lydia Fenwick's face.

As always the girl was beautifully groomed, and this time she looked lovelier than ever in a beautifully-tailored linen suit of the same warm, creamy gold as her skin. The wide eyes, always so innocent, now held sparks of spite though the voice, as ever, was beautifully modulated.

'I thought I recognized you, Melanie,' Lydia said, and glanced at the pile of goods on the counter. 'Shopping for a honeymoon?'

'I'm going on holiday after the Gala.'

'Of course, you're dancing for the Royals! I keep forgetting how famous you've become. You really have done fantastically well since you were – since the old days.'

'When I was a chorus-girl?' Melanie said bluntly, and had the pleasure of seeing Lydia change colour. 'Don't look so surprised at my remembering. You surely weren't stupid enough to think that dying your hair from blonde to red would stop me from recognizing you as the girl who ruined my marriage to Timothy?'

For an instant Lydia paused, then when she spoke her voice was as cool as ever. 'Why bother resurrecting such an old story? It won't bring Timothy back and it doesn't affect the future. Anyway, you acted very stupidly at the time.' The girl gathered her composure around her as though it was a visible mantle of support. 'You made a mountain out of a molehill. You interrupted a drunken kiss and you acted as though you'd found us in bed together! If you hadn't dashed off the way you did, Timothy wouldn't have had to chase you round the world. And if he hadn't done that, he'd be alive today!'

Melanie listened, astonishment replacing contempt. 'You really consider yourself blameless, don't you?'

'Yes.'

'And I suppose you're also blameless about the letter you found so unexpectedly?' The sudden sharpness of the question took Lydia by surprise, and she caught her breath and half turned away. Looking at the finely chiselled profile, Melanie was only conscious of feeling contempt. No longer was it important to maintain her pride or to pretend she was unhurt by what had happened. The reminder of Timothy's death had made her realize how fragile life was, and how little it mattered if Lydia knew that she still loved Gregory.

'What letter?' Lydia asked, her question – with its pretended innocence – only increasing Melanie's contempt for her.

'The one you conveniently found and gave to Gregory; the one that proved Timothy *hadn't* sold his shares to your father.'

'Oh, that letter!'

'Yes, that letter! Why did you do it? Was it just spite or was it the only way you could think of to try and get Gregory back?'

'I did it because it was the proper thing to do!' The red head tilted arrogantly. 'Gregory had a right to know what a rotten little schemer you are!'

'If anyone's a schemer it's you! You may be able to go on pretending with Gregory, but you can't do it with me. You know very well I never gave that letter to your father.'

Lydia shrugged. 'Gregory mentioned something about Anton trying to take the blame.'

'You didn't need Gregory to tell you that. You knew it already!'

'You're not suggesting—'

'I'm not suggesting anything,' Melanie interrupted. 'I'm *telling* you. From the moment your father had that letter, you knew about it. You knew it not only gave him control of the business but also the power to blackmail Gregory into marrying you!'

'You're crazy!'

'Am I? Then why did he break off the engagement as soon as his aunt died?'

The flush on Lydia's cheeks showed that the question had found its mark and, seeing it, Melanie suddenly became sickened by the whole scene. 'Can't you be truthful for once in your life?' she said wearily. 'Or are you still scared that I might try and get Gregory back?'

'If you haven't tried to do so before, you won't try now.' The approach of the assistant made her stop and she waited until Melanie had signed the account and the woman had moved away again to pack up the beachwear, before she continued. Only then did Lydia speak, her face no longer expressionless but full of malice and guile.

'All right, so I did know my father had Timothy's letter and I also knew that he used it to force Gregory into asking me to marry him. Then when his aunt died and he dashed off to New York, I made up my mind to show him the letter.'

'And tell him *I* had given it to your father?'

'Yes. It was the obvious thing to do.'

Although nothing Lydia had said had come as a surprise, hearing the words so blatantly and almost proudly uttered made Melanie more disgusted than she had believed possible.

'Is there nothing you would stop at to get what you want?' she asked.

'Nothing!' Lydia replied. 'That's why you're alone now and why I'll end up marrying Gregory.'

Melanie clutched at the counter, and seeing the movement, Lydia gave a delicate laugh. 'No, we're not engaged yet; but we will be. I can promise you that.'

'You're very sure of him, aren't you?' Melanie said, keeping her face averted.

'I'm only being logical,' Lydia replied. 'He hasn't got over you yet, but when he does, I intend to be there – waiting.' As though the sound of her own voice was giving her confidence, the girl came a step closer. 'You were very stupid to let him go. Why is trust so important to you?'

'Because without it, it means you don't know the person you're in love with. You may just as well be in love with a mirage.'

'Love *is* a mirage,' Lydia replied. 'No two people can ever completely understand each other.'

Melanie turned and looked at her. 'If you really think that, then I don't give your marriage much chance of success.'

'I'll have Gregory and I'll be his wife. That's all the success I want.' She gave a half shake of her head. 'If you wanted to, you *could* have convinced him that Anton had been the one to give Timothy's letter to my father.'

'Maybe,' Melanie said wearily. 'But he would still have believed that I knew about it – that I hadn't told him about it because I had been protecting Anton.'

'So what? You could always have pleaded that Anton had influence over you – that was one of the things Gregory didn't like.'

'I know. But it wasn't true. Anton never influenced me.'

'Whether he did or not isn't important,' Lydia said coolly. 'But Gregory believed it to be true, and if you'd played your cards properly, he would have forgiven you.'

'I didn't want to be forgiven for something I hadn't done!' Melanie flared.

'Then you're the loser and I'll be the one to wear his wedding ring.'

With a mocking gesture of farewell Lydia raised her hand and walked away, leaving Melanie to gather up her parcels and make her way blindly to the lift.

For the rest of the day she was able to forget her searing meeting with Lydia, for the dress rehearsal was unusually long and tedious, and by the time she returned to the flat she was so physically exhausted that she fell asleep the moment her head touched her pillow. Even the next morning she had no chance to think of her own personal problems, for another rehearsal was called and final adjustments made to costumes and scenery. But in the afternoon, on Verenskaya's instructions, everyone returned home to rest, and though Melanie knew she would not sleep, she lay in her bedroom with the curtains drawn to keep out the daylight and, as she had expected, thoughts of Gregory and Lydia flooded her mind.

Although he did not love Lydia yet, she knew that given time he would eventually marry her, as Lydia had so calmly stated yesterday. For the hundredth time she wondered whether she had been right to stop Anton from going to see Gregory. At worst, Gregory might not have believed him; at best he would have accepted Anton's guilt and – with the knowledge of how badly he had misjudged her – he would have pleaded with her to forgive him; begged her to let them start afresh.

She sighed and turned her head on to the pillow, acknowledging with bitterness that she was indulging in a daydream. So long as Gregory needed proof of her innocence, so long as his faith in her was so weak that it could not conquer the doubts put there by other people, then she would have had to live with the fear that one day someone or something else would have made him doubt her again.

With a sigh she sat up and, accepting the fact that she was not going to fall asleep, swung her feet to the ground and padded over to the window. She pulled back the curtains and stared into the square. A nanny was wheeling a baby in a pram and beyond them a young mother was walking hand in hand with a toddler. As they reached the corner of the street a man crossed the road towards them. The little boy ran forward and was lifted high into the air and then set down on his feet again. The mother stood watching, a smile on her face as she turned it up to receive the man's kiss. It was an ordinary meeting of a family, yet it made Melanie realize how different her own life was; how different it would always be.

'You should be sleeping.' Verenskaya's voice jerked her round and guiltily she moved back to the bed.

'I'm not used to sleeping during the day.'

'You should at least be resting.'

Dutifully Melanie lay down and Verenskaya went out, returning after a few moments with a pot of tea and a jug of milk.

Melanie smiled, 'I never ever thought a Russian would offer me tea without lemon!'

'I agree it is sacrilege to drink tea with milk, but you need fattening up. After tonight's performance you will start your holiday. If you don't rest you will collapse.'

'For once I'm not arguing.'

'There would be no point in it. Everything is arranged. Now drink your tea and rest. I will call you when it is time to go to the theatre.'

As Melanie was being fastened into her costume later that night, she was seized with such a fit of trembling that she could not hide it.

'Are you all right, mademoiselle?' the dresser asked.

'Yes, yes, it's just nerves.'

After a moment the trembling ceased and she was able to tie on her shoes, take a final glance at herself, and go to the wings where Anton was waiting for her.

At the request of the Palace they were not doing a full-length ballet, but a series of smaller works, and Melanie and Anton were to dance *Diana and Actaeon* which, though a short pas de deux, was so arduous that it required all their stamina.

'We've got a receptive audience, thank heavens,' Anton murmured. 'You can feel their excitement.'

'I hope I won't let them down.' She shivered. 'I feel as though I've never danced before.'

'You say that every time we give a special performance.'

'I know I do – only this time it's even worse. I can't go on, Anton. I—' The rest of her words were drowned by a burst of applause as the curtains swept back for their entry, and Anton gave Melanie's shoulder a reassuring squeeze as she moved past him to dance on to the stage.

The spotlight fell full upon her, and as she was bathed by its warm glow, professionalism overcame all her other fears and, drawing on reserves she had not dreamed she still possessed, her fatigue vanished and she danced with strength, vivacity and consummate skill.

As Actaeon Anton was superb, each leap drawing tumultuous applause, so that when they came to the end of their dance they were forced to give an encore, and even then, after innumerable curtain calls, the audience refused to be satisfied. The conductor, standing in front of the orchestra, looked up at Anton, waiting for his nod before beginning another encore, but after a fleeting glance at Melanie, Anton shook his head. Reading the signal correctly, the conductor put down his baton, the two men controlling the heavy curtains released their hold on the switches and the thick red velvet drapes swung across the stage, muffling the still thunderous applause.

Melanie stared at the curtains as though seeing them for the first time. The spur that had driven her all evening was now abruptly disintegrating and she felt curiously empty, her limbs so weak that she staggered and would have fallen had not Anton's arms reached out to catch her.

'What's wrong?' he asked, his voice harsh with anxiety.

'I'm tired,' she said simply, and then knew no more as she slipped into unconsciousness.

She was unaware of being carried to her dressing-room, unaware of the reporters who, clamouring outside her door for an interview, stopped in horror as they saw her inert figure and then, in one concerted rush, headed to talk to other members of the cast.

'Was this the first time the great ballerina had collapsed?' ... 'Was she suffering from an illness?' ... 'Was it incurable?'

Never short on histrionics, little dancers anxious to have their name in print made up answers as they went along, giving the reporters the dramatic replies which they felt would be most readily accepted. Truth never entered into any of the statements, and by the time Verenskaya – guessing what might be happening – left Melanie's side and descended on the corps de ballet like a force nine gale, the damage had already been done.

It was not until the following afternoon that Melanie, resting on the couch in the Bayswater flat, had an opportunity of reading the lurid stories which had been printed about her.

'England's greatest ballerina dying!' shrieked one headline. 'Leading dancer of Verenskaya ballet unlikely to appear again,' forecast another. 'A life of rest for Melanie – let the Queen make her a Dame,' ordered a third.

Melanie threw the papers on to the floor in disgust. 'Who printed all this rubbish?' she asked Verenskaya.

'If I knew that, there would be a noticeable pruning of my Company!'

'You should have let *me* see the reporters. Then this wouldn't have happened.'

'You weren't in a fit state to see anyone last night. The doctor says you're to take a complete rest for at least two months.'

'Two months!'

'Well, one month at least.'

'Two weeks,' Melanie said stubbornly. 'I'm going on holiday anyway, so it will work out all right.'

'One complete month,' came the insistent reply. 'I am not joking, child. The doctor was most emphatic.'

'But what about the season?'

'Tanya will dance more, and there is another dancer I can get from the Stuttgart ballet company. Believe me, no one is indispensable. And besides, all this paper talk is excellent publicity. By the time you dance again, everyone will be fighting to get tickets.'

'No doubt all waiting for me to collapse again,' Melanie said dryly. 'The public has a very macabre mind.'

'The public love you,' Verenskaya said simply, and indicated the mass of bouquets that filled the room. 'These are only a tenth of what have come for you. I sent the rest to the Middlesex Hospital.' The woman stood up. 'Rest again. I will be in the kitchen if you need me.'

Still under the effect of sedatives, Melanie lay in a state of semi-consciousness, drifting on dreams that occasionally gave way to reality. Gradually the sunlight faded and the dusty beams dancing into the room were replaced by blue shadows that crept over the carpet.

Verenskaya returned to the living-room, once more clad in her long evening dress and sparkling jet necklaces. 'A little supper before I leave?' she suggested. 'I have prepared some bortsch for you.'

'It's very kind of you, Madame, but I don't feel hungry.'

'You do not need to feel hunger to drink bortsch! I will—' she stopped in annoyance as the doorbell rang. 'No peace here! Always people coming uninvited!'

'It can only be Anton,' Melanie said with a faint smile. 'He always knows when you've prepared something special!'

'This time he will be out of luck. I have no intention of letting him in. You are to rest – not to be bothered with shop talk.'

'He doesn't bother me.'

'But he still reminds you of what you should be forgetting,' came the gentle reply, 'and for that reason alone I think it better if you do not see him.'

Melanie clenched her hands under cover of the light blanket that rested over her. 'My not seeing him won't help me to forget. Anyway, he's my partner.'

'Time enough to see him when you come back from your holiday.' The bell rang again, longer this time, and with a muttered imprecation, Verenskaya stomped out, closing the living room door firmly behind her.

Melanie lay back on the settee, but hardly had she settled herself when she heard Verenskaya give a loud exclamation. She sat up in alarm. It must be reporters, she thought agitatedly, and quickly patted at her hair with one hand while with the other she switched on a table lamp. Light flooded the room and the startling brilliance heightened the tension that swept through her as the door opened and she recognized the man framed in the threshold.

'Gregory!' she gasped. He came towards her and she shrank back with such a visible shudder that he stopped dead.

'I had to come,' he said jerkily. 'I read that you were ill ... very ill.'

Anger released her numbness, and furiously she lashed out at him. 'What for?' she mocked. 'Remorse before the requiem? You're wasting your sympathy, Gregory. You shouldn't believe what you read in the newspapers. As you can see for yourself, I'm perfectly well!'

He did not answer and though she tried not to look at him, she was unable to stop herself.

It was several months since their last meeting, and if its bitterness had left its mark on her, he too had not gone unscathed. The slight grey which she remembered at his temples had now become completely silver, and the glittering eyes were so deeply set that they made the lids appear dark and heavy, accentuating his saturnine expression. A devil in torment. From nowhere the thought came into her mind, and as it did, her anger against him died.

'I'm sorry you were misled,' she said gently. 'But I'm not ill. I fainted last night after the performance and the newspapers blew the whole thing up into a crazy story.'

Still Gregory went on staring at her and Verenskaya, sensing Melanie's torment, spoke for the first time. 'I am sorry, little one. I tried to prevent him from coming in, but it was impossible.'

'Nothing could have stopped me,' Gregory said harshly, not taking his eyes from Melanie's face. 'I had to see you for myself ... had to make sure. The moment I saw the newspapers I came straight here.'

'*Straight* here?' Verenskaya questioned.

He turned and looked at her blankly, then with an effort absorbed what she meant. 'I was away – abroad,' he explained jerkily. 'I read the newspapers when I was on the plane, and the minute I landed, I came straight here.'

Verenskaya's eyes took on their all too familiar gleam, and with a sense of doom Melanie knew what was going through the woman's mind. But it mustn't happen. At all costs Verenskaya must be prevented from turning this unwanted and painful meeting into some pseudo-reunion of blighted lovers.

Sitting up straight, Melanie forced herself to look at Gregory. 'It was kind of you to come here, but quite unnecessary. As I've just said, I'm perfectly well.'

'You don't look it.' He pulled the lamp round so that the light fell directly on her face, outlining the sharpness of the bones beneath the delicate skin. 'You're ill, Melanie. Don't lie to me.'

'I'm tired,' she admitted, and looked at Verenskaya pleadingly. But the look was ignored and Verenskaya walked to the door.

'You must have much to say to each other,' she said, and went out.

Alone with Gregory, Melanie fought down her desire to run from the room. Only by remaining calm could she make him believe that he no longer had the power to hurt her. Yet having to look up at him put her at a disadvantage, and pushing aside the blanket she stood up. It was not until she heard his gasp that she remembered she was wearing a chiffon negligée, the pink folds barely hiding the pearly gleam of her body. With shaking limbs she retreated behind the settee, aware that though she was now partly concealed by its brocaded back, her shoulders and breasts were still tantalizingly visible.

'There's no need for you to concern yourself about me,' she reiterated breathlessly. 'I was rather silly and worked too hard. That's all.'

'I've been reading a lot about you,' he said abruptly. 'Whenever we part you always become more successful.'

'All the more reason for you not to worry about me!' she rejoined. 'After all, seeing it in terms of my career, I owe you a lot. Without you, I might still have been in the corps de ballet!'

He gave a smile that held no mirth. 'Partings seem to improve my career too. Since our – since our last parting I've doubled my profits.'

'Then we can both be grateful to each other.' She put her hand to her throat, afraid that he would see the pulse beating there. 'And now you really must go. I'm expecting someone and I must change.'

'I have something to tell you first.' He took a step towards her. 'I love you, Melanie. No matter what happens in the future, I want you to know I love you.'

His look was so intense that she turned away from it. Coming after her meeting with Lydia, his admission did not surprise her. Never a man to give his feelings lightly, she had not expected him to stop loving her any more quickly than *she* had been able to stop loving *him*. Yet hearing him admit it himself, in no way abated her hurt or anger.

'Was it love or conscience that brought you here today?' she asked. 'Did you envisage comforting me as I lay dying?'

'Don't!' In a gesture of weariness which she had never seen from him before, he lowered his head into his hands. 'These last months have been a nightmare . . . there hasn't been a day or night when I've stopped thinking about you. No matter what I did – how hard I worked – you were always in my mind. Wherever I turned I saw your face . . . heard your voice. . . .'

'You haven't been trying hard enough,' she said coldly. 'Give yourself a little more time. I'm sure you'll eventually be able to forget me. Just keep reminding yourself how wicked I am.'

'Don't say that! I never thought you were wicked. Unthinking and childish perhaps – but only because of your loyalty to Verenskaya. Money was never important to you.'

'You didn't always think that,' she reminded him. 'You once

accused me of being a gold-digger.'

'That was the first time we met,' he said with something of his old irritation. 'You can't count that. I know you better now.'

'Better?' she retorted. 'That's an empty word, Gregory. You still think I sold Timothy's letter. That's one accusation you aren't so ready to take back.' The pallor of his face increased, but she was too angry to care. 'You shouldn't have come here. Nothing's changed and you're just making it difficult for both of us. I'm the same person I was when you last saw me – and you didn't believe I was unthinking and childish then. If I remember correctly, I was supposed to be treacherous, deceitful and money-grabbing!'

'That isn't true. I don't believe that any more.' Seeing her look of disbelief, he took a step towards her and then stopped. 'I know it's hard for you to understand what I'm saying, but at least hear me out. Give me a chance to explain.' Momentarily he stopped and then continued again, 'When I saw you that night, I was out of my mind with jealousy. Lydia had given me the letter the day before and I'd been up all night thinking about it. I went over the facts so many times that nothing made sense any more.'

Abruptly he stopped speaking and walked over to the window.

It was a blind, involuntary movement and he did not appear to notice the chair in his way nor hear it when it fell to the floor.

'When I remember what I said to you,' he went on, his voice so low that she had difficulty in hearing it, 'I don't blame you for not wanting to see me again. But I couldn't go on like this. I had to come here. Learning that you were ill was just an excuse. I was coming anyway.' He half turned but still did not look at her. 'Without you my whole life is a waste of time. Nothing is important to me; success, power, money don't mean a thing if I can't share it with you.' He turned fully and looked into her face. 'Do you understand what I'm trying to say?'

'Yes,' she whispered.

As he heard the word, he moved quickly towards her, but she held out her hands to ward him off. 'No! Stay where you are!'

'But I love you.' His voice was desperate. 'I know I should have come here sooner, but I couldn't. I kept remembering the things I said to you and I was afraid that you'd turn me away ... afraid that if we met again and you didn't forgive me. ...'

'I do forgive you,' she said softly, 'but it doesn't make any difference to the future.'

'Why?'

Though the question was a simple one, it cost all her effort to answer it. 'Because nothing's changed,' she went on 'I still think that trust is the most important thing in the world.'

'But I do trust you. Haven't you understood what I've been saying?' Ignoring that her hands were still outstretched to keep him away, he took another step forward so that they were only separated by the settee. 'Everything I said to you that night was wrong. That's what I came here to tell you. I don't believe you gave that letter to Fenwick and I don't even believe you knew about it.'

The unexpectedness of his statement took her by surprise and she fell back a step. 'Why?' she asked. 'Why have you changed your mind now?'

Once again he hesitated as though finding it difficult to put his thoughts into words. 'I've got to make you understand,' he muttered.

He came around the side of the settee, the swift movement rippling the folds of chiffon around her. For an instant he glanced at her body, then his eyes went back to her face, looking deep into her own eyes as though willing her to believe what he was saying.

'Try and put yourself in my place that night,' he repeated. 'We'd been parted for three weeks and every moment had been like a lifetime. I kept thinking of you with Anton – worrying that he was trying to part us – that he'd use his influence over you to—'

'He didn't have any influence over me,' she interrupted. 'You never had any reason to be jealous of him.'

'Jealousy doesn't need a reason. That's something you couldn't understand. You'd grown up in the Company and it was part of your life. I knew that and I was afraid that when it came to the final decision, you'd choose your career instead of me. And then Lydia gave me that letter.' He stopped speaking, his breath so heavy that it was a tangible sound in the room, an indication of the depth of his feelings. 'When I saw it,' he went on, 'I must have lost my mind. All I could think about was

Anton. The way he danced with you on the stage . . . the way he held you in his arms. . . .'

'But that's only on the stage,' she said. 'It was never real.'

'I know, but when I got that letter, I wasn't in a fit state to think properly. The only excuse I can give you for what I said is that if I hadn't loved you so much, I wouldn't have judged you so harshly. You were the first woman I've ever asked to be my wife. The first woman with whom I wanted to share my life. . . . I suppose I was scared.'

'Scared?' she echoed.

He nodded. 'Of knowing that without you I had nothing.' He came even closer so that their bodies were almost touching. 'Anton tried to tell me the truth that night, but I didn't believe him. I want to make you understand why. To make you believe that if it happened *now*, I wouldn't need *anyone* to tell me you were innocent. I'd know it for myself. You could never do anything that was underhand, no matter *what* was at stake.' He put up a tentative hand and then dropped it to his side. 'I'm not asking you for anything, Melanie. I don't deserve it. All I want is to be near you . . . to take care of you.'

She was silent, absorbing the wonder of something which she never thought could have happened. Not only was Gregory pleading with her to forgive him, but he was admitting that he believed in her innocence.

'I never thought I'd ever hear you say that,' she said tremulously. 'Sometimes I used to think you'd come back and say you'd forgiven me, but I didn't think you'd ever say I was innocent.'

'Why should you have thought it?' Gregory's voice was jerky and low. 'What proof have I ever given you that I could show any sympathy or kindness to you? From the first moment I met you, I—'

'Don't malign yourself too much.' There was a faint hint of laughter in her voice and hearing it, the anguish on his face gave way to a look of wonderment.

'Can you forgive me, Melanie? Do you think that in time we'd—'

'Not in time,' she interrupted, 'but *now*!'

With a swift movement she put her arms around his neck and leaned against him, her body trembling no less than his, her heart beating as fast.

'I love you so much,' he said huskily. 'I'll spend the rest of my life proving it.'

'Just hold me – that's all the proof I need.'

Her face turned up to his and his mouth closed over her own. No more words were necessary, for everything that had to be said was expressed in his touch and her own answering response.

Time passed without either of them being aware of it, and only the sudden opening of the door made Melanie draw back from Gregory's hold. Over his shoulder she saw Anton and colour flamed into her cheeks. But Anton did not look at her and his eyes, mocking and sharp, fixed themselves on Gregory.

'One more grand reconciliation?' he jeered. 'How long is it for this time?'

'For the rest of my life.'

There was a soberness in Gregory's reply that made Anton momentarily close his eyes, and watching the two men, Melanie knew that the hope of one had brought death of hope for the other. Realizing what Anton must be experiencing, she felt an overwhelming sense of sadness, but she knew better than to give any indication of it, and she remained silent, watching as he opened his eyes again and looked mockingly from her to Gregory.

'Does your being here mean that you have forgiven Melanie for her behaviour? Or have you suddenly found the sense to realize you'd been completely wrong?'

'I don't believe she knew anything about the letter.'

'Well, that's a step forward,' Anton said brightly. 'You can go to the top of the class.' Hands in his pockets he teetered slowly forwards and backwards on his heels. When Melanie went back to the flat to get her own love letters, I went with her. I found the letter Timothy had written and I was the one who gave it to Fenwick.'

'I'd already deduced that,' Gregory said.

'It took you long enough.'

'Don't talk about it any more,' Melanie interrupted. 'It's over.'

'It may be over for you, my sweet,' Anton replied, 'but there are still several things that have to be ironed out between Ransome and myself.' He looked at Gregory. 'I am referring to the Company. I can't see you letting Melanie be my partner any more. Not that I blame you.'

'Don't jump to conclusions,' Gregory intervened. 'As long as Melanie goes on dancing, I know she'll want to stay with Verenskaya. And as you're part of the Company. . . .'

'You mean you'll let her continue as my partner?'

'Yes.' Gregory turned and looked at Melanie, his eyes so full of love that she caught his hand and went on holding it as he turned back to Anton. 'If you can accept the fact that Melanie will be my wife, I can accept her continuing to dance with you.'

Anton's pale brows rose; an inimitable puckish movement which Melanie knew hid how deeply he was feeling. 'If you hadn't taken Melanie from me, I could almost like you, Ransome,' he said, and walked to the door. 'But this time make her happy. If you leave her again, I'll do my best to see you never get her back!'

'God willing, I intend to spend the rest of my life with her,' Gregory replied, and remained facing the door until Anton had closed it behind him. Only then did he turn and draw Melanie close again.

'I can't believe we're together,' he whispered. 'At night I used to dream you were in my arms and then I'd wake up and find myself alone.'

'I know,' she whispered. 'It was the same with me.'

'What a fool I was!' His breath was warm on her cheek. 'But now we're not going to waste any more time. I've got a special licence in my pocket and we'll get married at once.'

Startled, she lifted her head, and seeing the look on her face, he reddened with embarrassment. 'Yes,' he admitted. 'I sound like that damn fool Armand, but I came here determined to marry you even if—'

'Even if I were dying?' She gave a little giggle which turned into a sob. 'Oh, Gregory, what a waste of time it's all been.'

'A waste of time for you, my darling,' he said, 'because all it did was to make you unhappy. But at least it's taught me not to jump to conclusions.'

'You paid dearly for the lesson,' she said, and touched the silver hair at his temples.

'It was cheap at the price,' he replied and, catching her hand, pressed his lips against it. Then he dropped her hand and stepped away from her. 'If you feel well enough to get dressed,' he said casually, 'we can go to the register office now.'

'Today?' she gasped.

His eyes moved down her body and she flushed the same pink as the chiffon that barely covered her.

'I'm human, you know,' he said huskily, 'and I can only fight temptation for so long.'

'Then I'd better get dressed,' she said quickly, 'so we can make it legal!'

'What a pity,' he replied, and then added quickly: 'About getting dressed, I mean. It will be for such a short time!'

Laughter overcame her embarrassment and, giving him a swift kiss, she ran past him to the door, suddenly full of vitality. But on the threshold she paused and looked back at him. 'I can't believe it's really happening, Gregory. That I'm going to be your wife at last.'

'My wife for ever,' he replied. 'Hurry, darling. I'm waiting.'

Mills & Boon's Paperbacks

MARCH

WHO RIDES THE TIGER by ANNE MATHER

'There is an old Chinese proverb which says: He who rides the tiger dare not dismount. You are like that man, *senhora*. You cannot escape from your destiny,' a friend told Dominique with reference to Vincente, her husband. In her heart, Dominique knew she would never dismount – but what if she were thrown?

MARRIAGE BY REQUEST by LUCY GILLEN

'There's not a soul in Killydudden who doesn't think the doctor's a lovely man,' someone told Cerys when she arrived in Ireland, but Cerys had her doubts. After all, Dr. Kevin O'Rourke had made her look rather foolish on her arrival when (admittedly) she had spoken to him in rather a high-handed way, and he did keep on reminding her of the incident. Why then did she find herself also wishing to believe that the doctor was 'lovely'?

WIDE PASTURES by CELINE CONWAY

'When you feel like pulling up stakes, my dear, there's everything here a young woman could wish for, including a man who knows how to run a fruit farm and take good care of a wife,' had been the last words, written on a Christmas card, which Lucie ever received from Uncle Niall. And in his will Uncle Niall had seen to it that Lucie should have the opportunity of making his dreams come true. Uncle Niall's 'here' was a fruit farm in British Columbia and 'the man who knows how to take good care of a wife' was Norman Firland. But, after all, that was only Uncle Niall's opinion!

THE VALLEY OF ILLUSION by IVY FERRARI

'The Flower of Yarrow' was the title given to a fabled Border beauty in early Stuart times, but when Meg Linton was billeted at Scott Douglas's Border sheep farm during the making of a film she found that there was now a second Flower of Yarrow. Scott himself told her, 'The story goes about these parts that I shall never marry unless I can have the Flower of Yarrow, Mary Elliott in this case.' But why couldn't he have Mary? And why should Meg mind? Meg's own origins were in Yarrow. Dared she hope the title could pass on?

20p net per title

Mills & Boon's Paperbacks

EVE'S OWN EDEN by KARIN MUTCH

Joe Mannering was worried about his daughter Eve. If he sold Mangungu, what would become of her? He could not carry on for ever and ought to sell the farm, but it was Eve's whole life. Unlike other girls, Eve had no desire to dress up, go to dances or meet 'fellers'. So, when Lance Calandra arrived on the scene and showed interest in Mangungu – and Eve – the situation became piquant.

BARN DANCE by SARA SEALE

Selina was the latest of a long string of unsuccessful receptionists at Barn Close – some of them lazy, some of them trouble-makers, all of them imagining themselves in love with the owner of the hotel, Max Savant. When Selina arrived, Max thought her quite unsuitable, but she soon proved him wrong as she made friends even with the dragon Mrs. Bessimer, with cynical, neurotic Clive Williams, with little Paul Proctor, who was said to be such a difficult child . . . The reason was that Selina really *liked* people – she couldn't help it. So of course they liked her – that is, all except, perhaps, for one, Val Proctor, who was described to Selina by a friend as 'A honey! Got all the works, and then some! I'd marry her myself on looks alone, but I don't like tigers. *She means to have Max all right.*'

YET LOVE REMAINS by MARY BURCHELL

One of the most exciting romantic novels ever written by Mary Burchell!

AN EAGLE SWOOPED by Anne Hampson

When Paul Demetrius was blinded in an accident and his fiancée Lucinda walked out on him, her sister Tessa, who had always loved Paul, went to him, pretending to be Lucinda. Would her love be strong enough to stand the strain of living such a lie? And what if Paul found out?

20p net per title